GENE AMES, JR.

A WILDCATTER'S TREK

LOVE,
MONEY
and
OIL

For Coater Roberts the namesake of the greatest wildcatter his Great grandfather George Caater from

Gene Ames, Jr

January, 2017

DEDICATION AND DISCLAIMER

THE DISCOVERY OF the East Texas Oil Field in 1930 was the highlight of the golden age of the American oil industry. There were 2,475 automobiles sold in America in 1899. That number grew to 1,453,252 vehicles by 1929. The demand for gasoline skyrocketed and thousands of oil men, "wildcatters," spread across America to drill speculative wells in hopes they would discover the crude oil from which gasoline was refined. The sea of oil the wildcatters found in those days not only powered the engine of our nation's growth into the world's most prosperous economy, but provided the Allies the critical fuel on which to float to victory in World War II.

A Wildcatter's Trek: Love, Money, and Oil tells the fictional story of a young oil field pipe salesman named Jordan Phillips who risks everything to drill for oil in East Texas and discovers the largest oil field in the world at the time. He unwittingly joins the brutal, never-ending race of the oil wildcatter. Danger abounds as he's thrust into a conspiracy of murderous deception by those closest to him. The breathtaking core of *A Wildcatter's Trek: Love, Money and Oil* is fully exposed when Jordan Phillips learns that to preserve the treasure he has found he can never let his guard down and.... never stop drilling.

The oil fields in this story are real. The advances in geology science and geophysics over time really did happen, and, geoscience became a principal reason the wildcatters continued to find oil production deeper into frontier areas in their trek to expand the oil patch.

Jordan Phillips represents that generation of real oil wildcatters, who, during one short era of our nation's history, risked everything to join the drilling boom. Several made fortunes, but, many wildcatters went broke trying.

Few Americans are aware of the full extent of how much the great wildcatter oil fortunes have benefitted academia, arts, culture and science. Wildcatters built campuses of higher education and the oil royalties flow to this day subsidizing education costs for millions of students. Oil fortunes have filled entire museums and libraries with priceless works of art and artifacts of Western Culture. Endowed medical research has provided great advances in medical science and saved untold lives. Strategic plans continue to provide groundbreaking technological innovation and benefit mankind forever, from the bottom of the sea to the boundaries of outer space.

One indisputable truth is that the oil fields the wildcatters found made America the most prosperous nation in the history of mankind. Wildcatter's were brothers in arms and their common creed was 'My Word is My Bond'.

The words of the famous geologist Wallace Pratt stated exactly where America's oil began: *"Where oil is first found is in the minds of men."*

This story is dedicated to the following men mentioned in this story, and to all of their brother wildcatters:

Marrs McLean, Frank Yount, Tom Slick, Hugh Roy Cullen, H. L. Hunt, P.G. Lake, Neville Penrose, W. A. "Monty" Moncrief, John E. Farrell, Michael Benedum, Algur H. Meadows, J. W. Gilliland, Clint Murchison, Sid Richardson, Joe Zeppa, Ray and Bill O'Brien, Tom Gilcrease, Leonard "Mc" McCullum, George Coates, J. W. "Wordie" Gorman, Sr., Earl Rowe, Pat Rutherford, Sr., and O. W. Killam.

CHAPTER ONE

EAST TEXAS-1927

THAT'S ONE ANGRY river, Jordan Phillips thought, standing in front of his truck loaded with oil well casing, looking across what seemed like a half a mile of fast moving, rolling brown water to the other side of the Sabine. Ankle deep in cold flood water, rising higher on the bridge, keeping him from driving across, he didn't have the slightest idea how he was going to deliver his load of pipe to Beaumont. Mad as hell, he couldn't do anything but shake his head and spit at a swarming school of slithering water moccasins and wonder why in the world those stupid little snakes were trying to swim upstream in a river that was flowing so fast. Especially a river so choked with pine cones, and the rest of the usual trash the Sabine swept from the Piney Woods to the Gulf every spring when the rains came.

Being stopped by the Sabine was absolutely disheartening to Jordan. Even worse, though, he didn't want to be delivering pipe in the first place. Selling pipe made him feel like those water moccasins trying to swim upstream. He desperately wanted to become an oil man, knowing without reason but also without doubt that if he drilled for oil he'd find a big oil field and get richer than

God. So he took it that this flood was a sign. A benediction of sorts. Jordan had grown up in the oil field in Pennsylvania where he inherited the oil well pipe business that had been in his family since his granddaddy started it back in the 1880s.

After he was grown and learned more about the oil field, it didn't take him long to know that selling pipe was no way to get rich.

He worked hard, and at the age of twenty-five, he'd earned a reputation for doing what he said he was going to do. The staid oil men who bought pipe from Jordan were always surprised when they learned how young he was. He was more dependable and knew more about pipe than a man twice his age. You could take Jordan's word to the bank. And since he promised he'd get that pipe to Beaumont, that's what he had to do, even though he hated selling pipe.

His leather boots soaked, he turned the crank on his Model AA truck, started the engine, and climbed in behind the steering wheel to back the hell out of the rising waters and off the bridge, wheels spinning in the muddy ruts of the road. He drove the couple of miles back up to the crossroads and parked by the gas pump at the general store. Inside, standing behind the cash register, was an old man with reddish white hair that Jordan could tell was once flaming red. The few teeth the old man had left were stained as brown as the tobacco he was chewing. He looked at Jordan with a wrinkled red face. Big bags sagged under his eyes. He had a triple chin.

"Got any gas today?"

The man spit tobacco juice into a coffee can on the floor. "A little. 'Pends on how much you need," he quipped.

"Enough to about fill my truck, maybe twenty-five gallons."

"Yep, I probably got that much," he said as he put on a big straw hat and walked outside and stood next to the gas pump with the rain coming down in big drops, dripping over the side of his straw hat onto his sweaty neck.

"Where in the hell am I?" Jordan asked. "How can I get to Beaumont?"

Even with the rain slowing down, the old man had a hard time hearing what the young man was saying. He didn't even try to answer his questions. He pushed the pump lever down and pulled it back up slowly filling the gas tank.

He then hooked the gasoline hose back up on the side of the pump. The rain had almost stopped when he turned and stared at Jordan and pushed his hat farther back on his head.

"You sure askin' a lot of questions. Son, you're in the heart of the Piney Woods, in Gladewater. What are you doin' here with this here oil field pipe? Ain't no oil field 'round here."

"Delivering pipe. So how can I get to Beaumont with the water over the bridge?"

"If you don't want to wait for the river to go down, drive over to Longview and cross the high bridge, but you cain't make it through the Big Thicket less you watch out for stumps and holes."

"Thank you, mister. But tell me, why ain't there any oil fields around here?"

The old man shook his head and reached around behind him and scratched his butt. "No one ever drilled nothin' but dry holes in the Piney Woods. Who knows? Eleven or twelve dry holes maybe, but they tell me they're drilling good oil wells down at Corsicana, but not in the Piney Woods. If you ask me, Pine Trees is an oil field graveyard."

"How do you know that for sure?"

"Breathe deep and tell me what you smell."

"I don't smell a damn thing."

"That's what I mean. You cain't smell any oil like you can

smell down at Mexia. All you ever smell here in Gladewater is Pine Cones. They's not a damn smell of oil, not aroun' here."

"You're crazy, old man. If I started drilling here I'd find a big oil field and prove you wrong. But, hey, what would you do if you were me and stuck here on a Saturday night waiting for the rain to stop and the river to go down?"

The old man narrowed his eyes and frowned. It was like he couldn't believe Jordan was asking such a stupid question. "What a young man like you needs is a woman. You don't need me to tell you that." The old man chuckled. "When I's young like you, and I had to have a woman, I'd go somewhere like on the other side of the river down to Friendship and buy some white lightnin' from the colored bootlegger, and if it 'uz rodeo time, I'd head out to the rodeo and find me a gal that liked moonshine, and I'd take her down to th' river and we'd both get drunk and get nekkid. Yes, sirree. Heh, heh, heh." He chuckled and wagged his head. He spit again. "But I sure as hell wouldn'ta been looking for a woman in Gladewater. I'd been over in Shreveport where the action was back then."

Jordan didn't need any white lightning. But he sure liked the idea of finding a woman. He couldn't remember the last time he had been with a woman. "What about tonight, old man? There a Rodeo?"

"Rodeo started Wednesday. It's out thataway." The old man pointed west. "About a mile down the road to Big Sandy, jus' look to the right, and you'll see a field with a bob-wire fence 'round it, and that's where they's a rodeo. You better git your ass out there 'fore it's too late an' all the white gals git took."

"Thanks," Jordan said and he paid for the gasoline. As he was starting his truck, the old man raised his voice and said, "And don't you forget, son, if you decide you want to find oil, then don't you worry about findin' any oil 'round here."

Jordan drove on out to the rodeo. He wasn't much on cow-boying, but the gals at rodeos were often cute and looking to have a good time with a man.

It looked to Jordan like eighty-five or so folks were sitting on pine logs laid on the ground around the rodeo ring to form rows of seats. And eighty-five folks included everybody that came to watch the rodeo. The spectators, the rodeo cowboys, the clowns, and the cowgirl barrel racers.

As he walked through the gate onto the grounds, Jordan passed tables set up for anybody that had anything to sell to show their wares. A giant of a man with a huge stomach stood behind one of the tables. He was about six foot eight, Jordan figured, about five inches taller than he was. On the table in front of him, the tall fat old man had a bottle filled with putrid-looking green jelly with a hand-scratched sign leaning on it with big scribbly handwriting in red ink that said, "For Sale—Doc Angus Berry's Hoof Paste."

When Jordan walked past, the old man called, "Hey, Oil Field."

Jordan stopped and looked back.

"Yeah, you, Oil Field. Come back here. I got hoof paste for your horse, but you don't have no horse. I can tell you're an oil man 'cause you got so much grease all over your pants. Well, I got a big oil field for you to find."

Jordan walked back toward the old giant.

"Horse doctorin' is jus' my hobby. I make my real livin' finding oil. I'm a doctor of geology. I found the Cement Field in Oklahoma and Desdemona down past Abilene. An' I can find you a big oil field right here in East Texas." He held up a long rolled up piece of paper and said, "This here map is guaranteed to show you where to drill an oil well and hit it big, and I'll sell it to you cheap. It's guaranteed."

Jordan caught himself reaching for his wallet, and he stopped, thinking maybe this tall old fat man was the snake oil salesman his Daddy was warning him about when he told him to never drill for oil.

So he turned and walked away, eyeing a couple of girls in jeans. Brunettes. He decided a blonde barrel racer would be best or maybe she didn't have to be a barrel racer if she was a blonde. Blue jeans or a skirt, it didn't make any difference, as long as she was a blonde.

Then he smelled barbecue cooking. It was a damned good smell. He saw the smoke and the flames and the heat rising from a wood fire and the white-hot burning coals in a barbecue pit and the brisket sizzling on top of the grill, roasted to perfection and ready to eat, and he thought it must have been cooking a long time, probably since about four-thirty in the morning.

The cowboy cooking the barbecue handed him a big paper plate full of brisket covered with barbecue sauce and grilled onions and oversized French fried potatoes and two pieces of soft white bread on top. Jordan hurried to pay so he could start putting away the barbecue and all the fixings. Before he could dig into the barbecue plate, the barbecue chef handed him another plate filled with a big slice of chocolate cake with at least an inch thick cover of melting hot chocolate fudge icing oozing like a hot lava flow over the top and down the side of the cake. And on top were two big round dips of fresh turned frozen homemade vanilla ice cream. *Boy, does this taste good!* was all Jordan could think as he sat at a picnic table and ate every bite.

Then he was full, and now his only need was a pretty girl. He walked around and looked up and down the long pine seats. He found a spot with a couple of empty seats, squeezed himself down that row and sat down to watch the calf roping. His eyes never stopped scanning the crowd checking out each woman he saw, hoping to find an available blonde. Pickings were slim. The decent-looking girls were already hanging on the arms of cowboys.

Then down at the end of his row he saw a petite girl with sandy-colored hair in tight jeans, boots and a white Stetson. Her low-cut cowboy shirt was packed with whatever good looking gals filled up their shirts with. She smiled at him and took a seat on the aisle down at the end of his row. After the calf roping she stood up and started walking out of the rodeo stands. She looked back to see if he was still there. He followed her.

On his way to catch up to her, he walked past the horse doctor, or whatever he was. "Hey, Oilie! I really can find you an oil field."

Jordan Phillips came to a stop. "OK, I'm listenin'. Make it quick. What have you got?"

"A Geology map. Shows where to drill an oil well."

"How much do you want?"

"I'll make you a special deal. A hundred dollars, and you'll find your oil field."

Jordan couldn't get his daddy's words out of his mind: *Son, don't never drill an oil well.* So he looked Doc Berry straight in the eye and said, "No thanks, old man. Find yourself another sucker."

Then the gal turned and looked back at him. She smiled and pointed her index finger straight at him and swung it back pointing it in her own face, smiling all the while and nodding her chin up and down. Jordan knew he had it made with this one, and this let his mind focus one hundred percent on how rich he might get if he bought that oil field map.

In a flash of a second, the fear his father had put in him about drilling for oil left him. He peeled two twenties and a ten off the roll of long green in his pocket and flashed the money up to the so-called geologist.

"Fifty dollars for that damn map. You can take it or leave it," and he turned away from the old man and left him to go catch up with the rodeo girl.

"Wait. Young man. Wait. Give me that fifty dollars and this map is yours."

Jordan stopped, and turned back and looked at the old man. He felt a surge of excitement like nothing he had ever felt before. Something told him he was going to find a big oil field if he bought that map. He handed over the fifty dollars, and the old man gave him the geology map.

"That map won't do you no good 'less I take you down into the Piney Woods to the old widow woman's farm and you sign her up on an oil lease, and while we're down there, I'll drive a stake in the ground in the exact spot where you're gonna drill your damn oil well. I'll meet you at eight in the morning at the High Bridge in Longview."

Jordan nodded his head. "Okay, Mr. Geologist, I'll see you tomorrow morning at the High Bridge."

He turned away from Doc Berry and walked briskly to catch up with the blonde with his oil map tight under his arm. All night long the lightning struck and thunder claps rolled across the tops of the pine trees from Gladewater to Longview.

Early on Sunday morning he kissed his rodeo girl good-bye. They made plans to meet again next year at the Gladewater Rodeo. Carrying his oil map under his arm, he left for the High Bridge to begin a new life.

CHAPTER TWO

THE STORM FROM the night before lingered as they always do this time of year. Hard rain still pounded the earth. The old man was sitting in his truck parked on the Longview side of the bridge. Jordan parked his own truck and, with his geology map rolled up and stuck under his arm, ran through the rain and jumped into the old geologist's truck. Jordan felt like he'd been baptized and just lifted out of a river. His whole body shivered, and he shook his head like a wet dog. Water drops mottled the geology map he unrolled. "Show me where I'm supposed to drill."

"There, right there," the old man said, pointing at the middle of the map. "Those property lines show the fences of the farm owned by the widow woman I'm taking you to meet."

Doc Berry grinded into first gear and slowly drove his truck across the high bridge. He and Jordan looked down on the rising crests of the fast-moving dark-brown water, wondering how long before even the High Bridge was washed out. The river was already touching the bottom timbers.

"Old man, can I call you Doc?"

"Why not, son? Everybody calls me Doc."

"Are you a real geologist?"

"I am that for sure. Just look at all the oil fields and gold mines I have found. Up in Oklahoma, the Cement Field. And down in Mexico, President Carranza got me to come down there and write him a report on all the oil in Mexico. Check me out. I know how to find oil."

"Doc, how can I learn about geology?"

"Son, you got to read. Go up to Norman to the library at Oklahoma University and read geology books. You'll learn geology. Then, you got to go out on the ground and walk. You describe every rock you see and the faults and what they mean. Most of all you look for anticlines. That's where they's oil. Look under the car seat and see if they's not a geology book there."

Jordan reached down and felt under his seat and pulled out a musty, dirty old book with the title barely visible under the grease: "*Practical Oil Geology, The Application of Geology to Oil Field Problems*" by Dorsey Hager, Petroleum Geologist and Engineer.

"You got it. Take that book and read it. Dig wells and you'll eventually become a geologist, like me."

"Doc, how you know there's oil under that old lady's farm?"

"The rocks tell me, son, and, listen to this, you'll drill into oil in the Woodbine Sand at a depth of 3,500 feet, and you'll tap into an ocean of oil. What else do you want to know?"

What about this geology map?"

"What does it mean when it says on the map right here: Bradford Anticline?" he said pointing at the map again.

"Anticlines are what I was trying to tell you about. They's where you'll find you oil and my map shows they's an anticline on Miss Daisy's Farm. But they's another reason than geology that tells me about oil here in the Piney Woods, and it's because I went over to Van where the oil companies was drilling and played dumb. The oil guys thought I's a farmer an' not the scientist I really am. They ast me to find 'em find some good melons."

"What did watermelons have to do with finding a place to dig an oil well?"

"I'll tell you. I found a whole patch of Black Diamonds on the ground so ripe they 'uz ready to bust. I bought every melon on the ground for five dollars. Then I told the company men to follow me to the watermelon patch and we had a helluva melon bust. The roughnecks and drillers got so full o' melons they could pop, and I asked that company man if he'd tell me where I could buy a farm that had oil under it.

"He told me go to Arkansas to El Dorado and there 'uz lots of good watermelon patches for sale, and his company was sending him up there next to dig."

"Why didn't you go to Arkansas?"

"Oh, hell no, what I'm trying to tell you is you don't never drill where the big company boys say drill. It's the little boys like you and me that find the big oil. And the big company man said don't go to the Piney Woods. And for sure, since I found these anticlines there too, the Piney Woods is the place where you should go and drill for oil."

Jordan wagged his head with amusement. "Doc, you're a genius. An eminent scientist."

Doc Berry drove Jordan further down in the rain, down past the Kilgore Post Office, in the muddy ruts of wagon roads through the pine trees to the Carthage Road until he turned onto a muddy dirt lane and headed back north, up to the top of a hill where he came to a stop at the widow woman's farmhouse. The two of them walked up the steps of the front porch and Doc knocked on the door.

This old white-haired lady, standing on the other side of the screen door, said, "Come in this house. Git out of this rain."

Doc Berry said, "Hello, Miz Daisy. I'm sure glad to see

you again. This here's Jordan Phillips. He wants to drill you an oil well."

"Pleased to meet you, Missus Bradford," Jordan Phillips said, speaking loud enough to be heard over the noise of the rain hitting the tin roof. A bolt of lightning flashed and the sky was lit, and they heard the crack of the lightning striking a tree in the field down below her barn. A loud clap of thunder followed, rolling across the sky and shaking the house.

"Rain like this in East Texas don't stop till summer ends. The 'skeeters are so bad you can't stand outside. Not if you don't want to get the m'laria like people 'round here get all the time. Come in this house."

In her living room, Doc Berry told her if she would sign an oil lease, Jordan Phillips would pay her one hundred dollars and she would get a one-eighth royalty.

"What's a royalty?" she said.

"That's one-eighth of the oil. It's called royalty because the Queen of England got one of every eight trees that were cut down out of her forests."

"What am I gonna do with my one-eighth of the oil?"

"You're gonna sell it just like Mr. Phillips here is gonna sell his oil. In fact, if you're nice, he might just sell your oil for you."

"Well, better than pickin' melons, I suppose. Since my husband died, I learned that farming's too hard for an old lady. I cain't find any darkies any more to stay around here and plant and harvest. Used to be a dollar a week and all they could eat and I had plenty a he'p."

Doc Berry handed Miss Daisy an oil lease that said "Producers 88" in big black letters on top. She didn't take any time reading it, she just signed where he told her to.

"I do thank you, Missus Bradford," Jordan Phillips said as he unrolled a hundred dollars in cash from the wad of paper money in his pocket and handed it to her. "I'm happy to do business with you, ma'am."

Doc hugged the little old lady. "Miss Daisy, you gonna get rich from your oil royalty. I hope you buy some horses and let me take care of them for you, and maybe some mules to pull the plow."

"Well, I doubt if they's oil under my land, but I'll tell you this, Doc, I ain't never gonna have to work a watermelon patch again. And I want to thank you right now for what you've done."

"How's that, Miss Daisy? You don't need to thank me."

"Well, I do." Then she turned around and spoke loud enough for her colored maid in the kitchen to hear her.

"Marie, come here!" she yelled. "Bring some banana puddin' for these men."

In a couple of minutes, a little old woman at least ninety years old with snow white hair and pitch black wrinkled skin shuffled into the room. She was bent over, and she had a string of beads hanging down from her neck and a big lump of snuff puffing out her lower lip. With a smile of contentment on her face she sang a song that nobody could understand. She was bringing three serving plates of banana pudding. "Nana puddin', M'aam, with the blessin's of all the spirits protectin' you."

Miss Daisy said, "Marie's full of the same spirits her mama and daddy brought from Haiti a hundred years ago, back when my people bought them to work the Palmetto fields in Carolina. She cooks real fine and makes me happy bringing me the good news her spirits give her. In the years her spirits tell her I won't make a good crop, she saves me the money I'd have spent on seed and plantin'."

Doc Berry said, "Let's take Marie down to the watermelon patch so she can let her spirits bless the stake I'm going to stick in the ground to show Jordan where to drill. Her spirits can bring good luck to Jordan and, for sure, he'll drill into good oil sand."

With light rain falling, Doc Berry led them all down the hill to the watermelon patch. Walking behind the two men, Miss Daisy walked in front of the bent over old black woman, who shuffled down the hill slowly, singing as she went.

They stood in a circle around Doc as he hammered the stake into the ground. "Jordan Phillips, drill a hole right here, and drill it three-thousand and five-hundred feet deep in the ground. When you hit the Woodbine Sand, it'll be full of oil. And, Miss Daisy, it would sure help if Marie LeBlanc's spirits would tell you the same thing."

Before Miss Daisy could ask, the old black woman started chanting. "Halleluiah, halleluiah! Spirits speak, spirits speak. Stake in ground, stake in ground. Young man, young man, discover your treasure."

She raised her hands high and reached up to the sky, squeezing and releasing her beads, then she bowed all the way down to the stake. Tears started to flow out of her eyes.

Miss Daisy said, "Marie LeBlanc, what do the spirits say the future holds for Jordan Phillips?"

Wiping tears from her eyes, Maria said, "Spirits sing, 'River of oil, river of oil. Never stop drilling. Find river of oil.' Treasure found, then disaster—disaster and death. My spirits speak the truth. Hear me, hear me. Hear my spirits. Beware. Beware the future." The old black woman stopped talking. Her tears continued to flow, her old head wobbling on her scrawny neck.

Jordan turned to Doc Berry and whispered, "Good God, Doc, beware of a future of disaster and death? What does that have to do with finding oil? Good God!"

"Finding oil is hard and we need all the help we can get. Her spirits told her you'd find a river of oil. That's all you need to know."

The rain continued to fall in the watermelon patch on Daisy

Bradford's farm. Jordan said, "Her spirits said beware of the future. The only future I'm worried about is tomorrow. I'm ready to drill."

The East Texas sky turned black, and the wind blew hard and the four completely diverse characters standing together in a circle in the watermelon patch began to take cover as another flash of lightning shot across the sky and split in two. The two branches of the main lightning bolt were followed by a loud rumble of thunder, one heading toward Kilgore and the other rolling in the direction of Carthage.

Jordan turned and left Daisy Bradford and her black servant and her spirits. He took Doc Berry with him to return to Longview so he could begin his search for the iron he needed to drill a wildcat well in his search of his river of oil.

CHAPTER THREE

"CHIRP, WHAT'D YOU think if I shut down this pipe business and started drilling for oil? Would you come with me?" Jordan Phillips was back in Oklahoma in his pipe yard. Chirp Branscum was his superintendent, a Norwegian from Minnesota.

"Where you gonna drill, boss?" The hot Oklahoma wind blew grit in their eyes. They turned and the wind actually felt good on their backs.

"I thought about Beaumont," Jordan said looking at a stack of oil pipe.

"Beaumont? Isn't Spindletop about petered out down there?" Chirp spit into the red dirt.

"Spindletop's been reborn. When I was down there delivering my pipe, I heard the whole story. This man named McLean, Marrs McLean, talked an oil driller named Frank Yount into moving a drilling rig back to Spindletop and digging deeper, and Yount and McLean hit real pay dirt, better than the original Spindletop, and now they're producing eighty thousand barrels a day."

"Good for Spindletop, but where you need to dig is where no oil's ever been found. Look at Tom Slick. Just like you, Tom came from Pennsylvania and started out in the oil field as a salesman.

He dug dry holes everywhere. Then he struck oil at Cushing, and he kept finding oil fields all over Oklahoma that he sold out and got so much money that he quit drilling. But guess what? The other day I heard Tom Slick started drilling again in Oklahoma City, and he's already back up to eighty thousand barrels a day. Got the oil bug, and he can't stop. I'll tell you exactly where you need to dig is an oil field graveyard with nothing but dry holes, and you just dig and dig and dig 'til you find oil."

"I'm ahead of you, Chirpie. I got a place just like that. It's the Piney Woods in East Texas. It's an oil well graveyard."

"Good. You got enough money to keep digging long enough?"

"Enough to keep drilling for a couple of years anyway."

"We can do some good in two years."

"If I hit oil, Chirp, you hit too."

"That's not any worry to me. Good things happen in the oil field to good people who work hard."

The two men shook hands firmly, grinning at each other. Neither one of them asked the other for anything in writing.

"So, Boss, you going to look for that little Indian maid at the dance hall tonight?"

"I'm headed out to find her right now."

"It's a full moon. She'll be looking for somebody to take her to look at the moon out at the river."

"I'm goin' to find her and tell her she better dance with somebody who's about to become a real oil man."

"Tell her if she won't go with you, she's lost her big chance."

Jordan found the high-school Principal's daughter at the dance hall surrounded by a whole pack of men who were after her. Her name was Charlotte Sasakwa. Her mother was half-French, and her father was half-Osage. Everybody called her Miss Charlotte. Miss Charlotte was a striking blond with cinnamon complexion. A promise of a strong native passion exuded from every glance she gave, every gesture.

The fiddle music gave a rhythm to Jordan's walk as he approached her. A smile clearly directed at him cleared a space among her admirers, and half a dozen blue-jeaned hulks sulkily backed off as she shooed them away with a flick of her elegant hand. Jordan's confidence was boosted by this special attention. "Charlotte, I'm leaving to go to East Texas to become an oil man. Won't you dance with me one time before I go?"

"I'll give you one dance tonight, and if you go drill some oil wells, you can come back, and we'll dance again. If you're driving a real car and not a pipe truck, and you come back a real oil man, I'll go with you to the river to look at the moon."

CHAPTER FOUR

CHIRP COLLECTED A bunch of used iron parts trying to put together a drilling rig, but all he had was a pile of used iron that most oil folks would call junk. The string of old drill pipe was so worn out it just might break up into six-inch nipples if it was ever stacked up in a derrick.

"Boss, I tried to save you some money, but we damn sure can't start digging with a boiler that won't make any steam when we're down to burnin' green pine."

"We better go down to Lufkin, and find some iron that will get the job done."

So Jordan and Chirp drove to the Lufkin Foundry and Machine Company warehouse, and they bought the parts they needed and enough yellow timbers to build a derrick, and in August of 1927, they started drilling the well named the Jordan Phillips #1 Daisy Bradford Farm.

When it reached 1,098 feet in February 1928, Jordan and Chirp were standing together on the derrick floor with Chirp's hand on the brake. Where they were standing, they could see that the drill pipe was turning to the right, which meant that the bit was also turning at the bottom of the hole and with each turn of the drill bit, more dirt was dug out of the ground and the hole was dug deeper and deeper into the earth.

"Chirp, this well is sure digging slow. Do you think the bits wore out? Or is the dirt just rock that's too hard?"

"As long as it keeps digging and the mud circulates and brings the cuttings out of the hole, we cain't get in a hurry. Gettin' in a hurry in the oil field always brings trouble."

All of a sudden they heard a loud "pop!" They felt the derrick shake, and the drill pipe stopped turning.

"Goddamn it, Boss. This pipe is stuck." Chirp spit. "We'll have to junk this hole."

Jordan took off his hat and muttered a couple of cuss words and shook his head, looking at the drill pipe that had quit turning. Chirp shrugged. "We can skid this derrick down the hill and start over and drill the next well down to the Woodbine."

Jordan was learning that looking for new oil was a damn sight harder than working in an old oil field where the oil had already been found. They slid the derrick and all the machinery down the hill, and on April 14, 1928, they started drilling the second well on the Bradford farm.

All the time they spent drilling in the Piney Woods, Jordan and Chirp lived together next to the derrick in a bunkhouse slapped together with rough-cut pine boards. They called their bunkhouse the "doghouse." There was always a big pan of hot coffee simmering at a slow boil on a wood-burning stove. If you took a sip of boiling Hot Joe and your tongue was burnt and your eyes squinched, the coffee was ready.

One night Chirp came into the doghouse and found a young rookie roughneck snoring hard and catching some shut eye in Jordan's bunk bed. Chirp shook the boy and said, "Wake up, you little green ass. You're asleep in the big man's bed. Get your ass out of that bed, and go back home to Mama. You wore out your damn welcome on this here rig."

Chirp could look and sound fierce when the mood hit him or the occasion called for it. The kid woke up with a start. He was skinny and had a cowlick over the middle of his forehead, and his bleary eyes shined with the knowledge that he had lost his job and with the fear of what the red-faced Chirp might do to him. He flew through the doghouse door.

After drilling two wells in almost two years, Jordan was exhausted. When it came time for a meal, he could hardly eat. At the end of a day, he'd lie down in bed and couldn't sleep. He'd toss and turn and lie there and worry. When he'd fall asleep, he had a recurring nightmare—his daddy shook his fists at him and yelled, "Jordan, screw East Texas. Don't be an oil man. Go back to Oklahoma. No. Go all the way home to your mama back in Pennsylvania, and start over again. This time do like I told you, and don't drill for oil. Just sell pipe."

Then all of a sudden the sun would rise on a new day, and Jordan would jump out of bed and put on his coveralls and throw out yesterday's cold coffee and pour fresh water and coffee in the pan and light the fire and bring the new day's coffee to a boil. Through all this worry something kept telling him, if he would keep drilling, his dreams would finally come true.

CHAPTER FIVE

IN LATE FEBRUARY of 1929, it happened again. Trouble. The pipe twisted off in the #2 Bradford. Jordan had drilled another dry hole. He was standing on the planks of the derrick floor at the base of the derrick that stood taller than the tops of the pine trees around it. Looking straight down into the round black hole he had been trying to drill, he stalked to his superintendent.

"Chirp, go over to Shreveport and get that man they told us knew how to drill a well."

"Ed Laster?"

"If you get him to come drill, we'll try one more time."

Chirp knew his young boss had run up on a rock in the middle of the road.

"But, Boss, do you have the money to keep drilling?"

"I'll get more money somewhere."

"Where?"

"I can go to Dallas and hire me some money from a bank. I'm not selling a single percent of this business. That I am definitely not going to do."

"Boss, you got another choice."

"What's that?"

"See that rack over there? You can hang your tools on that rack and go back to Oklahoma. Least you'll be able to sleep at night."

"Don't talk to me like that."

Jordan had inoculated himself with the oil business. It was a known fact by a lot of oil wildcatters that if a man ever started drilling he would become addicted to it just as much as a man could become addicted to alcohol or to women or gambling. He would never be able to stop.

Chirp sighed and shrugged his broad, sloping shoulders. "Okay, keep drilling, Boss. But maybe we need to get away from these damn pine trees and go back to an oil field in Oklahoma or down by Houston, say, to Humble. My old buddy Smut Rymal runs Roy Cullen's drilling, and I've heard Smut tell how his boss told him when he calls him on the phone to tell him if he struck oil in a drill stem test, to never say he got oil 'cause the telephone operators are always listenin' in. He told Smut to always say he got water when the test flowed oil, and say oil if it made water, but when they dug through the heaving shale, and Mr Cullen struck oil at Humble, Smut got so excited that he yelled, 'Oil! Oil over the top of the derrick, up in the sky!' when he called Mr. Cullen to tell him about his oil well.

"The wildcatters are striking oil everywhere else around Texas, Louisiana, and Arkansas, and I want for you to leave these Piney Woods and go to the oil field, either down by Humble or one of those salt domes. Or, better still, let's you and me go back to Oklahoma."

"What's gotten into you, Chirp? You thought it was a great idea to drill right here. And Doc Berry is a world famous geologist. He says I'll find a big oil field right here under Miz Daisie's farm."

"Jordan, damn it. He's a veterinarian. He's not any geologist.

He's an old fat phony. How can anybody be a geologist if you drill two wells where he tells you to drill like we done and all you find is trouble and not one damn drop of oil?"

"We aren't through drilling here yet, and I believe him. I can't tell you why, but I believe him."

"Well, go get your money, and when you get back, I'll start the engines, and we'll skid the derrick down the hill and drill the #3 Daisy Bradford and drill it all the way down to the Woodbine. We'll drill it to China if we have to drill to China to hit the Woodbine."

In Dallas, Jordan found a new young banker at the Republic National Bank who laughed so hard he almost fell out of his chair. He told Jordan that banks didn't loan money to wildcatters to drill dry holes in the Piney Woods in East Texas.

The only way Jordan could get money to keep drilling was doing what he said he'd never do. He sold twenty-five percent of his company. The first thing he had to do was start drilling well number three.

Jordan drove back to East Texas from Dallas. He always got this good feeling driving from Dallas when he hit the Piney Woods at Terrell. It was like a horse must have felt when he saw his barn ahead and knew he was almost home. After a few hours driving around the Piney Woods, he sold his stock to three different men in three towns: Sam Knight who owned Knight's Drugs in Kilgore; Loyce Williams, President of the Overton State Bank; and John Henderson from Lufkin, who sold iron products fabricated by Lufkin Industries, a business in which his family was an owner. The main reason they bought his stock was that Jordan told them their cash registers would ring and their businesses would grow if he kept drilling and found an oil field in their neighborhood in the Piney Woods.

Jordan was a promoter, but he was a convincing business

man. He didn't want to oversell them on striking it big when helping their businesses was enough to make them want to invest.

Each of these businessmen invested five thousand dollars to buy stock in his new oil company: The Texas Oil Producing Company, TOPCO, for short. Jordan was the president of an oil company that didn't have any oil.

CHAPTER SIX

FOR THREE YEARS, he had been telling anybody in East Texas—his employees, farmers, share croppers, preachers, shop owners, school children—about the report that his world-famed geologist wrote that said an underground ocean of oil would be discovered when he drilled a wildcat oil well into the Woodbine Sand 3,500 feet on Daisy Bradford's farm.

Finally, after over a year of drilling, it looked like the TOPCO #3 Bradford Farm would actually drill into the Woodbine Sand, but Jordan kept running shy of a big enough crew to run the rig. He needed enough hands to cut enough firewood to keep the fires burning and the steam engines boiling. Chirp kept hiring farmer boys to help on the rig, and the first chore he'd give them was to cut brush and wood to keep the fires burning.

One day, all of a sudden, the string of drill pipe dropped ten feet and hit bottom with a sound like a pop. Jordan turned to his Superintendent. "We're in the Woodbine!"

"Sure as hell looks like you called this one right, Boss."

Pipe dropping like that meant that the bit had probably drilled into a sand and this could only be the Holy Grail that Jordan had been seeking, the Woodbine Sand.

Now it was put up or shut up time for Jordan Phillips. It was time for him to prove himself.

Doc Berry was up there standing on the derrick floor to direct the effort to find and identify the top of the Woodbine Sand. He told the young oil man to tell all the folks in the area that tomorrow was the time to come if they wanted to see an oil field discovered. Jordan figured that if these poor dirt farmers got wind of a chance to see oil discovered close to home they would come. He was right.

The next morning on October 3, 1930, at daybreak, the cock in Daisy Bradford's barnyard was crowing when the red ball of the sun peeked over the horizon announcing the arrival of another blue bird day. The farmers and their families began to gather along the old wagon road that passed by the pine forest that hid the lone oil derrick. They came with hope in their hearts of finding a new beginning, a way out of the poverty that had entrapped their families for generations.

A cloud of dust rolled in with all the people, and when the dust settled, there was a sea of mule-drawn wagons and Model T Fords and a crowd of hundreds that grew into thousands of people standing together with their automobiles and their wagons lined up down the road a mile or more.

Everyone was watching and waiting, the farmers with their wives and their children, their bent and weary old mothers and daddies, their friends and relations, standing there together in the panorama of the Piney Woods that stretched from fifty miles west of Daisy Bradford's farm to the Mississippi River and the Old South to the east. The land consisted of pine forests, red dirt, watermelon patches and cotton fields, patches of black-eyed peas, gardenias, dogwoods, cottonwoods, roses, and azaleas. The oil derrick was a singular thin structure, taller than the pine trees that engulfed it—the symbol of the new future that Jordan Phillips promised East Texas.

Jordan looked around, and he couldn't believe all the people there. Then back away from the crowd and standing alone in the trees was this friend he had made while he was drilling. He was a tall man from Arkansas. He liked to stand in the background and watch the goings on, wearing a straw hat, a starched shirt, and a tie with a thin cigar in his mouth. Jordan had first seen this man three years ago standing back in the trees behind the first well he drilled up the hill behind Daisy Bradford's barn. Naturally wanting to know who was scouting his well, he had introduced himself to this stranger, and they became friends.

Today Jordan asked him, "What d'you think, June?"

The man's name was Haroldson Lafayette Hunt, but he told Jordan to call him "June." "June" was for "Junior" because he was what most folks would call a "junior" since he had the same name as his daddy. However, in the case of the father and son, both named Haroldson Lafayette Hunt, "Junior" wasn't actually written in the family bible or on the Birth Certificate as an official part of the son's name. Instead, he was "H. L. Hunt (2)", and his daddy was "H. L. Hunt (1)," but everybody called the son June.

"Jordan, I can't figure you out," June Hunt said to him. "Here I am, feeling pretty good about your well, thinking you've got a chance of finding yourself a pretty good oil field. But, by God, you got yourself a problem, and I don't think you even know it."

"What're you talking about, June?"

"You've drilled two dry holes here on the Bradford Farm, and you're going to learn today if you're drilling a third dry hole."

"Or discover a new oil field."

"How many acres do you have under lease?"

"Nine hundred seventy-five and one half. I can probably drill a well on every twenty acres and that would be about fifty wells. You want to see a copy of my lease?"

"Well, even if crude oil flows over the crown block up there," he looked up, pointing his index finger up into the blue sky above the top of the derrick, "you have committed the oil man's greatest sin. You would have drilled a discovery well and not owned leases on enough acreage around it. Son, if you want to get rich in the oil business you'd better get in your truck right now and start driving. And drive up and down the roads through pine trees, and stop at every farm and buy yourself more leases. I already have four times as many acres leased as you. If you leave now and buy more leases, mark my word, you'll get rich."

Jordan motioned to the driller to start the engine and get the rotary table turning to the right and turn the drill pipe and the bit underground to the right too, so the drilling will dig out more dirt and drill the hole deeper and deeper. Everyone could hear the knocking and the clattering of the machinery. In about thirty minutes of drilling, pieces of sand and rock circulated up in the drilling mud from down deep underground at the drill bit and reached ground level. Doc Berry looked at a handful of the drill cuttings through his hand lens. He told Jordan he saw remnants of the rock that lay right on top of the Woodbine, a rock he said geologists called the Eagle Ford Shale.

Drilling for oil was a slow process. It always took longer than anybody wanted. But there was nothing Jordan and the folks could do but wait. And while they waited, they watched the ballet of the roughnecks that began when the derrick man high up in the derrick reached over into the cluster of pipe at the side and placed both of his arms in a bear hug slowly around three joints of pipe screwed together into one stand of drill pipe and rhythmically swung the pipe over into the space in the center of the derrick immediately on top of the drill string sticking up out of the hole so that the floor man at the bottom could "make up" the new string of pipe by screwing the end of the pipe sticking down into the long string sticking up out of the hole that ran all the way thirty-five hundred and twenty feet down underground to the bottom with the drill bit on the end. Making the drill string ninety feet longer by adding a stand of three thirty foot joints of pipe to the drill string sticking up and drilling deeper was the drilling ritual repeated every ninety feet in every oil well ever drilled. This ritual, happening over and over again in the hundreds of thousands of wells drilled for oil in the trek of American wildcatters that spread like wildfire across the country from Pennsylvania to the Southwest, was how the wildcatters opened up one new shallow oil field after the other and fueled the greatest economic engine the world had ever seen.

The excitement in the air around Jordan Phillip's derrick became electric. All the folks were ready and hoping and praying.

Jordan stood on the rickety wooden derrick floor, praying to himself that this would be the day when he would find oil, and his daddy would look down on him from Heaven and smile.

"These cuttings look like Eagle Ford Shale to me," Doc Berry said, looking at the chips of hard black slate-like rock through his hand glass. "I'd say we dug through the Austin Chalk and the black shale too, and the bit fell down into the top of the Woodbine."

"You're sounding like a real geologist, Doc."

"Goddamn it, Jordan, I am a real geologist. You've hit the Woodbine. Here, son, come here and let me show you I'm a real geologist." The fat old man scooped a handful of globs of something thick that was floating in the brownish drilling mud and he smeared the handful of drill cuttings across Jordan's open palm, and said, "Young man, look at this through my eye glass, and put it in your mouth and taste it."

The driller had stopped the drill pipe from turning to the right after slowly digging the hole deeper and deeper, inch by inch, to what might be the top of the Woodbine. Jordan held the old geologist's hand lens up to his eye and saw tiny grains of sand floating in the ooze he held, then he licked the mud off his hand and swished it around in his mouth.

His eyes suddenly opened wide. He took a swig of water and washed his mouth out clean and spit into a bucket. He looked over at Doc Berry, smiling as wide as a man can smile. "Doc, you know what that mud tastes like?"

"You tell me, son."

"It tastes like oil," he said, just as the engine blew such a loud blast that he had to yell louder to be heard. "We found oil, didn't we?"

All at once, the three years he had been drilling seemed like three days. He never doubted that, when he finally drilled into the Woodbine, it would carry oil, and the oil would flow out of the Woodbine reservoir as if it had been locked up in a bank vault, and the vault door had been opened like a dam had broken, and the oil inside the vault surged out and covered the world. He felt in his bones that was what he was about to see and what he wanted the whole world to see.

He turned to his well man. "Chirp, it's oil. Turn that engine off now." Chirp turned to Ed Laster, the driller, with his hand on the brake and gave him the word to shut down. Ed looked into the eyes of the roughneck standing closest to the steam-fired engine, and he pointed his own finger at his throat and swung it across his neck. The roughneck looked at Ed and nodded yes without a smile, and he turned off the engine and the engine's flames died and the folks were safe.

Silence followed the engine shutting down, and all anyone could hear was a soft whisper rising out of the open end of the drill pipe sticking up out of the hole. Jordan thought the sound was like the first cry of a newborn babe. Suddenly the air turned still, and the chatter from the crowd hushed, and nothing could be heard but that quiet little sound, and then a bubble appeared in the fluid standing in the drill pipe. The whisper changed to a gurgle, and the sound became louder and louder as the bubble in the drill pipe started to get bigger, and then the drilling mud in the pipe rose out of the pipe, higher and higher, and the sound increased to a crescendo that everyone could hear, and the pulsing of the muddy fluid repeated and repeated, and with each pulse, the fluid rose higher and higher until there was no longer any doubt. That first whisper from the drill pipe had grown into the wind of a coming storm, and the fluid in the pipe rose in a pulsating column of drilling mud, rising up in the derrick, a living, breathing geyser of fluid shooting higher and higher with each pulse, turning blacker and blacker until an explosion of oil shot over the top of the derrick into the East Texas sky, and the blue sky turned black. Black rain fell down on all the folks who saw what they came to see, history being made on that autumn day. When the black rain fell down on their faces, and they smelled the sweet petroleum, their voices joined together into a rousing cheer.

Jordan looked over at Doc Berry and saw his eyes open as wide as they could open, and his head shaking back and forth left to right in complete disbelief, and Jordan knew he was looking at the most surprised person in Rusk County. "Doc, thank you. Thank you, Doc," Jordan said with tears in his eyes.

More than a thousand folks were now out on the road. Daisy's nephews, the Miller boys, had a land office business squeezing lemons and selling lemonade at their lemonade stand. Those standing close to the rig were either laughing or crying— Jordan, Chirp Branscum, Ed Laster, Daisy Bradford and the oil field scouts, and another independent wildcatter named Neville Penrose from Fort Worth, who brought his own map maker, W. W. Zingery, so he'd have a map to buy his own oil leases from the other farmers around Daisy Bradford's farm, and of course, H. L. 'June' Hunt who brought his friend Pete Lake, who made a lot of money selling clothes in his store in El Dorado, Arkansas, where June Hunt lived. They all were all there, all smiles, and congratulating Jordan.

Jordan watched his superintendent direct the crew to keep digging trenches so the new oil could flow into more and more pits that they dug to hold and save the new black gold that kept on gurgling and flowing out of the ground. The oil kept flowing, and they kept digging, and Jordan kept pinching himself, not believing what he was seeing.

"Congratulations, Boss. Might be a good one. It's sure a damn good start. But like I've said, you'll never find any rest from drilling for oil once you're an oil man."

Jordan thought, *Maybe he's right, but right now, I'm here, and I'm happy, and I can't believe it. How did I get here in the first place? Maybe June Hunt will turn out to be right. Maybe I've found something good.*

Jordan couldn't stop thinking about June Hunt's warning: *Start buying more leases. This is a bigger oil field than anybody knows. Leave now. Spend every dollar you got buying more leases.*

So Jordan Phillips left his oil well, got in his truck, and started driving around the Piney Woods, stopping at every farm. He leased more land as fast as he could crisscross the Piney Woods from Kilgore up to White Oak, leasing small and large farms from farmers named Bumpus, Arthur Christian, Allan Tooke, and T. W. Lee. By the time he stopped talking to farmers, he had more than nine thousand acres of land leased for oil. When he drove into Gladewater, he took the road south to Tyler and came to the bridge over the Sabine where something hit him square in the face. Right here was where it all started.

He parked his truck on the town side of the bridge and walked down to the river and looked at the dark brown water.

He began to reminisce to himself about the time three years ago, when the river was flooding over its banks, almost a half mile wide, and he looked at that school of water moccasins struggling to swim upstream. Then he thought about the rodeo where Doc Berry had sold him his oil map, and he decided then and there to become an oil man, and how it all came true today. This was truly a day he would never forget.

Jordan got back in his truck and drove back to his oil well. The sun was setting and only a couple of hundred folks were still there. They were standing around smiling and talking and laughing, watching the black green oil belch out of the well and flow through the trenches into the mud pits. This had been a day that would change all of their lives.

So the #3 Daisy Bradford was completed, and the stock tanks were built, and Jordan sold ten thousand barrels of the oil that had flowed into the mud pits. The sale of this oil at one dollar a barrel gave him ten thousand dollars of new money. The Deep Rock well and several other wells were started in October around the Daisy Bradford Farm, and two other important wells were started: one near Kilgore and the other as far north as Longview. The world would soon know Jordan Phillips had discovered a real oil field.

CHAPTER SEVEN

JORDAN FELT LIKE he needed to tell his three investors how he had spent their money. He asked them to join him for breakfast in the coffee shop of the Gregg Hotel in Longview. John Henderson, the iron salesman and part owner of a company called Lufkin Industries, sat slouched in a rumpled suit across the table. "Jordan, I need some good news. The stock market is at 155 this morning, down from 297 in eight months. The fastest decline on record. It would sure be nice if my oil investment with you works out."

"Partners, keep this to yourselves, but the real story is that we have an oil well. It started out flowing 6,500 barrels a day, and the production fell off fast. It looks like it stabilized at 250 barrels a day. I'm expecting we'll have room to drill lots more oil wells. It looks like we've found an oil field."

Loyce Williams, the old bank president from Overton, sat straight in his chair with his white hair impeccably groomed, his tie bright red. "Well, somebody must agree with you. They're buying leases up and down the road from Overton as far as Kilgore, even up toward Longview. I had the best week of deposits in the history of the bank."

Jordan Phillips nodded. "The Deep Rock well about a mile

west of the #3 Bradford came in flowing 3,000 barrels a day of forty and a half gravity oil. H. L. Hunt has started a well to the south. We may have found a really big oil field."

"What does this all mean for our company, Jordan?" Sam Knight asked.

"We don't know how big of an oil field we've found, but I bought about 8,500 more acres of leases, and if it's a big oil field, we could have over a thousand oil wells to drill, maybe thousands. I don't know where I'll get the kind of money our company would need to drill all of those wells, but that's a bridge I hope I have to cross. I'll find the drilling money somewhere, and we'll keep drilling until we don't have any more places to drill."

The skin of Sam Knight's face was taut and sweaty. "Look, Phillips, I need cash. When can you start paying a dividend? I still got bills to pay from my wife's illness."

"I told you when you bought your stock that, as long as TOPCO was drilling wells, we were not paying any dividends."

"Okay, Phillips," the druggist said, "just remember, goddamn it, when you take money out of the company for yourself, don't forget we want money too."

"Sam, don't be so hard on Jordan. He's done what he said he would do. He found oil. We've got to give him time to see if he can make any money," John Henderson said. "What we're already seeing is the birth of an oil boom, and your businesses and mine will make a lot of money with all the people flooding in."

CHAPTER EIGHT

JORDAN PHILLIPS LIKED to daydream about the little part-Osage, part-French high-school principal's daughter coming to live with him in his oil field. She was so beautiful with her curly strawberry blonde hair and her cinnamon skin.

On a Saturday night back in Seminole County in Oklahoma, he went looking for her at the dance hall. When he didn't see her right away, he started worrying. Maybe she had forgotten him and had already found her oil man. Maybe she didn't think he had what it took to become an oil man anyway.

Then he saw her on the other side of the dance floor, laughing and pretty, stomping her feet, dancing and singing along with the dance hall band as it played "Cotton Eyed Joe."

Jordan felt goose bumps all over as he walked over to where she was dancing and tapped the shoulder of her dance partner, who frowned and shook his head "*no*" and kept dancing.

Jordan looked straight in Miss Charlotte's eyes, saying "please" with his. She looked at him and smiled and backed away from her partner and put her arms around Jordan, and without missing a step, she kept dancing and singing along with the band: "*If it hadn't been for Cotton Eyed Joe, I'd been married a long time ago. Where did you come from, where did you go, Cotton Eyed Joe?*"

She swung Jordan around the dance floor until the music was finished. She looked up into his face and asked him, "You an oil man yet?"

"Yes, I'm an oil man. Dance with me, and we'll go and look at the moon over the Canadian River. I'll tell you about the oil field I found in East Texas."

The fiddler started playing the "Kentucky Waltz," and Miss Charlotte grabbed Jordan again, this time pulling him closer and swinging him slower.

"What kind of music do they play at dance halls in East Texas? I like Oklahoma music, but I don't know about East Texas music."

"They play the 'Kentucky Waltz' down there too."

"How do I know you're really an oil man?" she said as they waltzed.

"Honey, I don't lie. Come go with me to look at the moon, and I'll tell you what happened. I'm not driving a pipe truck anymore."

After a few more dances, they left the dance hall, and he drove her to the banks of the Canadian River in his shiny new black Ford Model 'A' coupe with a rumble seat. They were in the middle of the Seminole Oil Field. It was nighttime, and the sky above was pitch black except for the large round bright yellow moon rising in the east and the flickering yellow flares of the oil wells as far as they could see in both directions along the river.

"I found an oil field down by Kilgore. Folks that know about those things are saying it could be the biggest oil field in the world. All these oil wells you see pumping right here on the river aren't nearly as many oil wells as I'm going to drill down in East Texas. Charlotte, come with me to my oil field. I'll get you a new car, and I'll build you a big house. You'll be the wife of the biggest oil man in Texas."

Standing with her in front of his Model 'A,' under the light of the moon and the lights of the oil well flares, he could almost see her blush. She put her arms around him and hugged him and said, "Jordan, are you asking me to marry you?"

"Yes, Charlotte, I am asking you to be mine. Will you marry me?"

"I always thought I loved you, and now you're an oil man, and I know I love you. If you're really an oil man, you need me. I got a good head for business, and I can help you run our oil company." She hugged him tight and covered him with kisses.

With the full moon high in the sky, Jordan took Charlotte home. They woke her parents and Jordan asked her father for Charlotte's hand in marriage. Charlotte's mother sat in a wing-back chair in her robe, her hair in curlers, yawning, while the two men sat on the sofa talking. Her father said, "We're happy Charlotte found you. She'll make you a good wife." He looked over at Charlotte, who was too excited to sit, standing by the fire-place, fiddling with photos of herself displayed on the mantle, rearranging them. "Her mother and I have taught her about the duties of a wife both at home in the kitchen and in the family business and everything that makes any difference. She will love and respect you. Right, Charlotte?"

"What, daddy?" she said, not really listening, but studying a picture of herself with long hair and taken when she was eleven or twelve in Indian dress dancing at the annual Osage celebration every August at Pawhuska.

"You're going to make Jordan a good wife."

"Sure, Daddy. Of course."

CHAPTER NINE

ON SUNDAY, DECEMBER 28th, Mrs. Lou Della Crim was in church praying at 11:30 AM when the Ed Bateman #1 Lou Della Crim Well came in on her land outside Kilgore. The well flowed at the rate of 22,000 barrels of clean pipe-line oil a day. Wallace Pratt, the head geologist for the Humble Oil and Refining Company, with one of his geologists, G. M. Knebel, had written a geological report a few years ago that the Woodbine in East Texas might be a big shoreline trap, a geological theory which was now turning out to be true. Pratt made a phone call to Bateman after the test of his well on the Crim land was public knowledge. He offered for Humble to buy Bateman's leases for one and a half million dollars cash and a payment out of oil in the amount of eight hundred thousand dollars or one million eight hundred thousand dollars total. That was the most money anybody had ever seen in the Piney Woods of East Texas—until a few weeks later.

At the end of January, 1931, W. A. Moncrief and John E. Farrell opened the master valve of their #1 Lathrop well north of Longview, and with 18,000 people watching and a sea of automobiles lined up on the road by the Lathrop well, history was made again. It flowed 320 barrels of 39.6 gravity oil in an hour, and if that well had been opened up, it would have flowed more than 20,000 barrels in one day. A week and a half later, Monty Moncrief and John Farrell and their partners sold out to Yount-Lee Oil Company for three million dollars cash.

Everybody started calling Jordan Phillips's oil field the "Black Giant." It was soon recognized that it was the largest oil field in the world at forty-five miles long and thirteen miles wide. No one could imagine how many tens of thousands of oil wells would be drilled in this enormous oil field.

There were many oil fields discovered in America by wildcatters drilling all over the country during that brief era of the most wildcatting for shallow oil in America. Sid Richardson and Clint Murchison from Athens decided more money could be made trading oil leases than trading cattle, and they drilled wildcat discovery oil wells not just in Ward and Winkler Counties in West Texas, but in other parts of Texas too. O. W. Killam used his doodlebug in South Texas near Laredo to find the purest crude in the shallow Mirando Sands.

None of the wildcat wells would discover more oil than Jordan Phillips discovered when he completed his #3 Daisy Bradford well and discovered the East Texas Oil Field. East Texas was bigger than Roy Cullen's Tom O'Connor Field and Tom Slick's discoveries in Oklahoma, including his new oil wells flowing 80,000 barrels a day in the Oklahoma City Field. It was larger than the prolific Yates Oil Field discovered by Mike Benedum and Joe Trees, wildcatting on a surface anticline in Pecos County in West Texas. There wasn't another oil field anywhere in the world as big as the 'Black Giant' until 1948 when Ghawar Field was discovered in Saudi Arabia.

Tens of thousands of people flooded into East Texas: lease hounds, major oil company men, independent oil men, land speculators, drillers, bartenders, merchants, gamblers, pimps, whores, as well as the bank robbers Bonnie Parker and Clyde Barrow and their gang and the lawmen chasing them. The white folks and the colored folks would get together at the joints on the Tyler Highway or on Highway 80 between Shreveport and Dallas, and they'd listen to The Ink Spots, Louis Armstrong, Nat 'King' Cole, Glenn Miller's and the Dorsey Brother's Orchestras, and Jack Teagarden's too. Many celebrities-to-be of that time got their start in show business in the bars in East Texas during the boom.

Jordan Phillips also became famous as the wildcatter who discovered the oil field and started the boom. A tent village was built between Henderson and Carthage, and they named it Phillipsville.

Thousands of wooden derricks were built almost overnight in the pine trees. The oil world was turned upside down. The boom was on.

CHAPTER TEN

J ORDAN HAD FOUND the oil field, but he didn't have any cash in the bank. When he brought Miss Charlotte to Kilgore, he didn't know how many oil wells he would have to drill or how long it would take him to drill them, but he told her he expected to become a very rich man in the next few years. She thought she was very rich when she said "I do." She never stopped asking him to give her money or to build her a large home or to buy her everything she ever wanted.

"But, honey, living is going to be tough at first in the oil field. With the boom on now, the only place I could find for us to live is a garage apartment, but it's got two bedrooms, and it's nice. It's got indoor plumbing."

"You said you were going to build me a big house."

"I will soon, darlin', but I can't yet. I've got to drill the oil wells first and get the money coming back to me. It won't be long before you'll have a house like you never dreamed."

So TOPCO drilled one oil well after the other. Chirp Branscum brought three more drilling rigs in to East Texas, and TOPCO had four rigs drilling all the time.

Oil men drilled 3,612 oil wells in Jordan's oil field in 1932.

That was just the beginning. The rigs weren't the only thing moving into East Texas. The rains came too.

Rain and mosquitos were everywhere, but the iron moved around in the oil field in spite of the rain, rain, and more rain and all the mud and all the trucks stuck in the mud. TOPCO and all the other oil companies would keep drilling until they drilled 27,000 or more oil wells to develop the Black Giant.

Spindletop oil field was discovered in 1903, and the State Fathers gave the authority to regulate oil wells in the state of Texas to the Railroad Commission of Texas because oil was sold and moved out of the Spindletop oil field by railroad train. That is why the Railroad Commission was regulating the East Texas Oil Field. The Railroad Commissioners ordered all the wells in the oil field to be opened up and tested for one hour. They produced at the combined rate of fifteen-million seven-hundred and seventy-seven thousand barrels of crude oil in one hour. Everybody knew that producing all the wells wide open like that would cause billions of barrels of oil reserves to be lost forever left underground, and if the wells were produced wide open, there would be no way the market could take all that oil. The price of crude oil collapsed to ten cents a barrel anyway without the wells being opened wide up, if an oil producer could even sell a barrel of oil. So the Governor of Texas shut down all the oil wells in the East Texas Oil Field. He declared martial law and called up the Texas National Guard to enforce the shutdown of the oil field.

The Governor let the oil field open up again to produce oil after the Railroad Commission issued an order that oil wells in the field could produce only a restricted amount of oil, which was two hundred and sixty-five barrels a day.

Jordan Phillips slammed his fist on the scarred-up old pine desk in his TOPCO office in the yard out in the field and growled, "It's communism to tell a man how much oil he can produce. Communism." He looked out his window at a sea of mud and oil.

"Maybe we ought to sell out and go back to Oklahoma," Chirp said.

"Oh, shut up, Chirp."

CHAPTER ELEVEN

ORDAN WAS GETTING richer with new oil reserves deep underground, but he was cash poor up at the top of the ground. He still couldn't afford to build the big home that he had promised Miss Charlotte that he'd build.

All she knew was that she was home alone and the oil wells in downtown Kilgore kept getting closer and closer. She'd stand outside the front door and hold the screen door open and watch a truck dumping steel for a derrick in the empty lot across the street where only a week ago a feed store stood, then she'd close the screen door and walk back upstairs into their apartment and look out the front window and see that the derrick builders had already started assembling the new derrick, and the derrick next door to the derrick being built was literally touching it. That derrick next door was supporting a drilling rig with the bit turning to the right down in the bottom of the hole, and in the derrick next to that one, a flare had been burning all day. A new flare, according to Jordan, was oil burning from a new oil well coming in.

Sometimes Charlotte would sit on a big couch in the living room and look out the window and watch the circus which was the oil boom. The big couch was comfortable and soft, with down padded cushions and a table beside it holding a bright lamp so she'd have good light when she wanted to read. She had some books there she always wanted to read like *The Great Gatsby* and *A Farewell to Arms*. But with all the noise of the engines and the clanging of the pipe in the derricks, she never could concentrate enough to read her books, so she'd wander around the three rooms of the apartment looking out one window and then the next thinking, *I hate this oil field. Why did I let myself get into this mess?*

She was totally dismayed when she saw the steeple of the Church of Christ being torn down across the street where just last Sunday, people were praying in church. It wouldn't be long before another oil well was drilling where all the Christians were praying. Soon, there would be more than a thousand oil derricks inside the city limits of Kilgore, and then every Christmas people would come from all around to see the derricks in downtown Kilgore all lit with strings of colored lights and bright stars representing the Star of Bethlehem on the tops of the oil derricks.

Jordan would come home at night, and he and Charlotte would walk outside in the dark. She would always count eight or nine fires. She could never forget her uncle being burned to death in an oil field fire when she was a child growing up in Seminole.

"Jordan, I'm scared," she told him one night when they were standing outside. "I can't believe there are all these fires. I hate fires, and I hate the oil field, and I want my own house. With all these oil wells you're drilling, I don't understand why you can't find the money to build me a house."

"Charlotte, drilling all these oil wells takes more money than I have. If you can be patient, it won't be long before I'll build you a fine home, and you'll never see another oil field fire. But, you know, those fires are good fires. New oil wells coming in, signs of growth and more money someday for you and me."

"But you're always gone all day. I need something to do. I want to help you run your business. Let me go with you and show you how I can help you make money. Then we can go out and have some fun at night."

"Well, Charlotte, darling, where would you go to have some fun?"

"You could take me out dancin' to Mattie's Ball Room. I hear that's where everybody has fun in Kilgore."

"How about tomorrow night?"

"Jordan, let's go right now. Tonight."

So Jordan showered and shaved and changed into a clean white shirt and some clean khaki pants. Miss Charlotte put on her best dress and her high heels and was as beautiful as any young curly haired blonde girl could be going dancing with her young husband.

Mattie's Ball Room was full of people having a good time. As many as four hundred oil field people were drinking beer and talking loud and dancing to the music of Jack Teagarden's band. The crowd turned quiet when the most famous couple in East Texas walked into the room. Many whispered, "There he is. That's Jordan Phillips, the young millionaire wildcatter, and look at that beautiful blonde on his arm. She must be the Indian Princess he brought from Oklahoma." If there was royalty in the East Texas Oil Field, Jordan Phillips and his bride were it.

The band was playing Jack Teagarden's old favorites, "After You've Gone," and "The St. Louis Blues." Jordan took Miss Charlotte to the dance floor, and she was smiling and warming to the beat of the music, and she liked having all the eyes of the crowd on her. She was becoming excited about having a night of fun. Jordan held her tight and swung her around the dance floor.

All the couples dancing and sitting at the tables around the dance floor were from the oil field. One of the men sitting with his wife and watching Jordan and Charlotte dancing was a tall and handsome fellow, a member of a roughneck crew drilling for Jordan's company.

The roughneck must have wanted to make some kind of impression on his boss and on the crowd too. He walked up to the first couple of the oil field while they were dancing, and he tapped his boss's shoulder to cut in and dance with Miss Charlotte.

Jordan, surprised but smiling, was, as usual, very polite. He shook hands with the tall roughneck and handed Charlotte over to him for the next dance, and he returned to their table. Charlotte was never a girl to be shy. She wrapped one arm around the tall roughneck's back and the other around his neck. She held him close and looked into his eyes. In complete control, he swung her around, dancing to the beat of the "Muskrat Ramble."

She never stopped looking into the eyes of her new dancing partner, and he looked straight into hers. They danced at least four songs holding each other close and staring into each other's eyes, without a smile and never saying a word.

Jordan sat alone at his table drinking a beer. He ordered a second. He stared at the dance floor, obviously not happy, and he began to think about making his rounds in the oil field the next day. He didn't show any emotion about the attention his wife was giving another man, but on the inside he reached a slow boil.

Miss Mattie witnessed the flirtation not knowing what to do until the wife of the roughneck came up to her and said, "Miss Mattie, that woman is hot for my husband. You go up there and break them up, and tell my husband I'm gone. Tell him I went home by myself."

When Jack Teagarden's music stopped the flirtation ended. Miss Charlotte went back to Jordan sitting at his table drinking his beer. When the music ended, Jordan stood and silently walked out of Mattie's Ballroom with Charlotte walking behind him.

"Well, I hope you had your night of fun dancing at Mattie's Ballroom with your roughneck."

"Jordan, he was a fine dancer, and I'll bet his wife has a home bigger than mine."

CHAPTER TWELVE

IN 1933, THE oil men drilled another 5,560 oil wells in the East Texas Oil Field. That brought the total number of wells drilled in the field to 9,372 oil wells. At the end of the year, TOPCO was producing fifteen thousand barrels of oil a day out of the hundred and twenty-five oil wells it had drilled. Jordan and Chirp were on the way to establishing TOPCO as the largest independent producer in the oil field, and possibly, in not too many more years, the largest independent oil company in Texas.

"Jordan, what'll you do when it's over?"

"When what's over? What are you talking about, Chirp?"

"When the drilling's done, I'll bet you'll have almost two thousand oil wells, then the bad stuff will begin to happen. You're going to wake up and wonder how in the hell you're going to replace all the oil you've been producing."

"Why talk about that now, Chirp?"

"You oil guys are always too late to learn that nothing in the oil patch is forever."

In the real world of East Texas, the oil market was flooded. On some days, oil couldn't be sold for ten cents a barrel. All Jordan could worry about was how was he going to sell a barrel of his oil, and he decided he had to have the option to refine his own oil into gasoline. Sometimes it was easier to sell gasoline than oil, especially when you couldn't give a barrel of oil away.

"Chirp, find us a piece of land and build a gasoline plant. We can sell gasoline to the folks easier than we can sell crude oil to those damn major oil companies. Build the refinery on a railroad, so when we have to, we can move our gasoline or even our crude oil out by train."

In a few days, Chirp Branscum told his boss, "I found twenty acres over in Gladewater next to the railroad track on the east side of the school house. We can build a twenty-five-hundred-barrel-a-day gasoline plant for about fifty thousand dollars. We'll have four flowing oil well Christmas trees inside the plant, and we can open those wells up and rent us a train load of tank cars and fill 'em with crude and ship to wherever you want."

"We can ship to New Orleans and store it in a tank farm and sell it into the market at a hell of a profit when the price comes back."

The only tank cars the railroad company could find to lease were in Canada. When the train of empty tank cars pulled on the train tracks next to the refinery yard in Gladewater, most of the empty tank cars had bottles of bootleg whiskey hanging on a string from the top, swinging loose down inside the empty tank. The bootleg entrepreneurs in Canada thought they had found a way to market their rot gut into the United States.

"Boss, who do you think was supposed to buy those bottles of booze?"

"We'll never know, Chirp, but I bet whoever was supposed to sell it would have got a hell of a lot more money than the ten cents a barrel we'd be getting for crude oil. It's probably worth about fifty dollars a gallon, and that, my friend, would be more than two thousand dollars a barrel of bootleg booze."

"Something's got to happen. We can't run this oil field on

ten-cent oil. Something has to happen or this oil field will be a total bust."

"Something will happen. The Commission's going to shut down the whole damn field again on the first of the month. I'm getting a thirty-day injunction in Federal Court against the Railroad Commission so we can open up our wells and fill this train full of oil."

Standing between the main boiler and the tin door into the refinery laboratory with his grease-covered Stetson in his hand, Chirp said, "I guess it's either we move it to New Orleans or become bootleggers ourselves. Thank God for your brains, Boss. I'm glad one of us has brains."

Once again, the Railroad Commission shut down the East Texas Oil Field, and the Texas National Guard was again called up to enforce the shutdown. When they opened the field back up the Commission ordered that a producer was allowed to produce only an allowable prorated amount of oil from an oil well. There was still so much easy oil to produce in the East Texas Field that a five-year-old child could fill a thousand-barrel tank by just turning a valve open, not any harder to turn open than the faucet of a bathtub. Good church-going people believed, right or wrong, that the law of capture gave them the right to capture and sell any oil that they could put in a barrel, but the state had the right to restrict the number of barrels of oil produced, and if any oil was sold without a State Allowable, it became illegal "hot oil."

Texas Ranger Manuel "Lone Wolf" Gonzaullas was on the lookout for "hot oil" traders and bootleggers. He usually worked alone but holstered a pair of Colt .45s to help keep the peace. He'd traced one bypass pipeline delivering secret oil from four oil wells. Lone Wolf discovered that the mysterious pipeline disappeared underneath one side of a home and came out on the other side. When the Ranger searched the suspicious home, always a gentleman, he waited two hours for the lady of the house to come out of her bathroom. When he finally went into the master bathroom, he opened a cabinet door, and instead of finding bath towels, he found a large valve. Gonzaullas opened the valve inside the cabinet in the bathroom and heard the "hot oil" flow through the hidden pipeline at a rate that he soon discovered to be five hundred barrels of oil in one hour.

CHAPTER THIRTEEN

HOUSING WAS SCARCE, and oil men looking for a place to sleep often showed up unannounced at Miss Charlotte's door, sometimes telling her that Jordan had invited them to stay overnight in their extra bedroom.

Late one afternoon, a young man and an older man knocked on the door and introduced themselves to Miss Charlotte. At first, she wondered whether they were a grandfather and his grandson, but they didn't look alike at all.

The young man said, "Mrs. Phillips, my name is Algur Meadows, and Jordan told me you all had an extra bed if we couldn't find any place to sleep. This is my partner, J. W. Gilliland. We would sure be glad if we could spend the night in your extra bedroom."

They wore nice suits and had clean fingernails.

"Please come in. I'm always glad to have company around. Mr. Gilliland, I am from Seminole County in the oil field in Oklahoma, and it seems like I heard of Gilliland Oil Company before."

"Yes, ma'am. I was at Wewoka and Allen in Seminole and at Papoose too. Then there was Cushing and Drumright. This must be about my eighth or ninth boom," the older man said.

Charlotte wondered how two men with such an age difference ever got together as partners, but she guessed that maybe since they were business partners, they didn't mind sleeping in the same double bed. She knew they weren't oil field workers thinking about a day job. They were obviously successful businessmen driven to make money in the oil field.

She didn't mind having these clean, well-dressed men around. She listened to them talking about starting a new oil company, and she heard them say they would name the company the General American Oil Company of Texas. She agreed with what they were saying, and just listening and agreeing made her feel that she had as much business sense as any man.

One evening, Algur Meadows and J. W. Gilliland sat around the table and talked after eating Miss Charlotte's fried chicken and mashed potatoes. They were talking about selling some oil wells to pay off some debt and clean up their company's balance sheet so they could use it as a platform to grow what Al Meadows kept saying had potential to become a large oil company.

The older man didn't seem as interested in building a big company, but he was agreeable to selling those oil wells. J. W. Gilliland loved drilling oil wells, and he was more interested in talking about these two scientist brothers from France he had heard about, Marcel and Conrad Schlumberger, who had invented an electric method for locating underground deposits of iron. "But," Mr. Gilliland said, "they have figured out a way to lower this electrical recorder down into an oil well and pull it out as they shoot an electric shock out to the side, and they have someone up at the top on the ground recording by hand the electrical measurement of the rocks underground as the gadget is pulled up, and, listen to this, Al and Jordan, they say it actually takes a picture of the rock formations." Jordan was sitting there listening to all this talk. He was more interested in what they said about selling some oil wells to get cash and clean up their balance sheet than he was about hearing of these French doodlebuggers electrical well recorder.

Miss Charlotte stood next to the sink doing the dishes while she listened to everything the men said as they sat and talked in the area next to the little kitchen in the Phillips' garage apartment where there was a sofa and a couple of chairs, which let Charlotte call it her living room. At the end of the conversation Al Meadows and J. W. Gilliland were having, Jordan told them that if they'd let him, he'd like to buy the forty-six oil wells the two partners wanted to sell, and with that, Jordan's two guests were freed to start their new oil company. TOPCO had another forty-six oil wells to operate.

The next morning at breakfast, Charlotte said to Jordan, "I'm tired of doing the cooking, and you making the business deals. I heard you buying those oil wells last night. Why can't I do business deals too? You gave them their price, but I would have bought those oil wells for less money. Anyway, I want my half of those forty-six oil wells. You bought them with both our money."

"C'mon, Charlotte, get serious."

"And I want a home—a big home. Now. I'm not waiting any longer. I can't stand this garage apartment. We've visited all your oil field friends in their new stone mansions with huge lawns and gardens and white board fences that run around their property for miles. If you won't build me a mansion, I'm going back to Oklahoma."

"Honey, be patient. The money is finally starting to roll in. Give me just a little time."

CHAPTER FOURTEEN

ONE NIGHT IN March, when springtime started to show its head, and the flowers were blooming, Miss Charlotte met Jordan at the door with fury in her eyes. "I can't be left here in this apartment any longer by myself. The noise of all the drilling never stops."

She was waving her arms around, and Jordan thought she might be ready to smack him. "Honey, I want to go dancing again. I saw in the paper that Mattie's Ballroom is having this colored horn player from New Orleans playing tonight, and he's supposed to be something special."

"You want to go back to Mattie's so you can dance with that roughneck. That tall guy. That's what you think is special."

"You get jealous, and you might just get what you worry about."

"What you need is a baby to keep you company."

"We'll see about that. I want to go hear that colored trumpet player tonight."

The tall roughneck and his wife weren't there. The colored jazz singer and trumpet player from New Orleans was Louis Armstrong, and Charlotte loved his gravelly voice singing "When it's Sleepy Time Down South," and, with the crowd clapping and singing along, he gave his rendition of "Ain't Misbehavin'."

Jordan, however, seemed distracted and sat gazing off into space.

'What's wrong with you?" Charlotte asked.

Jordan looked at her, smiled. "I'm sorry. Just thinking about some deals I need to close."

Charlotte pinched Jordan on the cheeks and looked him in the eyes. "If you really want to make money, you ought to turn your deal closing over to me."

"But you've never closed any deals. You don't know—"

"Honey, take me home, and let me show you how I can close a deal with you. You've never had anyone be as friendly as I'm gonna be tonight."

In August, the dog days of summer were too hot for Miss Charlotte to spend much time outside, so she stayed inside their garage apartment with the window fan on high. One August day, she woke up feeling low and didn't get out of bed. She just lay around in her nightgown and picked up *The Great Gatsby.*

In my younger and more vulnerable years my father gave me some advice that I've been turning over in my mind ever since. "Whenever you feel like criticizing anyone," he told me, "just remember that all the people in this world haven't had the advantages that you've had."

She put the book down. It made her angry to think of how Jordan had brought her to East Texas making her think he was so rich and had all these advantages. Like he was this wealthy oil man, and she would have whatever she wanted, including a fine home. She couldn't concentrate on Scott Fitzgerald or Gatsby or West Egg, Long Island, or wherever in the hell this man named Gatsby was from, so she turned on the Victrola, put on a record, and listened to Tommy Dorsey's band.

After all morning in bed and nothing but a peanut butter

and jelly sandwich for lunch, she was feeling sorry for herself and she felt weak. She called the drug store and asked to speak to the pharmacist. The druggist picked up the phone and said, "Hello, pharmacist. May I help you?"

"Well, I hope so, or I wouldn't have called you."

When he learned that his caller was the wife of Jordan Phillips, the man that had sold him stock in his company, he wanted to talk to her. The more oil wells that were completed on the block with his drug store, the madder Sam Knight got. He couldn't stand thinking that the biggest oil field in the world was discovered with his money, yet he had never made a single dime. Maybe there would be some way he could get word of his anger through her to her husband.

"Oh yes. Missus Phillips, what can I do for you?"

"I'm feeling low with all these oil wells drilling all around me."

"Well, you're not the only one bothered, ma'am. How do you think I feel? There's twelve drug stores in Kilgore now with this oil boom and another one being finished. You must know that I know your husband."

"I don't know who my husband knows, but I have a backache. Do you have something in your drug store that could make my back stop hurting?"

"We have a tonic should make you feel real good and a liniment you can rub on your back. It's best you start right away, a tablespoon now, and then another one every three hours until you feel better."

"Can you bring it over?"

"I have a delivery boy. He can bring it over in a couple of hours."

"Why can't you bring it now? I want to meet you, and I'm feelin' so low that I'm still in bed."

He paused and thought about the possibilities. He'd seen her, and the possibilities were damn attractive. "Well, alright. I'll get there as soon as I can get away from the store."

In fifteen minutes, Charlotte heard a knock downstairs on the front door. She raised her voice loud enough for to be heard down there. "Is that you, Mr. Knight?"

"Yes, ma'am. Drug store."

"The door's unlocked. Come on upstairs. I'm back in the bedroom."

Sam Knight went in the apartment up the stairs and all the way back to the bedroom. He found Charlotte Phillips in bed under the covers, still in her nightgown. 2:00 P.M. was awfully late to be in bed clothes, he thought.

"Sorry, took me longer than I thought it would to get here from the store. Main Street was blocked with all those trucks bringing in another drilling rig. I guess I'll have to move. H. L. Hunt will pay anything to buy my property. He wants to tear down the store and all the buildings on the block so he can drill four more oil wells. Sorry you are feeling bad, ma'am."

"Don't sell him your property. We don't need four more of those awful oil wells. What did you bring me, Mr. Knight? Something for my back, I hope."

"This tonic will fix anything, Mrs. Phillips."

You can call me Charlotte. Isn't there a Mrs. Knight?"

"And you call me Sam. My wife got malaria and died when Sam, Jr., was only a baby."

"Oh, Sam, I'm sorry. I didn't realize."

"Don't worry about that. She was so sick. Sam and I are making it just fine. You know, I am an investor in your husband's company, TOPCO. Now, ma'am, tell me where does it hurt?"

"Well, I knew that Jordan had to sell some stock to keep drilling, and I didn't realize you were one of the ones who invested. But, as far as me, it's my back, my lower back. Come over here and let me show you. Jordan doesn't talk business with me, and I hate this oil field." She was still lying face down on her stomach. She reached around behind her back and pulled the sheet down to her waist.

"Well," the druggist said, "you don't need a tonic. You need some ointment rubbed into your back. I brought this liniment that should stop the pain if you rub it on your back."

"Why don't you rub it on my back?"

"I do most anything that helps a person. You know, a country druggist is almost like a doctor. Trying to heal people is all we think about." He started rubbing the liniment into her back, and she moaned.

"Sam, it's feeling better. Don't stop."

From then on, he'd come to the Phillips' apartment every Wednesday afternoon.

CHAPTER FIFTEEN

ON JANUARY 1ST, 1934, a daughter was born to Charlotte and Jordan Phillips. Her name was January. They called her "Jan" for short. Nine months earlier, Charlotte hadn't known Sam Knight, at least not in the Biblical sense yet, so she knew Jordan was the father. The baby had Jordan's curly hair.

Jordan found a colored mammy named Annie, who lived in the black community known as Friendship. She was married to Sully, and they had a son named Herman, and every day, Annie would ride the county bus into Kilgore to help Charlotte with the baby.

Charlotte was as unhappy as ever. She complained to Jordan about everything, especially about the wives of the oil field service and supply salesmen.

"Erle Halliburton's cement salesman's wife asked me to play golf on Tuesday, which she said was Ladies Day, and since I don't play golf, she said, 'Well, how about playing bridge with my bridge club on Wednesdays?' So I played bridge, and she and all those other salesmen's wives got tight as ticks on Tom Collins.

"I'm never playing bridge with them ever again, but the pipe salesman, Mike Hazel's wife, asked me to play Mah Jong with her on Friday."

"Bridge is good exercise for the mind, and Erle's salesman's wife is just trying to help her husband cell cement," Jordan said. "I never heard of Mah Jong. Why don't we go out to eat tonight, Charlotte?"

"I'd have to take the baby."

"Get Annie to take the baby home for the night with her, and we'll go out on the town."

"You mean let her take my baby to Friendship?"

"Sure. The blacks love babies, and they'll take good care of Jan. You and I can go get a steak over at Casey's. Who knows, maybe we can come home and see if we can make another baby."

"You shut up. You must be kidding. I love Jan, but I don't want another baby, not here in this oil field. And listen to me, Jordan Phillips, I'll never do anything like you're talking about with you ever again unless you build me my own home."

"Well, honey, I was going to tell you, I've made plans to build you a mansion. It's going to be bigger than any of the other homes in the oil field."

"It's about time you built me a home, but you've got to take me to Neiman Marcus in Dallas. I need some decent clothes if I'm going to have a new house, and when we got engaged, you never bought me a diamond, so when we go to Dallas, we'll go see that man from Linz Brothers, Clarence Badt, who comes around here trying to sell me rings, and you can take of that little obligation too."

Driving Miss Charlotte to Dallas turned into a fiasco. Jordan thought he was taking her just to buy a new dress at Neiman's and a diamond ring at Linz Brothers Jewelers. Little did he know how much money she would end up spending and how much this trip would end up costing him.

On the way to Dallas, he told her, "Honey, I told you I was building you a home."

"Yes, and I told you it was about time."

"Well, I bought the land in the River Bottom on my oil lease from Allison Money next to where I have eighty-five flowing oil wells in his watermelon patch. I've got the plans for the house already, and here's the best part: it's going to be a log cabin."

"What are you talking about? Why would I want a log cabin? You aren't Abraham Lincoln, and I'm not dumpy old Mrs. Lincoln. I want a home, not a log cabin. Heaven forbid."

"It will be a big log cabin built out of pine tree logs. Twelve thousand square feet. The first air-conditioned home in East Texas. I want it to be a home that you will love and will make you feel good about life in the oil field."

"I'll try to learn to like it, but I don't know how I'll ever learn to live in this awful oil field. Will we have help at this cabin? I didn't marry you to kill myself being my own maid."

"Honey, of course there will be cabins for the help."

"I want room for a piano. I was pretty good playing Cole Porter and George Gershwin back home."

"You can have a piano too. You can have anything you want."

When they got to Dallas, Jordan opened a charge account for Miss Charlotte at Neiman's. He had never seen five thousand dollars charged so fast. He was far more astounded at what happened at Linz Brothers Jewelers. Clarence Badt, the manager of Linz Brothers, was there. Charlotte had seen Clarence before in East Texas, when on one of his regular trips he would call on her or Jordan showing jewelry he had for sale.

When they went into the Linz Brothers Jewelry store, Jordan said, "Show us some rings, Clarence? Like I have been telling you back home, it's time for Charlotte to have a diamond engagement ring,"

"Here's a nice selection of diamond rings on gold settings that match Mrs. Phillips's wedding band. We can easily find a nice gold setting for the loose diamonds. Look at these, Miss Charlotte, and tell me what you think." Clarence Badt placed three diamond rings and two loose diamonds on the counter in front of them.

Charlotte frowned. "They're all so small."

"This stone is two carats, and this one is four and a half."

Jordan peered at them and asked, "How much they cost?"

"The four and a half carat stone is $2,500."

"Since it's the engagement ring I never got Charlotte, let's get that one. Put that biggest one on your finger, honey, and see how it looks."

Without even putting it on, Charlotte said, "It's too small. I can hardly see that diamond. Don't you have a real diamond?"

The Linz Brothers manager went to the back of the store to look for a larger stone. He returned with a ring with a real rock mounted on it. "This is the biggest stone in the store. Twelve-carats."

Charlotte's eyes lit up at the size and shine of it. "I want it, Jordan."

"Clarence, how much is that one?"

"Twenty-four thousand dollars. Two thousand a carat."

"Honey, why don't you wait for the rock, and let's take the ring with the four and a half carat stone for your engagement ring, and you can wear it home. It looks good on your hand. I'll write Clarence the check for $2,500."

"If I can't have a real diamond, I don't want a diamond." She walked out of Linz Brothers as fast as she could and headed down Main Street to the parking lot where Jordan had parked his car.

With a frown on his face and shaking his head, the wildcatter was left standing alone next to the counter in the jewelry store. He turned to Clarence Badt and said, "I don't know what to tell you, except on your next trip to East Texas, Clarence, bring both of those rings. Of course you must know, I'll be buying them both."

In a few months, Jordan would be ushering his wife, with her diamond engagement ring on her ring finger and her new twelve-carat diamond ring on her right hand, into the finest new home in East Texas. "I hope you enjoy your log cabin, Charlotte. It gets hot on the Sabine in July, but you don't need to worry about the heat, this will be the first air-conditioned home in East Texas."

"The air conditioning will help, but I'll never be here in this God awful mosquito-filled hell hole of heat and humidity in July. We could move to Dallas and run our oil business from there, but if I must live in this oil field, I'll admit, life would be better in a home like this."

"Sit down with me here, Charlotte, and let me talk to you about our new life." Jordan motioned for her to sit beside him on the large red leather couch in the Great Room.

"We'll have enough servants to keep the Log Cabin clean, and they'll take care of the stables and raise a big vegetable garden too. Chirp built four cabins behind the barn where four families of help can live: all painted light brown with wood shingle roofs and two of the nicest outhouses between them, both two-holers."

"I hope you're not making me treat these colored people like slaves. How many coloreds are coming? Is Annie's husband joining her too?"

"Yes, he's coming. His name is Sully. He will be my man. He and Annie are bringing their boy, Herman. He's smart, and he can help his dad with the horses in the stables and with my things. They are fine folks, and, at first, there'll be seven adults, including Sully's brother Earl and his wife Minnie B and their kids and two other families of their relatives from the Friendship colored settlement. You won't have to raise a finger to do anything. You can take up oil painting, you can ride horseback, or you can play the piano. Charlotte, I hope you'll give life in the Log Cabin a chance."

"I'll try, Jordan. I'll try."

Waiting for dark on the deck around the pool became the best time of day for Jordan after he and Charlotte moved into the Log Cabin. Some nights Charlotte would sit with him.

"Can I get you a drink, Mistuh Phillips?" Sully in his clean and starched white jacket would ask him when he was sitting on the deck with Miss Charlotte at sundown.

"Dewar's on the rocks, Sully."

"And what can I bring you, Miss Charlotte?"

"Sully, bring me a martini—a vodka martini—straight up with an olive, but bring it in to the piano. I'm going inside to play."

While Sully went to the bar to get their highballs, Miss Charlotte went inside to play the piano. Sometimes she would sing the words to the George Gershwin songs she played.

As the sun would set, Jordan would sit outside on the deck and sip his scotch and look at the flares of his eighty-five flowing oil wells in the field south of the Cabin where watermelons used to grow. Then, as darkness came, all of a sudden millions of fireflies would appear from nowhere, blinking and flashing, an overture preceding the raising of Mother Nature's curtain, exposing for all to see, a symphony of light rolling across the heavens in full-color presentation of yellows, reds, and, eventually, the solid orange of the burning nighttime sky of East Texas from the flares of 20,000 oil wells producing a half a million barrels of oil a day—a spectrum of light merged into one solid bright glowing sky, visible as far as Jordan's eyes could see.

Only one man in the world could watch this symphony of light and know that he alone was responsible for the nighttime sky in East Texas. Only Jordan Phillips could experience that feeling of ecstasy and the pride of what he had accomplished.

Sitting there under the bright yellow oil field sky he would hear Miss Charlotte's playing her piano, singing Gershwin, *"Someday he'll come along, the man I love,"* and he'd wonder if he was really that man who had come along for her to love.

He was comforted by the peace and security that he felt his oil field brought him forever, never giving any thought to the possibility of his tranquility ever coming to any surprising end.

CHAPTER SIXTEEN

J ORDAN SAT BEHIND his desk in his office in TOPCO'S one story wood frame office building in front of the refinery. There were now 22,000 oil wells in the East Texas Oil Field producing a regulated limit of 470,000 barrels of oil a day. He had expanded the TOPCO Refinery to run 5,000 barrels a day.

Twenty-four hours a day, tank trucks with the TOPCO'S bright red spinning top logo painted on their doors and the words "Rich-Tane" painted below the spinning top, were lined up in two rows at the refinery gates patiently waiting their turn to either unload crude oil or to pick up a load of gasoline. TOPCO now had 227 filling stations across Texas, Arkansas, and Louisiana. In 1937, Jordan expected to deposit over a million dollars cash in the bank from TOPCO'S crude-oil refining and gasoline marketing activity.

Jordan's secretary, Merle Francisco, came into his office and said, "Jordan, is it okay to take a hundred dollars cash out of the safe to send down to the loading dock so the guys can pay for a delivery of crude oil?"

"Why cash? The freelance crude buyers are on a monthly pay schedule."

"Not this guy. He told our man that the only way he'll unload his truck is C.O.D. His name is Eddie Scurlock, and he says he's buying more trucks, and if we want his business, it's C.O.D, take it or leave it."

"Sure, Merle. Take out the hundred bucks and send it down to the loading dock, and pay that guy."

"I'll do it, Jordan. But something else, I was going through the files, and I found that you started drilling the first well on the Bradford Lease ten years ago."

"So?"

"It seems to me that the tenth anniversary of an event so important is a milestone you ought to celebrate."

"Maybe so. Too bad Daisy's gone. She'd love to throw a barbecue for us down on her farm right there up the hill from the discovery well."

"Her Miller relatives are still around. And there're folks all over Texas as far away as San Antonio and Houston and even in Louisiana at Shreveport living better lives because of you. Gregg County is the richest county in America. Does it ever make you feel guilty about us in East Texas being so prosperous when the rest of the country is still in a deep depression?"

"I don't feel one twinge of guilt. I feel proud. Our success has made the whole country more prosperous. We're building new schools and new highways all around the state. The highways in Gregg County have been paved with the whitest cement anyone has ever seen. Here in East Texas, we're paving the way for a new beginning for the rest of the country."

"That's why you need to celebrate. There hasn't been prosperity like this anywhere in the country since the prosperity in the South before the Civil War. My hometown, Charleston, was one of the most prosperous cities in the world, before the War of Northern Aggression."

"You're right, Merle. That's a good comparison. Our country

had never seen prosperity like the South before the Civil War, until now, right here in East Texas.

"Well, you did it, Jordan, and you need to have a party and celebrate! We'll decorate the tables with cornucopias of fruit and vegetables and happiness flowing out of horns of plenty, and the guests can say thanks to you."

"I don't want to be thanked, but I wouldn't mind a little partying, raising a glass and celebrating. It's a great idea, but she'd never let me do it."

Merle paused to think. "Charlotte? But it's not her celebration, it's yours. It was your discovery, not hers. And, besides, I think you may be wrong."

"Why?"

"She's happier. She likes The Log Cabin. She might like the idea of helping you host a big party, especially if you invite celebrities."

CHAPTER SEVENTEEN

THAT NIGHT AT dinner, Jordan and Miss Charlotte sat as they always sat at either end of the long dining table at the end of the Great Room in the Log Cabin waiting for Sully to serve dinner. The ceiling of the Great Room was two and a half stories high. Heavy, oversized dark red leather chairs and couches in the center of the room invited all who were there to sit and relax in front of the flames of the crackling fires that would burn in all three fireplaces during the months of the winter. The Great Room was large, and the dining room table was long, and the man and his wife had to raise their voices when they talked to be heard.

The walls of the Great Room were covered by several works of Western Art that Jordan had been buying, including three Charles Russell oils he had acquired from Kennedy Galleries in New York. "Meat's Not Meat 'Til it's in the Pan," "A Doubtful Handshake," and "A Strenuous Life" were scenes of cowboy life in the Old West that highlighted the pioneer spirit of the cowboy. Jordan believed that was the spirit oil wildcatters possessed, a spirit he wanted to memorialize in his art collection. Two Frederic Remington Bronzes were resting on tables in the Great Room, "The Bronco Buster" (Number 25) and the small version of "Coming through the Rye" (Number 5) all contributed to a feeling that Great Room was an inviting place to relax.

"Sully, what's Annie serving for dinner tonight?" Mrs. Phillips asked her servant as he poured her tea.

"Ma'am, Annie's servin' fried chicken and mashed potatoes an' fried okra and corn pone. She jus' took the corn bread out of the oven, and it's all hot and sho' does smell good. Y'all goan like yo' supper, Miz Phillips," Sully said, standing there, proud, in his white jacket.

"Thank you, Sully."

They sat there waiting for dinner. Jordan said, "Charlotte, in a few months, ten years will have passed since I started drilling the first well on Daisy Bradford's farm."

"Time passes, doesn't it, Jordan?"

"For some of us around here, this ten years is an important milestone."

"It means I've lived in this oil field longer than I ever thought I would."

"Merle thinks we ought to celebrate the tenth anniversary with a party out here at the Cabin."

"I'm not much on big parties, Jordan. You know that. Who would you invite? Those oil field workers from the company camp?" Sully put plates of Annie's soul food in front of them.

"I'd invite everybody I know in the oilfield and their wives too, from Gladewater and Kilgore, Arp, Longview, Greggton, and White Oak. Even the folks all the way down to Carthage," he said as he reached for a steaming piece of Annie's legendary cornbread. Fresh out of the oven.

The secret recipe had been passed down from her great-grandmother. "Made with huh love," Annie'd say. Its wonderful aroma filled the room as Sully placed a large plate of fresh churned butter next to the cornbread. As was his custom, Jordan cut the bread down the middle, then took a large dollop of soft fresh butter with his knife and slowly spread it down the middle of the piping hot bread. Always from left to right because it was better that way. He waited a few seconds to make sure the bread was thoroughly lathered. Jordan smiled. There were never any leftovers of Annie's cornbread.

"Would you even invite those pipe salesmen?"

"Charlotte, these people are wonderful folks, the salt of the earth. I'd have TOPCO'S field hands and their wives and everybody from the oil company camps and everybody we do business with in East Texas."

"Good God. So you'd invite all those people who live in those camps?"

"Of course. I could have never found this oil field without Chirp Branscum, Maria Julia, and their kids, who have grown up in my company camp, and I was thinking I might invite some of the politicians from Austin. Last week when I was down at the Commission, I ran into this lawyer from St. Augustine named Ed Clark. He was on the Governor's staff, but the Governor appointed him Secretary of State. He was really a nice guy, and he's an East Texas boy. He might enjoy coming and helping me celebrate."

"But, why would you invite him, Jordan?"

"Well, why not? He's the Secretary of State in Texas, and Governor Allred must have liked him or else he wouldn't have appointed him Secretary of State. I'll bet if we invite Secretary Clark to come to East Texas, he'd bring the Governor with him."

"The Governor? Would he come?"

"Governor Allred's a politician. He wouldn't miss the chance to celebrate the biggest oil field in Texas. I bet he'd come and bring half the state government with him."

"Well, that's different. If the Governor comes, I might like it."

"I'd also ask June Hunt to come from Tyler, and maybe Monty Moncrief would come from Fort Worth and Ray O'Brien from Shreveport. They were all big in the boom, and they need to celebrate, too. Our neighbors down the Tyler Road, County Commissioner Shepperd and his wife and their son John Ben, can come too. John Ben's received all those honors and is a young leader in politics, you know. And we'd ask Lindley Beckworth and the other local politicians, and we'll hire a good band. Somebody like Bob Wills and the Texas Playboys, and maybe some other celebrities will come."

"If you want to do it, I guess I could try to enjoy it."

CHAPTER EIGHTEEN

*L*IFE MAGAZINE WOULD call it "The Party of the Century" and would proclaim that Jordan Phillips was one of the richest men, not only in Texas, but in America and maybe even the whole world, and his rags-to-riches story would be told over and over again.

Jordan was obviously enjoying himself, standing on the pine planked deck that surrounded the swimming pool, laughing and talking and greeting the guests as they arrived. Dressed in a new Khaki Pendleton shirt with a string tie, he was wearing khaki pants and a shiny new pair of black handmade Lucchese boots from San Antonio. Charlotte stood beside him, looking beautiful with her shiny pink lips and caramel skin and curly blonde hair, dressed in a floor length brown and white western dress. Jordan would say hello to each guest and then introduce them to Charlotte. She seemed to enjoy welcoming the most important people in Texas to her celebration.

The contingency from Austin were among the first guests to arrive with the Secretary of State, Ed Clark, in the lead. Considering the importance of this group, they were where they should have been, first in line. The music started at seven o'clock. Jordan could see that Ed was obviously a leader in the power structure of the state, shepherding his flock of the state's most powerful to the celebration of the tenth anniversary of the discovery of the East Texas Oil Field.

"It's good to see you again, Ed. Thanks for coming to East Texas to our party and bringing your Austin friends. I'd like you to meet Charlotte, my wife, and," he turned to her, "Charlotte meet Ed Clark, our Secretary of State."

"It is nice to meet you, Mr. Secretary. Welcome to East Texas."

"Thank you Missus Phillips, but please call me Ed."

"Thank you, Ed. I will do that. And remember, I am Charlotte, not Mrs. Phillips. I hope you have a good time tonight. I want to get to know you better, and I'd love to have an opportunity to talk to you. Sometime soon."

"Yes, ma'am. That's for sure. Jordan, I've brought some folks with me that you and Charlotte need to meet. First, meet Governor Jimmie Allred and Mrs. Allred."

"Governor Allred, welcome to East Texas."

"Jordan, Joe Betsy and I wouldn't miss this chance to be with you and Charlotte on this important day in the history of Texas."

"Thank you for coming, Governor," said Charlotte.

"Governor, I was hoping that maybe you could take the microphone later and make a few welcoming remarks to the folks," Jordan said.

"That would be an honor for me. I'd be proud to tell the folks how important you are to the State of Texas."

"Oh, Governor, please. Please don't say a word about me."

"Jordan, tonight, you are the man. This is the time for Texas to congratulate you and thank you for what you did for the State of Texas."

Bob Wills and the Texas Playboys began playing Bob's famous rendition of "The San Antonio Rose." The partygoers started dancing and singing along, and the Governor and his wife moved from the receiving line into the party, continuing to shake hands and meet the guests as Bob Wills crowed "Ah hah, San Antone!" Mr. Clark stood back with his hosts to introduce the other important people he had brought to the party.

The receiving line grew longer.

"Jordan, meet our new Congressman, Lyndon Johnson," Ed said, introducing Jordan to a tall young man in cowboy boots, proudly holding his Stetson Open Road in his hand.

"I'm sure proud to meet you, Mr. Phillips." The young politician had a good firm handshake, and Jordan immediately liked him.

"It's good to meet you, Congressman. We hope you'll stay in Washington a long time. We need a good Texan like you taking care of us up there."

"Don't forget, Jordan," Ed said, "one of my jobs is to keep Lyndon in Washington, and I'll need your help in the campaign."

"You can come by my office anytime. Talk to Merle. I'm always here to help."

"Lyndon, meet Jordan's wife. Miss Charlotte is the secret of the success of Texas's greatest oil finder."

"Ma'am, it's sure nice to meet you," said the congressman. "I always say a man is only successful if he has a strong and beautiful woman like you helping him, ma'am. Thank you for what you have done to help Jordan and the State of Texas too."

"It's so nice to meet you, Congressman Johnson," said Miss Charlotte. She looked him up and down, and Johnson gave her a grin and a wink. She watched him as he moved into the room, taller than most of the other men and radiating something she couldn't describe but that she liked.

Later, Governor Jimmie Allred, holding a microphone, stood in front of Bob Wills and his Texas Playboys band. He picked up an empty glass and tapped it several times with a spoon and began speaking speak loudly into the microphone.

"Welcome, fellow Texans. Welcome to the celebration of the tenth anniversary of the discovery of the East Texas Oil Field. The great oil discovery we celebrate tonight originated as an idea in the mind of the man we honor tonight: Jordan Philips." He paused before continuing after the cheers and applause died down. "Tonight we celebrate a man who had the desire and the determination to keep drilling and never quit until he discovered the largest oil field on Planet Earth!" The partygoers cheered louder. "Come on up here, Jordan. And Lyndon, you come up here too."

The crowd cheered and flashbulbs were flashing as the photographer took the photo that would become famous around the world on the cover of the next week's edition of Life Magazine, a close up photograph of three of the most prominent men in Texas: Jordan Phillips in the middle with the Governor of Texas and Congressman Lyndon B. Johnson on either side, raising their glasses in a toast to the great wildcatter, all three with wide smiles from ear to ear.

After the flashes from the flashbulbs died, the Governor continued to speak. "If we were residents of the moon looking down on the Earth, all we would see tonight would be the bright yellow light of the East Texas Oil Field. I toast the man who discovered the world's greatest oil field, the great Wildcatter, Jordan Phillips."

Jordan Phillips shook his head, not comfortable with such adulation, yet, finally, he smiled in appreciation as all the voices broke out singing "For He's the Jolly Good Fellow."

Among the guests standing back in the crowd, were the three men who had bought the stock in TOPCO, and, in doing so, enabled Jordan Phillips to keep drilling and make his great discovery. Two of the three investors were not happy, and they did not come to the party to celebrate. They were mad as hell, and they came to complain to Jordan Phillips about how they thought he had cheated them.

After the ceremony, Jordan ran into Loyce Williams, the President of the bank at Overton. "Jordan, you were nice to invite the three of us, but Sam Knight's mad as hell. He's not waiting any longer for you to pay us a dividend."

The music and the voices of the partygoers made it hard for Jordan to hear exactly what Loyce was saying, but he answered as best he could. "Tell Sam I don't talk business at parties. If you guys want to talk to me about your deal, come to my office. Call Merle and get an appointment. The number at the refinery is 189. Come by my office, and we'll talk about what's bothering you."

"Sam told me to tell you that he wants money or you can see him on the courthouse steps."

Inside the Cabin in the Great Room, Miss Charlotte was playing her piano. As she was sitting on the piano bench playing Gershwin's "Rhapsody in Blue," her druggist from Kilgore, Sam Knight, Sr., walked over to the piano and stood next to her. When she saw him, she kept playing, then as she continued to play, she turned to talk to him.

"Sam, how are you? I didn't know you were here."

Sam sat down beside her. "Charlotte, when can I see you? I miss you, and I need you."

She turned and looked at him, smiling, and, continuing to play, she said, "I've missed you too, Sam, and I need you."

"Call me at the drug store," he said as he walked away.

Charlotte went back outside to the party where she ran into Ed Clark. "It's been so good to finally meet you tonight, Ed. I have heard so much about you. Thank you for coming."

"It is a great time to celebrate this discovery with you and Jordan. It's a success Jordan would have never achieved without you, Charlotte. The way I see things, the best is yet to come in this life that Jordan's carved out for you."

Charlotte looked away. Ed could see her shaking her head. She looked back at him, and her smile was gone as she said, "You're right. He would have never found this oil field without me, and let me tell you, I hate this damn oil field. There is no way that I can live here in East Texas forever." She turned and returned inside the Log Cabin to her piano.

Ed was in shock after that conversation. He needed to talk to Jordan, and he found him next to the bar talking to a group of the party guests.

"Jordan, I need to talk to you."

"What's up, Ed?"

"What's going on with Charlotte? I'm just learning about your personal life, and I have to tell you that you need to watch out for her. With all this publicity, spending all this money on this party, the cover of Life, for God's sake, you could be getting problems from others. What about your shareholders in your company?"

"Well, I told them I'd meet them at the office on Monday. I'll take care of them. They have to stop telling those lies about me. Ed, let me tell you something you need to understand about me, if you don't already know it. I'll never double cross a partner."

"I know that, Jordan. My advice to you is that you better get your house in order—both at home and on the business front. I'll get you a good people problems attorney because you are damn sure going to need one. You know, I'm starting up a new law practice in Austin. I'll do your contracts and represent you at the State Capitol, and I have connections with the kind of litigator you'll need—like everybody needs—to help with problems that arise with most people in their lives."

"Whatever you say, Ed, I'll do, but I'll always take care of my partners. I just want them to trust me and leave me alone."

At midnight, the crowd was leaving. The last couple to say good night was Jordan's closest friend, his well man and his superintendent, Chirp Branscum. Chirp was with his wife, Mary Julia. About fifteen years older than Jordan, Chirp was approaching sixty. "Boss, we've had a great roll these past ten years. I'm proud that you let me join you down here from the very beginning."

"It wouldn't have happened without you, Chirp. I hope we're stuck with each other for a long time. And, who knows, we may cut a hell of a melon before it's all over with. I don't know how to thank you enough, brother."

"You thank me every day, Jordan. I'm the one that needs to do the thanking. Are you coming out to the yard Monday?"

"I got to run by the office Monday morning. My investors are coming by to eat my ass out. I'll get out there around one thirty."

"I'll be there. There are some real problems I need to talk to you about."

"Problems. I thought I knew all your problems. What's going on?"

"The *ice cream* is turning to *shit.*"

"What? What the hell are you talking about?"

"Come see me Monday."

Sirens started blaring inside Jordan's head. Chirp Branscum was a man of few words and hearing him say "The ice cream is turning to shit" scared the hell out of him.

Jordan's thoughts flashed back to Daisy Bradford's ninety-year-old Creole maid's words: "My spirits sing, 'Treasure found, then disaster—disaster and death.' My spirits speak only the truth."

CHAPTER NINETEEN

ON THE SUNDAY morning after the big party, Jordan was out in the stable with his little girl trying to teach her how to ride a horse. Jan's horse was a small paint. Her daddy had thought it would be easier for her to learn how to ride a little horse than it would be a big horse or a pony. Jan was dressed in a cowgirl outfit with leather chaps and cowboy boots and a cowboy hat. Jordan was wearing his usual khaki shirt, but this time with his honorary Texas Ranger badge on the left pocket. His khaki pants were stuck in the tops of the Western boots he always wore when he went horseback riding, and he wore his Stetson Open Road on his head. Herman was in the stables with them. He had saddled Jordan's white stallion.

"Honey, you hold your hand on the front of your saddle like this, and put your foot in this stirrup," Jordan said. He placed her left foot in the left stirrup and helped her swing her right leg over the saddle to place her right foot in the right stirrup, and then he helped her get comfortable in her saddle. "Now you're ready to go for a horseback ride with Daddy by your side."

Jan held the reins and said, "Daddy, this is fun!" Her daddy held the front of the halter above the bit and led her pony from the stable over to the log fence surrounding The Log Cabin.

"Jan, you're a real cowgirl." He wanted to show Charlotte how Jan could ride.

"Daddy, what's my pony's name?"

"Honey, he's not a pony. He's a little horse, and you can name him whatever you want."

"Can I name him Tony Boy?"

"Sure. That's a great name."

"Mama," Jan cried out. "Come out and look at me. I'm on my horse, and his name is Tony Boy. "

Jan's mother opened the back door of the Log Cabin. She looked across the fence at Jordan standing next to the pony their daughter was riding.

"I don't want my daughter on that animal."

"He's not just an animal. He's a horse."

"Mama, his name's Tony Boy."

"Jan doesn't know how to ride and she's too young to be taught. Young lady, get off that horse, and come in this house right now."

"But, Mama, Daddy wants me to ride with him."

"You are not riding a horse until you grow up. That's that. Get down off that horse right now, young lady."

Jan started bawling. "Mama, I wanna ride. I wanna ride with Daddy," she cried, but she slid off the side of her horse, landing hard on the ground below, crying harder and harder. With tears flowing she rose from the ground and ran through the gate into the back yard and up the steps into the house. Jordan stood there in disbelief, holding both horses' reins.

He looked at Charlotte. "I was going to lead Jan through the cypress trees along the river. There's no danger in that for her. That's how a child learns to ride."

"I don't want my daughter being around horses."

"I don't understand. I just don't understand."

Charlotte turned away and followed her daughter into the Log Cabin. Jordan stood there shaking his head in disbelief.

CHAPTER TWENTY

JORDAN FINISHED HIS breakfast at home on Monday morning and went to his office at the refinery. As he usually did, he arrived at his office at nine o'clock. He parked the 1937 DeSoto pick-up, with its Beaver's Motor Company frame attaching the license place to the rear bumper, in the parking space reserved for him and walked into the office. Merle was waiting for him. She stood up and pointed her index finger in the direction of the reception room and told him in almost a whisper that his three visitors were waiting.

"And they're not happy," she said.

"I told them to come by the office and talk to me. I might as well get this over."

Merle brought the three men into her boss's office. Jordan greeted each of them and invited them to sit down in the three red leather chairs in front of his desk.

They sat down without saying a word, waiting for Jordan to be the first to talk. He looked down on them from his higher chair behind his desk, remaining silent. Nobody said a word.

Finally, Sam Knight said, "Jordan, that's a nice picture," referring to the photograph of a tall wooden derrick in the piney woods of East Texas hanging on the wall behind the desk. It was the famous photograph of the #3 Daisy Bradford Well with hundreds of automobiles and wagons lined up on the dirt road running by the derrick.

"It certainly is a nice picture, Sam," Jordan said looking at the photo. "A picture of a historic moment. A historic moment that you all can be proud to have played a part in." Jordan paused and turned back to his partners. "I understand that you're not happy with the deal we made eight years ago."

Sam Knight's face was tight and flushed. "I don't give a damn about history. I want some cash. How can you take that kind of money out of this business and spend it on a party for yourself like you did Saturday night? How can you do that in good conscience?"

"I told you when you made your investment that as long as I was drilling, you would never receive a return. Well, in case you didn't know it, I'm still drilling, and I'll be drilling for many more years."

"Bullshit. You're taking all the money you want out of the company and letting us pay for twenty-five percent of everything you do, not just your oil wells, but for this refinery and this office building, for your mansion and for that party and, goddamn it, for everything you buy."

The other two men looked at Jordan, waiting. Jordan turned back around and studied the photo again.

Loyce Williams cleared his throat. "Jordan, why don't you expect us to want a dividend?"

"I can't pay dividends and keep drilling," Jordan said, as he turned, stood up, and walked around in front of his desk and pointed at the map of the East Texas Oil Field on the wall. "And I don't know how many new wells I'll have to drill this year. One thing's for sure: I'm not paying dividends. You guys ought to forget your griping and hang on to your stock. Someday it may be worth a lot of money."

Sam Knight jumped up from his chair. He was shaking. "I need money now."

"I think it would be a mistake for you all to sell out, but if you really need money and you don't like my deal, why don't you sell out to me? Tell me, what you would sell your stock for?"

"How would we know what your company is worth? Stock in a closed corporation isn't worth the cost of the paper the certificate is printed on," said Loyce Williams. "Based on what I know, I would say my stock in TOPCO would be worth something like $50,000."

"Fifty thousand would be a ten-to-one return on your investment. What's wrong with a ten-to-one return? But you're a banker, and you're right: there's no market for stock in a private company. That makes the real value of your stock more like zero."

"Damn it, Jordan, either write me a check right now for $50,000, or I'm filing a law suit tomorrow," said Sam.

"Sam, for a druggist, you are a tough guy. I'm not stupid. What would you really take?"

"Okay, Jordan, write me a check for $40,000, and hand it to me right now."

Jordan quietly looked at all three of them. "Sam, let me tell you something. If I bought you out for $40,000 or even $50,000, that would be highway robbery, and let me tell you one more thing: I would never steal my partner's interest in a deal. Besides, I owe you everything for saving my ass back when I needed the money to keep drilling. Let me tell you what I'll do. I'll pay you more than you asked for. I'll pay you each $75,000 in cash for your TOPCO stock. That's a fifteen to one return on your money, and I'll give you a year's option to cancel the sale and buy the stock back from me for what I pay you, but you'll have to agree in writing that this is a fair and square deal."

John Henderson had not said a word until now. "Jordan, I couldn't care less. I don't agree with Sam and Loyce, and I don't want to sell, but I appreciate what you've offered." Pointing his finger at each man in the room, he continued, "It would be best for you,

Jordan, and it would be best for Sam and for Loyce too, and for me, if we accept your offer and went our merry way."

Sam Knight's face dropped, and he shook his head. "Jordan, this proves you're an honest man. I accept your offer."

"I will too. Thank you, Jordan," said Loyce Williams.

"I'll have the papers drawn up, and you can all come back into the office Wednesday and sign the papers and pick up your checks."

No one was happier than Jordan. He finally owned one hundred percent of his oil company again. His investors left his office happier than they ever expected to be.

After the meeting, Jordan grabbed a hamburger at his favorite burger joint, the Green Hut.

For some reason unknown to him, he was so nervous he almost swallowed his hamburger whole. Perhaps, he was worried about what Chirp might be going to tell him out at his office in the field. He didn't know yet that his fears were not unfounded.

He headed for the middle of the oil field, driving five miles east of Gladewater past oil derricks standing above Christmas trees oil wells on both sides of Highway 80. He passed Lake Devernia and then he turned left off of Highway 80 on to TOPCO Road, which was identified by a large sign on the highway which said "TEXAS OIL PRODUCING COMPANY, EAST TEXAS DIVISION, 1,759 OIL WELLS."

On TOPCO Road, Jordan drove past nine Christmas trees up the hill to TOPCO'S field office in the heart of the Fairway of the East Texas Oil Field. East Texas Fairway oil wells were as good as any oil wells in the world. Petroleum engineers had estimated that Fairway wells would flow for another hundred years, but opening up those oil wells wide would suck in the salt water and ruin the oil field. That was why the Railroad Commission restricted the flow of oil from an oil well in East Texas to a low rate, but state conservation didn't keep Jordan from worrying every day about the salt water that was relentlessly encroaching across his oil field.

Jordan pulled into his personal parking space. He went into his superintendent's office and sat down in the chair in front of Chirp's desk. Chirp had his feet up on his desk, swatting flies with a fly swatter. He was talking on the phone.

He put his hand over the phone receiver and whispered to his boss, "Good to see you, Jordan. This is Bobby Manziel. It'll only take a second." He turned back to the phone. "Sure, Bobby, he just walked in." He handed over the phone saying, "Jordan, here's Bobby Manziel. He says he has to talk to you."

Jordan took the phone. "Hello, Bobby…It's good to talk to you too. How's everything in the prize-fighting world?" After another pause, he said, "Well, we missed you and sorry you couldn't make the party…No, I can't come to New York, but if you want that farm-out, write me a letter, and we'll work something out for you. Thanks for calling. Send me that letter and you'll have your deal signed up in a couple of days. Tell the Champ hello…Good to talk to you, Bobby, and I look forward to seeing you when you get back home. Bye."

"What'd Manziel want?"

"He wanted me to come to New York to meet with Jack Dempsey at some restaurant on Times Square called Lindy's. He said that's where Dempsey did his business."

"The Champ's his money man. No telling how much money the Champ has invested with Bobby, and they've got some damn good oil wells right in the middle of town."

"Well, this farm-out he wants won't be much of a well. He wants to drill on that eighty acres we hold by production west of the old Starnes plant south of town. To me it's a cinch to be a water well. It'll go down in history as the well that proved the exact oil water contact in the Woodbine."

"Farm it out to him, Boss. Even if it would have once produced, it's too far off structure now."

"Look, I am here because you told me my ice cream had turned to shit. What the hell is going on?"

"It's like this. The damn salt water is flooding out your oil field."

"That's nothing new. I stay awake nights worrying about the salt water."

"Well, Boss, I never thought the West Side would water out as fast as it has. Five of the wells on the Money are cutting water, and two of them died last week: numbers 79 and 84. When the Governor made his speech and said you had yellow flares burning on all eighty-five flowing wells on the Money Lease, I didn't want to tell him he was wrong. You didn't have but eighty flares burning on the Money. It won't be long before all of those Money flares will be history and all those wells will be on the pump, and there won't be eighty-five wells left either. The damn salt water is flooding us out. I didn't want to worry you with it, not at your big celebration. What I'm telling you now is you better get ready to buy at least a hundred pumping units in the next six months."

"What are we doing with all that salt water?"

"I wish we could dump it into the Sabine, and let it go down to the Gulf of Mexico."

"We can't do that. The salt water would ruin the Sabine."

"I know that. I'm digging bigger and bigger pits, and we'll put the salt water in pits and hope it'll evaporate fast. I heard the Commission is talking about building a drainage ditch all the way to the Gulf of Mexico, but that won't work."

"Of course not," Jordan replied, shaking his head and trying to decide what the news he was hearing meant to him. "What are we going to do?"

"Jordan, let me tell you, there's a hell of a lot more oil to produce here in East Texas in the Fairway if we can handle the salt water.

Those engineers in Dallas will say that the Fairway wells will last another hundred years, but you're going to lose those fairway wells too unless you talk to your politician buddies down in Austin and get them to pass a law that requires underground disposal of all the salt water."

"We'll damn sure try. We got to get the right folks on our side and speaking up. I'll talk to June Hunt and Pete Lake and Joe Zeppa. We'll ask the Commission to call a hearing and pass a rule that requires the operators to handle their own salt water disposal. We can do it ourselves. We don't need the state taking it over."

"Jordan, I been thinking. What are you going to do if these engineers are all wrong and instead of a hundred years of oil you only have fifteen or twenty years left for East Texas?"

"Branscum, don't talk to me like that. That sounds like what you were telling me when the #3 Bradford was flowing over the crown. You were saying then that I'd found a one-well oil field. Don't do that to me again."

"Jordan, every barrel of oil you produce you got to replace, and you are producing a lot of oil."

"How much oil did you make today?"

Chirp opened his ledger book and read out loud, "March 18, 1937, seventeen-thousand and three-hundred and twenty-five and sixty-seven one hundredths of a barrel. That's how much we put in the tanks."

"Then today all the new oil I need to find is 17,325 and sixty-seven one hundredths barrels of oil, right?"

"And tomorrow and the day after tomorrow. When you add it all up, you need to find another damn big oil field. Doesn't that chill your bones?"

"You're right, Chirp. It looks like I'm going to be busy if I want to keep being an oil man. I've got to find me another East Texas Oil Field."

CHAPTER TWENTY-ONE

WHEN THE BLAST hit, they jumped out of their chairs, and Chirp was yelling profanities. It was like an earthquake. The wooden building shuddered and swayed. Its windows rattled, and the sound and vibration from the explosion lasted for several seconds before rumbling away like thunder. The blast was so loud that it hurt both men's ears. They wondered if they would ever hear again. When things quieted down, they stood there and looked at each other, their ears ringing.

"Down that way," Chirp said pointing toward Kilgore. "We gotta get there." Chirp raced out of his office with Jordan right behind.

"Get in your truck and follow me. We both need our trucks."

Jordan followed bumper to bumper. They turned at Clarksville toward Kilgore. A police car with sirens blaring and a fire truck flashing red lights passed them.

When they arrived in downtown Kilgore, Chirp stopped so Jordan could park his truck and ride with him. Jordan saw an old man standing beside the road and he asked him, "What happened?"

"'Splosion. Down by New London. The schoolhouse done blown up. All the law done gone down there. They say all the school kids are dead. It's terrible."

Chirp and Jordan headed for New London. When they got to the edge of the town, they saw the most devastating sight either had ever seen. Nothing remained of the new school house. It was a smoking ruin. The road was packed with ambulances, police cars, and men running back and forth.

Jordan and Chirp got out of the truck and joined all the oil field workers who were running through the ruins looking for anyone still breathing. Jordan ran into John Henderson, who had heard the blast in Lufkin and had come to see if he could help. John joined him and Chirp and they carried stretchers filled with burned remains of children's' bodies. They stacked the bodies and body parts one on top of the other.

"What happened?" Jordan asked the Sheriff as he and sheriff were on opposite ends carrying a stretcher loaded with gory hunks of flesh, bones, and tattered clothing.

"Gas explosion. We don't know the whole story yet, but we'll find out. Someone from the school said they thought there had been a slow gas leak from a new connection in the basement and either someone struck a match or an electric short ignited it when a switch was turned on."

"I bet I know what happened. It was that free casing-head gas that they always get from the oil wells. There's not enough odor in that gas. I bet they couldn't smell the leak."

Back in the Great Room of the Log Cabin, Miss Charlotte was sitting on the long couch reading when she heard the explosion. She thought it was thunder at first. It was too loud and it lasted too long to be thunder, then the walls of the Log Cabin started shaking.

"Sully, was that an explosion?"

"Yes'm, Miz Phillups. It was a s'plosion, for sure."

Later that afternoon, Jordan hadn't come home at his regular time. Sully said, "Miss Charlotte, Ah'm worried. Ma'am, don't you think you bettuh check on Mistuh Phillips?"

Charlotte picked up the telephone and cranked the ringer. "Operator," she said, "Please ring 189...What? Operator, did you say it was the school over at New London? 500 children were killed? Good Lord! Ring 189."

"Hello."

"Merle, I'm sorry to call you, but where is Jordan?"

"I don't know, Charlotte. He left the office for lunch on the way out to the Camp for his Monday meeting with Chirp."

"Call the sheriff, and ask him if he knows anything about Jordan, then call me back."

As she hung up the phone the front door of the Log Cabin opened and she heard a voice saying, "Charlotte. Help us." It was Jordan staggering into The Log Cabin with Chirp Branscum leaning on his shoulder, his face and his khaki shirt and even his blue jeans covered in dried blood.

Charlotte could hear Jordan moaning, "Get Chirp some towels and some alcohol and help him clean the cut on his head. The stupid bastards. It looks like they must have tapped a flare line to get free gas to the school, and then they piped the gas into the school in a leaky pipe. Finest new school in the country and those cheapskates were saving a little money moving free gas through junk pipe and the gas didn't have enough odor so anybody would know it was leaking. Those poor kids." Jordan threw his dirty Stetson Open Road down on the table and literally fell into his big leather chair and laid his head in his hands. "It makes me sick. I'm going to call the sheriff and tell him to put those guys in jail."

"You got to get your buddies in Austin to pass a law that

anybody giving free gas away to a school or a business or somebody's home has got to put an odor in it," Chirp said.

"I'll call Ed and have him draft the bill and push it through the legislature."

"Tell 'em they can get the chemistry right if they mix alcohol with sulfur and make something like skunk pee or garlic that smells terrible."

"Sully, bring Mr. Branscum an Old Charter on the rocks and my usual to me."

"Yessuh, Mr. Phillips. They's both on the way,"

"Thanks, Sully, and bring Mrs. Phillips a martini."

"I can't believe you finally remembered me."

"Sorry, darling. Got a lot on my mind."

"I hope I'll be on your mind someday," she said as she exited the room and left the men to their conversation.

When she returned a half hour later, Jordan said, "What about another martini, honey?"

"Sully knows how I like my martinis. Of course."

"Sully, the usual for Mrs. Phillips. Straight up with a drop of Vermouth and an olive."

"Yessuh," Sully said from the bar as he shook another martini for Miss Charlotte and fixed another Dewar's for Jordan.

Jordan and Chirp sat there and drank. They talked about the day. Charlotte got sick of hearing the two men talk about the blood and body parts, the mangled bodies of children, so she left the room. Later, she came back and listened to them some more and drank another martini. The men kept talking and drinking and getting drunker, and they talked until they figured out what was needed in a new state law.

Miss Charlotte was feeling no pain either when she heard Chirp say, "It's after midnight. I better head home."

"Why don't you let Sully drive you?"

"I can drive myself home."

"You drive slow, and get yourself a good night's sleep," Jordan said. After they were alone, he turned to his wife and said, "Honey, are you okay?"

"No."

"Let's go to bed. Tomorrow'll be a better day."

Miss Charlotte and Jordan walked up the stairs together. He had been sleeping by himself in their bedroom the last four months, and Charlotte slept in the guest bedroom. They parted at the top of the stairs to go their separate ways when Jordan stopped and turned back to her and said, "Honey, why don't you sleep with me tonight? I want your arms around me."

"Jordan, you're too goddamn drunk. This has been the worst day of my life. When I heard that explosion I knew you had blown up. Thank God, you're okay, but I hate this life. Jan's only playmates are the children of your coloreds. I'm going to Beverly Hills, and I'm taking my daughter with me, and I may never come back."

Jordan couldn't believe what he was hearing. He raised his voice, "God, Charlotte, I can't believe you're treating me this way. Why in the hell did you marry me anyway? I've given you everything. I found this oil field for you. I built you the finest home in East Texas, and you treat me like dirt. The fires and the explosions will soon be only a memory, and this will be the finest place in the world to live. This oil field is a special place. It has its own special sweet smell. I love the sounds of the oil field. The people here are the salt of the earth."

Charlotte listened and stared at him with the steely cold eyes of a snake. After he finished she said, "You can have your damn oil field." She walked into the guest bedroom and slammed the door.

"Go on out to California!" he barked. "You'll come back when you see that the real world is here in East Texas."

CHAPTER TWENTY-TWO

THREE DAYS AFTER the New London School explosion, Jordan received a call from Austin. Ed Clark was on the phone, and he said, "Jordan, everybody in the country and from around the world is contacting New London and Austin, giving their condolences. The Queen of England sent a telegram, and so did Adolph Hitler, giving his sympathy for the loss of all the poor children. And we have a draft bill. Let me read the preamble to you: 'REQUIRING INTRODUCTION OF MALODORANT AGENT IN NATURAL GAS. H. B. No. 1017 Chapter 364. An Act amending Article 6053 of the Revised Civil Statutes of Texas of 1925 by empowering and authorizing the Railroad Commission of the State of Texas to investigate the use of malodorants by persons, firms, or corporations engaged in the business of handling, storing and selling or distributing natural gas and liquefied petroleum gases including butane and other odorless gases for private and commercial use.' How's that for a start, Jordan?"

"That sounds great, Ed. Go for it. We've got to do whatever it takes to see there's never another tragedy like New London," Jordan Phillips said.

Thursday's other big event for Jordan Phillips was Miss

Charlotte's leaving. She was going to Los Angeles, determined to change her life. Jordan, with Sully driving, took Charlotte and Jan to the train station with as much luggage as two redcaps could load on a train. Charlotte didn't give much thought to the fact that Jan was also Jordan's daughter as she hurried to get herself and Jan in the train without really saying goodbye to Jordan.

In the time-honored tradition of the Old South of keeping the help in the family for generations, she took a colored servant girl—Annie and Sully's niece—to be Jan's nanny. As soon as the train pulled out of the station in Gladewater, Charlotte would no longer force herself to tolerate the environment of the oil field. No longer would she be subjected to the smells so awful to her, those pungent and sweet smells from the refineries where the crude oil would be refined into gasoline. No longer would she have to listen to the grinding noise of the pump jacks going up and down all day and all night long. She was looking forward to inhaling the air of southern California. Beverly Hills smelled really nice.

In her suitcases, she was taking everything a self-proclaimed independent woman of means would need to become part of the Hollywood scene of beautiful people: bags filled with make-up, and five or six bathing suits, tennis shorts, and tennis shoes.

Charlotte stayed in Beverly Hills. Her home was next door to a man named Temple who was an attorney. The Temple's had a curly haired daughter named Shirley who was a child movie star. Shirley Temple and Jan Phillips became great playmates. Charlotte rarely talked to Jordan except when she needed big money. It became a long-distance relationship that worked for Charlotte. It worked especially well because she received checks from Jordan every month.

One month, Charlotte called Merle and told her to send a

million dollars so she could buy the mansion next door to the Temples that she had been renting.

Jordan sat at his desk and rubbed his face with both hands. Then he ran his fingers into his hair so that it stood up straight. "Good God, Merle. It was fine for you to send her twenty thousand a month without bothering me, but a *million?*"

"That's what she said, Jordan. A million dollars. But if she was still living in Texas, wouldn't she be asking for that much money or more?"

Jordan nodded, chagrined. "Of course. Of course she would. She might spend more. Send her the check."

CHAPTER TWENTY-THREE

BY SUNDAY, DECEMBER 7, 1941, almost 27,000 oil wells had been drilled in the East Texas Oil Field.

On Monday, December 8, 1941, in Jordan's office, Chirp said, "Now that we're at war, I guess they'll open up the oil field."

"Yeah, they will. Ed Clark said he heard that Roosevelt told Harold Ickes to build a 24-inch pipeline from Longview to the East Coast."

"That means for sure they'll open up the field."

"They're calling it 'The Big Inch.' A big pipeline will move a lot of oil. Damn Nazi submarines have been sinking tankers in the Gulf. That pipe line will get the oil to the East Coast and the tankers will get it across the Atlantic to the battlefields in Europe."

"You'll see more money than you ever dreamed, but the water will move in so fast there's no telling how much quicker this oil field will be history."

"Chirp, there is an old proverb that says, 'A fool only gets one chance to fix a problem.' We'll figure out a way to make that problem an opportunity."

"Well, I sure as hell don't know what to do. Thank God for your brains, Boss."

*

One October evening during the war, Jordan was sitting alone in the Great Room of the Log Cabin, reading. He always sat in the leather chair with the table next to it where the Remington bronze 'The Bronco Buster' rested. He noticed the bronze was gone.

When Sully brought him his Dewar's on the rocks, he asked him, "Sully, what happened to my bronze cowboy?"

"Miz Phillips called me and tole me to ship it to her. She said you didn't want it anymore, and you didn't care. Ah sho' hope that wuz alright, Mistuh Phillips."

Thinking about Miss Charlotte turned Jordan's mind to Jan. He made a long-distance call to Beverly Hills.

"Charlotte, I want to see my little girl. I want her home for Thanksgiving. I'll send you her tickets, and you can put her on the train. And what about my Bronco Buster? When are you sending it back?"

"Jordan, damn it, half of everything in the Log Cabin is mine. You need to send me half of those Charlie Russell's and another bronze too. As far as Jan coming to see you, absolutely not. I'm taking her to the desert for Thanksgiving at Thunderbird Golf Club. We're going with some new friends, the McBurneys. You know, shovels. Their daughter is one of Jan's best friends."

Jordan's heart clenched like a fist. "Charlotte, the Remington bronze is one thing, but you can't keep my little girl from me."

"I'm sorry, Jordan. We have plans, and she has no business traveling on the train alone."

When Charlotte hung up the phone, she turned to see the pretty little nine-year-old brunette standing there looking up into her eyes.

"Mama, why can't I go see Daddy? I want to see my daddy."

Charlotte sighed. For the life of her, she didn't know what Jan saw in her father or why she'd want to spend time in that smelly oil field, but she wasn't going to have Jan grow up resenting her. "Well, alright. This one time I'll let you go spend a week with your father, but you'll have to take care of yourself on that train to East Texas."

"Mama, I love the Pullman cars. Those conductors are so nice. They take good care of me."

When Jordan met Jan at the train station in Gladewater on Monday, November 22, 1943, she ran into his arms.

"Daddy!"

"Jan, baby, welcome home. I have missed you so much." He squeezed her and didn't want to let go.

"I love you, Daddy."

"Not any more than everybody in East Texas loves you," he said into her soft hair.

When he finally let her go, she asked, "What happened to all the oil derricks, Daddy?"

"They've been torn down. Now there are those pump jacks on the oil wells. See over there?"

"They look like horse heads rising up and down and eating."

"Jordan squinted at the pump jacks. "You're right. They do look like horse heads, but they aren't eating oats. They're pumping oil out of the ground."

Jan loved staying at the Log Cabin with her daddy. She loved riding around the oil field with him in his truck checking on his oil wells and stopping to say hello to Merle and everybody at the refinery. She missed East Texas, and she had especially missed her little horse. On the day before Thanksgiving, she asked her daddy if he could take her on a horseback ride.

"Darling, I'd love to take you, but I can't do it this afternoon.

A cool front is blowing in. I have some work to do. The weather will be better tomorrow, and I'll go riding with you then."

"I can go by myself. I remember how to ride."

"But where would you ride, Jan? I don't like you riding alone."

"I'm going to ride in the pine trees up in the river bottom. Please won't you let me?"

"Alright, just let Tony Boy take you for a little ride up the river bottom into the pine trees and back."

At the stable, Jordan was happy to see Jan cinch the saddle tight on Tony Boy's belly and gracefully mount the saddle. He watched her with pride as she rode away toward the pine trees.

"Honey, be careful not to ride the wrong way. Let Tony Boy take you where he wants to go. He'll always return to his barn, and you'll be fine if you let him have the lead."

So she rode off toward the pines, holding the bridle and the saddle horn with both hands. She turned and smiled and said, "Daddy don't worry, Tony Boy and I will be fine." She waved goodbye. He couldn't believe how his little girl had grown up.

Shaking his head in disbelief, he walked back into the house and ran into Sully outside the back door of the Log Cabin. "Sully, if my little girl doesn't return on her horse in an hour, I want you to send Herman to find her."

"Herman's done rode down to Friendship, but if youah not heah and she doan come back, doan you worry, I'll saddle up. I'll find her."

Tony Boy walked Jan through the watermelon patch with all the pump jacks rising and falling. The little horse decided to trot in a circle around one pump jack and then around the next pump jack and then the third one, and Jan loved going around and around, and she kicked her horse and sped him up circling the pump jacks faster and faster until she was dizzy.

All of a sudden, Tony Boy turned and headed for the cypress

trees and trotted along the river until he passed through an open gate onto Lovelady Road. She loved the freedom of her horse trotting fast with a cool north wind at her back, and when Tony Boy's trot turned into a gallop, she loved the feeling of speed so she reached behind her saddle and slapped Tony Boy on his rear and clicked her mouth to make him run faster.

When she realized the horse was racing and out of control, she pulled back on the reins trying to slow him down and started yelling, "Tony Boy, slow down." As she bounced on her saddle with each gallop, her black hair blew straight back, and she was glad when she remembered that her Daddy had told her not to worry because Tony Boy would take care of her. Holding on tight to the saddle horn and with her horse in control, they ran through another open gate into a pasture. He kept galloping for what seemed like another mile and he headed for a group of houses on top of a hill and a chapel with a tall steeple where Jan saw all a crowd of people standing outside a barn in front of a burning fire, a plume of black smoke reaching high into the sky.

As her horse galloped closer to the fire, she saw at least ten colored men and boys butchering a large hog on a long wooden table. The closer she and Tony Boy got to the gathering the more she could smell the smoke and then the strong odor of burning pig skin. Some of the boys were scraping skin off the hog, some were cutting the fat off, and some were working a meat grinder. Two men were carrying another whole hog carcass and sticking it into a cast-iron pot full of boiling water hanging over a pine-log fire. Tony Boy ran straight up to the fire and turned and skidded to a stop. Jan almost pitched off the saddle into the pot of scalding water. She grasped the saddle horn tighter than anything in her life and let out a little squeal of fright.

"Why, Miss Jan, be careful," a voice from the crowd spoke up. "Don't fall in the fire."

After seeing his little friend was okay, Herman smiled at her and said, "Miss Jan, what are you and Tony Boy doing here?"

"Oh, Herman, I'm so glad to see you. Tony Boy ran away with me, and I didn't know where he took me."

"This is Friendship, Miss Jan. I try to be here every year on the day of the first cold front. I meet up with my brothers and cousins, and we have our hog killing."

"Hog killing?"

"It's what you're looking at. The fatback and the skin make wonderful cracklin's and the loins and the shoulder are ground up into sausage. Every piece of the pig gets eaten except the oink, and there's nothing better to eat."

"I need to get back to my daddy."

"I'll take you. I know he must be worried."

So Herman got on his horse and Jan rode behind him on Tony Boy all the way back up Lovelady Road to Tyler Road and then the two miles to the Log Cabin gate.

Jordan was preparing to go out to find Jan when she and Herman rode into the stable. Jan jumped down from Tony Boy and ran to her daddy.

Jordan squeezed her hard and blinked back tears. "Jan, I should have never let you ride alone."

"Tony Boy took me to Friendship, and we found Herman. I watched the pig being cooked. It was really a lot of fun. I love you, and I love East Texas. Why won't Mama move back here? I want to come back and live with you and Annie and Sully and Herman and Tony Boy. Why can't I come home? This is a lot better than Beverly Hills."

Jordan tried to blink back more tears but failed. As they ran down his face, his voice broke as he said, "I know, honey. I know. You tell Mama you want to come home."

CHAPTER TWENTY-FOUR

THE ALLIES FLOATED to victory in Europe in a sea of East Texas oil. A half billion barrels of oil flowed out of the Woodbine Sand reservoir. Jordan Phillip's share of that oil made him richer than ever. Yet, in gaining all these riches defeating tyranny and saving freedom for the peoples of the world, Jordan and the other oil producers in East Texas paid a dear price. A half billion barrels of salt water encroached into their Woodbine Sand oil reservoir as one more signal of the ultimate depletion of the oil.

"Jordan, you damn sure need a new oil field, what with all that salt water moving in," Chirp said.

"I know it. I don't have any choice. I've got to find a new oil field at least as big as East Texas, but I'll move to Dallas and look for oil with the big boys if I want to find one. June Hunt moved to Dallas, and I hear he's already found a big new oil field in Louisiana. I've got to do the same thing."

In Dallas, Jordan leased a whole floor in the tallest building west of the Mississippi. It was the building with the Flying Red Horse on top: the new Magnolia Petroleum Company Building.

Sully and Annie and their boy Herman went with him. This was the first time anyone in Sully's or Annie's family had left

East Texas since their grandparents had walked to Texas as freed slaves behind the covered wagons carrying the white folks who had owned them before they were run off their ancestral farms by carpetbaggers.

Jordan bought a Southern plantation-like mansion on White Rock Lake on the northeast side of Dallas. With a fifteen-acre lawn of St. Augustine grass along the shoreline of the lake, his home was one of Dallas's finest. He built a servants' cottage for Sully and Annie and their boy with their first indoor bathroom.

He rented a cottage in Highland Park for Merle. Merle did everything for Jordan. She paid his bills, and she sent Miss Charlotte and Jan their checks every month. The most important thing Merle did for Jordan was to hand him a slip of paper every Friday afternoon with only two numbers on it. There was a dollar sign in front of each seven or eight digit number.

One of the two numbers was the company's bank balance, and the other number was the balance in Jordan's personal bank account. Those two numbers were all Jordan needed to run his business and his personal life.

Jordan joined the Dallas Petroleum Club and the Dallas Country Club. He started having lunch at the Petroleum Club on Tuesdays, Wednesdays, and Thursdays.

He'd sit at the round table reserved for the independents and an occasional company man. The waiter quickly learned that Jordan's favorite lunch was a club sandwich. Sometimes he'd have an ice cold Lone Star in a frosted beer stein.

Like some of the most successful wildcatters, Jordan was a listener and not a talker. One day, a wildcatter who had just moved to Dallas from Midland was telling the group he was drilling a wildcat in Scurry County. When that guy asked the table if anybody wanted to buy a piece of his deal, Jordan raised his hand and without expression of any emotion he said, "I'll take half," and he pulled a check from his wallet to write the wildcatter a check.

"Don't worry about paying me now. I'll send you a bill when we get down on the well."

In a couple of months Jordan received a letter with an invoice to the Texas Oil Producing Company for payment in the amount of $337,500.00 for "Turnkey Drilling costs for the Al Ferguson #1 Wesson, Dry Hole, drilled to a Total Depth of 10,001 feet, Scurry County, Texas."

"I thought that guy knew what he was doing," Jordan said to himself. "This is a no way to find oil." When Merle walked into his office, he handed her the approved invoice and said, "Take this damn bill down to accounting and tell them to cut a check and mail it today. I want that guy to know I'm a quick pay."

"Boss, I ran a tape on how much you have spent on the deals you've bought at lunch at the Petroleum Club since we moved to Dallas."

"I know it's at least a couple of million."

"Since you've been in Dallas, you've spent 2.75 million dollars at the Dallas Petroleum Club looking for a new oil field. "

"That's about what I had mentally calculated. There's got to be a better way to find oil."

"It's sure time for you to do something different, Boss."

"I need to build the right team right here in Dallas. I need petroleum engineers and an attorney to manage all the lands I've got to lease. You'll be busier than ever running the office, Merle, but what I need most is an oil finding geologist and to spend the money it takes to find oil."

"But, Jordan, can't you drill dry holes and lose all your money drilling wildcats?"

"Right now I have the time and money. I've got to find another East Texas Oil Field, or else one morning, I'll wake up to a call from Chirp Branscum, and he'll tell me my oil field is history. I'd be as broke then as I was when I started. The only way to keep that from happening is to start drilling and never stop drilling until I find more oil."

CHAPTER TWENTY-FIVE

RADUATION DAY AT Rutgers School of Law was a blue bird day without a cloud in the sky. After the ceremony, the Paternos and the Lambrisis drove to David Paterno, Sr.'s summer home at Highlands, New Jersey near Sandy Hook. They were all proud to see David Paterno, Jr., walk across the stage, graduating third in his class.

After a mid-afternoon lunch at the Paternos', most of both the Paterno and the Lambrisi families said their goodbyes to all their family and returned to their own homes. As the afternoon turned into evening, David Paterno, Sr., was sitting at the gazebo by the water's edge with his son, David, Jr. The father was a founding partner of the law firm of Paterno and Lambrisi, which he and his brother-in-law, Angelo Lambrisi, Sr., had formed years ago. Their offices and primary residences were in Newark, not far from the Rutgers Campus.

"David, your uncle and I need help at the firm. Your cousin Angelo will join us next year after he graduates." Except for their low voices, the only sound was the water lapping against the boardwalk.

"I don't know what I want to do, Dad. I've been thinking it would be better for me to get away from here."

"Why is that?" His father sipped his cognac.

"Sure, you and Uncle Angelo have a million-dollar law practice, but you never know how long it will last. Things may change."

"What makes you say that, David?"

"I've never known much about your clients—who they are and what they do."

"They're in trucking and distribution of food and beverages, wine and spirits. Most have been very successful, and now that the war is over, they're expanding across the country and getting more into the travel and entertainment business."

"It's no secret that several of them started selling liquor back in Prohibition days. Haven't you been with them since the beginning?"

"Atlantic City had its own laws and special waivers of the federal law. Everything my clients did was legal. That was my responsibility. We were able to take advantage of the laws that made it legal to distill alcoholic beverages in Atlantic City for medicinal purposes, and it was legal to broker and transport the medicine the pharmaceutical companies were making. Many sick people were cured and their quality of life was improved by medicines that could only be made in Atlantic City by my clients during those difficult times."

The son thought his father sounded like a politician delivering a well-rehearsed speech. "I was proud to have been part of that major benefit to the health of mankind. I took every precaution to see that all that work was accomplished legally and for the benefit of all."

David forced himself not to smirk. "Your law practice has been good to you, Dad, but I want a different life."

David Paterno, Sr., stood and turned toward his son and shook his index finger at him. "Don't you ever forget that my law firm financed the finest legal education for you that money can buy. You have a family obligation to repay the firm the costs of your education, and if you don't join the firm then you'll carry the obligation forever."

"Dad, I understand my obligation to repay the firm, but I don't plan to come with your firm. I'll repay my debt with referrals."

"You'd be passing up an enormous opportunity if you don't join the firm. What are you going to do if you don't come with us, David?"

"I want to learn new businesses. I've decide to move to Texas."

"The only thing Texas has is oil. You don't know a thing about oil. You can't even change the oil in your car. How're you going to learn the oil business?"

"I've applied for a job as an attorney for the Texas Railroad Commission."

"You don't have to go to Texas to learn the railroad business. I can get you a job with the New York Central."

"I know this sounds crazy, but the Railroad Commission in Texas doesn't have much to do with railroads. It regulates the oil business, and Texas has more oil wells than anywhere else, and the only reason this state job is available for a lawyer from New Jersey like me is because the job doesn't pay anything much, but it could help me learn oil and gas law, and it could lead to something bigger."

"Somewhere along the way you'll need help. Mark my words, David. When would you start this job?"

"I have an interview June 15th in Austin. If I get an offer, I will accept it and stay there and start work as soon as I can. But, Dad, I'll never need any help from your firm."

"Dammit, David, only because of your youth and inexperience do you say that. You'll need help, and when you ask for it, you'll get it. That's the way our family works. I can assure you that when you see where the money really is, you'll be back in Newark.

Put off starting your new job for a month. Come to Havana with me. Meyer Lansky asked me to be there to help run a meeting between the family businesses of several of our old clients, Albert Anastasia and Joe Bonnano and the three other families. I can use your help. They want to branch out around the country, and they want me to facilitate an agreement on the division of their businesses into these new areas."

"Don't you mean 'mediate' instead of 'facilitate'?"

"Mediate may be a better word, but it makes no difference. These families have businesses that compete with each other. They are hardnosed and aggressive business men. They have all learned to respect me and your uncle. We have kept them from tearing each other's throats apart for many years. Their joint respect is an asset of your Uncle Angelo's and mine. We will use that asset as long as we can. Meyer Lansky keeps them all working together and he knows all of the players. Most of the time, Lansky has kept the peace between them, but when he knows he needs help he calls on your uncle and me, and he has asked us to help him run this meeting in Havana. We will referee inevitable arguments as they expand into tourism and gaming across the country into Florida and Nevada and California and into Cuba and the Caribbean."

"Dad, isn't 'dividing up the markets' the same as what the law calls restraining trade?"

The sun was setting, shadows lengthening. David Paterno, Sr., rose and walked in circles around the gazebo taking more frequent sips of his cognac.

"Son, goddamn it. You've got a lot to learn. There's no 'restraint of trade' in what your uncle and I do. There's plenty of opportunity to spread around, and it is good business to help your clients organize how to satisfy the consumer demand in the new tourist markets. For example, they're talking about this god awful little bus stop in Nevada called Las Vegas. Ben Siegel is selling them on investing in this large tourist court where no tourist in their right mind would want to be in August when it's a hundred and twenty in the shade, but it might work because the state regulations could let gaming become an attractive draw.

"And," he continued, "Lanksy has them meeting in Havana because it is neutral ground, but your uncle and I think that Lansky may want Cuba for himself, but that's okay. He'll make them all happy, and they'll listen to him as they have for many years as their business advisor who saw to it that they made money, not war.

"I need you to come help, David. It'd be good experience for you. I need young new blood. These old guys are turning their family businesses over to their sons. You are my son, and you could bill lots of hours for the firm and the firm would make a lot of money if you would come to Havana. If you're going to be a lawyer, the first thing you need to learn is how to add the hours on to your billings."

"Dad, what you're describing is exactly what I don't want to do. I don't want to get involved with your old clients. I want to make my own fortune—fair and square and honestly."

David Paterno, Sr., stopped crisply. He turned and looked with his steely eyes into the eyes of his son. He lit another cigarette and inhaled deeply and cried out, "Son, goddammit, don't cross that line. Don't you disparage my legal career. My job has been to guide my clients in honoring the law in all their businesses. That's what I've always done. I have kept them legal and out of jail. Don't ever accuse me of doing otherwise. Never. Do you understand?" He inhaled again and blew the smoke out.

"Dad, I understand."

By now dark had fallen. The breeze from the Atlantic had become stronger, and father and son stood there in silence looking at each other by the gazebo next to the ocean, the father remembering his son as he grew from childhood to manhood and now into adulthood and into a legal career. The son was thinking about how he wanted to make his own fortune away from the dark, secret world of the waterfront of New Jersey and New York.

The two of them rose and raised their glasses to take the last sip of cognac before they turned their gazes into the darkness of the sky over the Atlantic, and they swung their heads to the west across New York Harbor and the bright lights of Manhattan.

CHAPTER TWENTY-SIX

S IX MONTHS AFTER being sworn in as an attorney for the state of Texas, David Paterno, Jr., was assigned to brief the commissioners on the law of field-wide unitization. This was in preparation for a hearing the Commission had called in four months on the petition of the Liberty Oil and Refining Company to unitize the nation's largest oil field: the East Texas Oil Field.

David needed most of the four months to become an expert on the law of oil field unitization. Approval by the Railroad Commission of Liberty Oil's proposal to unitize the East Texas Oil Field would mean all the thousands of properties on which the oil wells were located in the East Texas Oil Field would be consolidated into one property: the East Texas Oil Field Unit, and the one property would be operated by the company that operated the most wells in the field before unitization. In the East Texas Field, the operator of a Fieldwide Unit would be Liberty Oil.

Great economic distress would occur in all the towns in and near the oil field would suffer great economic distress as thousands of oil field workers would lose their jobs. The new Railroad Commission attorney from New Jersey began reading the law on unitization, and overnight, David Paterno, Jr., found himself becoming an important person in the regulation of oil and gas in Texas.

Jordan Phillips flew down to Austin in his DC-3 to join about four hundred persons expected to attend the hearing. This crowd would include the top management of most every independent operator, representatives of all the major oil companies, and the leaders of all the communities and towns in East Texas, all of which were fearful of becoming economically distressed if the East Texas Field were to be unitized.

The testimony was presented by the major oil companies supporting unitization and by the smaller companies opposing it. Then, the Chairman of the Railroad Commission called on the Railroad Commission's attorney, David Paterno, Jr., to summarize the case.

"Mr. Chairman, thank you for the opportunity to testify today during these oral arguments before the three commissioners on the question of unitization of the East Texas Oil Field. As Staff Attorney for the Commission, it is my privilege to summarize for the commissioners the arguments in this case for both the proponents and the opponents of unitization. It is also my charge to present to the commissioners the conclusion of the examiners of the Texas Railroad Commission who heard the cases presented by both sides at the Public Hearings."

After an hour of detailed testimony, Paterno closed his remarks by saying, "This oil resource in East Texas is one of the great treasures of the state of Texas, and the question before you today is whether or not this field should be unitized and operated by one operator instead of several thousand operators as it is today. With all this testimony you have heard today in mind, commissioners, I hereby hand you the joint recommendation prepared by the six Commission examiners. The examiners unanimously agree that unitization will decrease the ultimate oil recoveries of oil. They agree with the engineering report of Thomas Calhoun, of DeGolyer and McNaugthon, engineering consultants, Dallas, Texas, that the status quo of the East Texas Field today should be maintained, and the field must not be unitized. If the field produced as it is today and not unitized, more wells will be operated to ultimate depletion and more wells means more oil. In conclusion, the examiners unanimously recommend to the Railroad Commission of Texas that the East Texas Oil Field not be unitized. Thank you for this opportunity to speak."

The four hundred people in the ballroom of the Stephen F. Austin Hotel sat in stunned silence, then they stood and broke out in applause.

Ernest O. Thompson, the chairman of the Railroad Commission of Texas, hammered his gavel repeatedly, saying, "Ladies and gentlemen, this hearing is adjourned."

Jordan Phillips turned to Ed Clark, who standing by his side, and said, "Ed, what do you think about the Commission's young attorney?"

"I am not impressed easily, but, Jordan, that boy impressed me today."

A week later, Ed called Jordan to report that the Commission had voted unanimously against unitization. "Jordan, you need to thank that young Commission attorney. He is responsible for you not being forced to give up the operations of your oil wells, and you'll operate your wells as long as they keep producing, and you can capture all the oil reserves you're entitled by the law to produce."

"Ed, what would you think if I offered that boy a job as my attorney here in Dallas?"

"I don't know anything about his background, but if he checks out okay, you could use somebody like him."

Jordan failed to check David Paterno, Jr.'s background. He

did not learn anything positive or negative about him that could impact his oil business if he hired him. He did not learn that his candidate for in-house attorney was part of a family of law-yers whose law firm was the legal counsel to the five Mafia fami-lies that controlled not only the sale and distribution of alcohol, but were the power behind all the construction and shipping along the waterfront of New York and New Jersey. On the other hand, Jordan was thrilled to offer the job as in-house attorney for TOPCO to a young lawyer he thought would be an outstand-ing general counsel and help him to build his company. David Paterno, Jr., had come to Texas specifically to get such a posi-tion in the Texas oil business. He accepted the offer and agreed to move to Dallas to join Jordan Phillips as TOPCO'S in-house legal counsel.

Jordan called Chirp Branscum on the phone. "I wanted you to learn straight from me, Chirp, that I just hired the young Commission attorney that whipped Liberty's ass."

"That's good, Jordan. You darn sure need the help."

"Yes, I do, and I'm going to need an engineer in Dallas too."

"Things are changing out here in the field, and I've been thinking, Jordan...Well, I kinda hate to talk about it, but I got to tell you, it's about time I hang my tools up on the rack."

"C'mon, Chirp, you can't retire. What's the matter with you? You feeling bad?"

"Not bad, just old. I'm not quittin' life. I'm just changing what I do. Producing the easy oil is over in East Texas. We're plugging water wells every month. You need to spend your time finding a new oil field, but you also need new blood out here in this oil field. I have a lead on a young buck Aggie with math smarts who can come in and produce the 'hard' oil. He's an East Texas boy, and he worked summers for us when he was going to White Oak. He did a good job. Not too many of those young boll weevils would climb down inside a tank and clean out the bottoms when it's a hundred and five degrees outside. He's graduating from A&M at College Station with a petroleum engineering degree, and I hear he wants to come back home to East Texas and work."

"What's his name?"

"Sam Knight Jr., son of the druggist in Kilgore, one of your original investors."

"Oh, sure. I remember Sam talking about his son, but hell, Chirp, I don't want you ever to quit, but, if it makes you feel better, go ahead and hire that boy, and tell young Knight not to forget that I'll want him to spend some time in Dallas. Tell him I'm going to find me another East Texas Field, and I need him to engineer all the wells I'm going to drill. Tell him that you will be his boss too and still running the oil field for years to come, I hope."

"Boss, you are the greatest optimist I have ever seen. Thank you, Jordan."

CHAPTER TWENTY-SEVEN

OIL WELLS DIE when the water hits. They won't flow, and then pumps have to be run down to the bottom the oil well to pump out the oil and all the water, and there was nothing that reminded Jordan more of the personal money trap he was facing with his oil wells going to water at the same time Merle was telling him of all the money Charlotte was spending.

"Jordan, we just got a bill for another car from Beverly Hills Cadillac—a new black Fleetwood Limousine, one that she can't even drive. It has to have a chauffeur."

"There's not a damn thing in the world I can do about her except to find a new oil field and keep up with her spending."

CHAPTER TWENTY-EIGHT

"MERLE, WILL YOU call David Paterno, and tell him to be in my conference room next Monday morning at eleven? And Sam Knight, Jr., too. Call him at the field office. Tell him to get to Dallas and be in my conference room Monday."

Sam Knight, Jr., had worked his way up to be Chirp's assistant, and when he walked into Jordan's conference room the next Monday, Jordan Phillips greeted him warmly. "Sam, it's good to have you as a member of the TOPCO family. I hear good things about your work out in the field. Tell me, how's your dad? I hope he's doing okay."

Sam stared straight at his boss without smiling. He didn't want to talk about his father's investment in the TOPCO stock. "Dad sees Chirp, and so do I. I saw Chirp and Mary Julia last night at the Green Hut. Chirp never forgets to let me know what I need to be doing, and I get it done fast, or he'll never let me alone."

"Sam, I need you to move to Dallas. You better start looking for somebody to take your place in East Texas."

"Why would you want me here?"

"We'll talk about that in our meeting."

When David Paterno, Jr., entered the conference room, Jordan said, "David, I think you've met Sam. I asked him to be here."

"Sure, Sam. It's good to see you here in Dallas." Sam and David shook hands, and the three of them sat down around the conference table.

"I called this meeting to tell you both about how I plan to find another East Texas Oil Field, and I want to tell you why I want Sam to move to Dallas."

"Sam move to Dallas?" David's his jaw dropped.

Jordan stood and went to the blackboard. "Before the war, I first saw the water encroaching into the west side of the field," he said, picking up a piece of white chalk and drawing a rough outline of the East Texas Oil Field in the shape of an upside down boot. Then he changed to a piece of red chalk to draw a wiggly red line showing the salt water encroachment in the west quarter of the field. "This water encroachment has been like the Chinese water torture for me. Then the war and the Commission, at the Fed's request, opened up the field, and we produced a half a billion barrels of oil, but it pulled in the salt water, and in '46, the salt water production was up to over 500,000 barrels a day."

He put down the chalk and sat back down at the conference table. "So, I am going to find another East Texas Oil Field. I am going to convert TOPCO into the finest exploration company in the history of the oil and gas industry. I asked you to meet with me so I can enlist your help in achieving this goal." Jordan took a sip of his coffee, which had gone cold, and he made a face.

The two young managers were stunned. "How are you going to find a new oil field the size of East Texas, Mr. Phillips?" asked Sam.

"This business has changed. Oil finding is improving with the advances in geological knowledge. We need to hire geologists, and I mean oil finding geologists. Sam, get me interviews with the top geological candidates, and I'll select my oil finder. You will also need a staff of engineers. Merle will show you the suite of offices for you and your new engineers."

David thought his boss was losing it. Sam was mystified at what he was hearing.

Jordan continued, "We need to drill smart. Many people say Doc Berry's primitive geology found East Texas by accident, and that will always be a debatable question, but there's no question about it. Today, there are more scientific ways to find oil. It boils down to the creativity in the mind of the earth scientist. There's new research by a Frenchman Maurice Allais on applying the Monte Carlo simulation method to determine the probability of a prospect finding oil, but the real secret is to start drilling behind the best geology and keep drilling until you hit oil. "

David Paterno broke his silence. "Is it the science or the drilling that finds the oil? How much money do your probability studies show you would need to spend to find these new oil fields, Mr. Phillips?"

"Fortunately, David, I have the money. I'm ready to budget whatever it takes to find a giant oil field. If we need to spend thirty million dollars, we'll spend thirty million, or if we need to spend fifty we'll spend fifty million dollars."

"Sir, you're losing me. I'm not allowed to see any financials. Do we actually have thirty to fifty million in the bank?" David said.

"Oh, and I didn't tell you anything about how we can use seismic to help find oil. Did you know that the German army figured out how to use seismographs to locate cannons in the First World War? They'd set up three seismographs to record the vibrations in the earth when a cannon fired, and with the seismic, they could pinpoint the location of the cannon, and wham! They'd destroy that cannon. Then after the war, when seismic reflections were being used to show the anticlines underground, two brothers, Scott and Dabney Petty, decided how, by using a vacuum tube, the measurements would be more accurate.

"But," David Paterno repeated, "Mr. Phillips, sir, how about the money? Do you have the fifty million in the bank?" As he spoke, he looked over at Sam Knight, Jr. Sam stared back with his eyes wide open, and shook his head at David. He looked bored as hell.

Jordan paid no attention to his not-so-captive audience and continued his lesson about the science of oil finding. "Seismic took off for finding highs to drill and find oil. We'll use as much seismic as our geologists say they need to help nail down the prospects to drill."

"Mr. Phillips, I know you know how to find oil, but what about the money? Where will you find it?"

"Forty million barrels of Fairway reserves in East Texas should provide all the collateral we need if we have to borrow money. The major oil companies borrow money from the public. They borrow from banks. They find oil. If we need money to keep drilling we can always go to the bank and borrow on our Fairway reserves."

Sam was leaning far forward across the table. Sweat beaded on his forehead. "I don't understand it. I guess I'm just a dumb Aggie engineer."

"We need to start by hiring the best oil-finding geologist. Sam, get those resumes on my desk next week."

"If that's your orders, sir, I'll sure do it."

"That's what I want, so do it. Well, gentlemen, you've heard all I had to say. I'd like for you to think about what you've heard today. I expect you to give me your thoughts on the plan I have laid out when we meet again next week." Jordan Phillips stood up from the table and walked out of his conference room.

Sam and David were left alone, staring at the door Jordan Phillips had closed behind him.

"David, what the hell's going on?"

"I'm in a state of shock. Fifty million dollars. Did you hear what I heard?"

Sam nodded. "I sure did. I need a drink. It's Carousel Club time. I need a drink right now, but I can't get there 'til four thirty. Can you join me?"

"I'll be there. A broke wildcatter won't make a payroll very long, and for somebody who appreciates a pay check, that's not a happy thought."

Sam got to the Carousel Club before David and ordered a double Dewar's on the rocks. *Good Lord*, he thought, *I hate the ground that old bastard walks on. He screwed Dad when he forced him to sell his TOPCO stock back to him too cheap.* Listening to Jordan Phillips in that meeting today convinced Sam that Jordan Phillips had really gone crazy. *I'll never be happy until I can figure out a way to get back at that son of a bitch for fucking my old man.*

The smoke and the other putrid odors in the back of the Carousel Club could only be described as Bus Station Urinal Fragrance #5. The bartender's 78 inch Victrola was scratching out the strains of an early Duke Ellington version of "Mood Indigo."

Sam was on his third Dewar's when David showed up. The drunker Sam got, the louder he talked, repeating over and over how spending fifty million dollars wildcatting was a sign that his boss was falling into some form of early dementia. David didn't say anything. He just nodded and listened, sipping his Tanqueray martinis.

CHAPTER TWENTY-NINE

"SAM, THANKS FOR getting me the resumes of those geologists. I like this Mike Wharton. Could you arrange for him to come to Dallas for an interview? He looks like the right man to build an oil-finding program."

"But, Mr. Phillips, do you really want to hire a PhD?"

"What's wrong with a PhD?"

"PhD's will break you trying to prove geological theories. Sir, I guess it's none of my business, but I don't understand why you can't be happy with all those Fairway Wells in the East Texas Field. They'll last another hundred years. And, Mr. Phillips, you have so many Fairway Wells you can forget about the salt water encroachment. This is none of my business, but if I were you, I'd sit back and enjoy my life."

Jordan had a hot cup of coffee in front of him today. He liked coffee hot to the point where it nearly burned his tongue. He took a sip, felt that pleasant burn. "Sam, thank you for your concern, but let me tell you something about me that you may have missed. There's no feeling like the euphoria a wildcatter feels when he brings in a new oil discovery, and I want to feel the elation again like what I felt under those pine trees on Miss Daisy's farm back in 1930 that day the oil flowed over the top of the derrick. Just one more time. The East Texas Field will be depleted someday. I can never stop drilling." He paused, looking straight into Sam's eyes until Sam looked away. Jordan continued. "Mike Wharton's doctoral dissertation *Probability Studies in the Exploration for Giant Oil Fields* tells how he will discover new giant oil fields, and he concludes in his dissertation that there may be no better place to look for a giant oil field than in Alaska. There's nothing I'd like better than finding an oil field in Alaska. From what I can read about Mike Wharton, he sounds like the man to lead our oil finding effort."

In two weeks, Jordan Phillips made a rare Saturday trip downtown to his office to interview Mike Wharton. At the end of the interview, Jordan Phillips was not pleased when he was forced to say, "So, Mr. Wharton, you won't take the job as Chief Geologist? I'm the largest independent in Texas. I don't understand it."

"Sir, it's an honor to meet a great wildcatter, but I'm not just looking for a paycheck. I wish I could accept your offer."

Sam Knight, Jr., had been in the room with Jordan and Mike Wharton through the entire interview.

"Sam, thank you for arranging for Mr. Wharton to come to Dallas to meet us. I'm sorry we couldn't sell him on joining us. We have offered him as much salary as anyone, except me, in the company is drawing. Mr. Wharton, before you leave, I'd like a chance to talk to you alone. Sam, would you mind excusing yourself?"

"Of course not, sir. Mike, drop by my office on your way out," Sam said. "Give me your expenses, and I'll have accounting send you a check."

"Thank you, Sam, but I don't have any expenses; I was

coming through Dallas anyway on the way home to Sherman. Thanks very much. It was nice to meet you."

After Sam left, Jordan Phillips asked, "Mr. Wharton, do you really think you could find a giant oil field?"

"Mr. Phillips, could you call me Mike?"

"Sure, Mike."

"Thanks. I'm just not that formal."

"Do you think you could find a giant oil field?"

"I've devoted myself to learning about the earth. My entire education has been focused on learning the science of the generation, migration and the accumulation of oil where it is found trapped, deep underground. It would help me answer your question if you could tell me how you define a giant field."

"Mike, I compare everything to East Texas. I want to find another East Texas Oil Field. East Texas looks like it's going to produce maybe six billion barrels. I'm not greedy. If I can end up with TOPCO owning a one-billion-barrel oil field, then I'd have found a lot more reserves than I had in East Texas. That's how I define a giant field—one billion barrels."

"I don't see any problem with that."

Jordan was amazed at the confidence of this young man. "Mike, you're serious, aren't you?"

"Sir, I am serious. There are many billion-barrel oil fields left to find in this world, but the fact is, we'll have to look outside of Texas. Shallow oil above six thousand feet has been drilled up in Texas. Deeper wells are finding mostly natural gas."

"You think big, and I like that. You're a dreamer, and it takes a dreamer to find a giant oil field. That's why I want you to join me."

"Thank you, sir. Hearing you say that makes me even sorrier I can't work with you."

"Why won't you work for me? We offered you a large starting salary and good benefits."

"Mr. Phillips, I'm not interested in just a salary and benefits. I am going to find a giant oil field, and I want a piece of the action. I want an overriding royalty. Sam Knight told me you wouldn't give anybody an override."

"Well, that's right. No oil company I know gives overrides. I certainly don't give overrides, never have, and I can't start doing that."

"Mr. Phillips, I couldn't accept a job with you anyway. I'm headed back to Alaska in July for my last summer with the USGS mapping crew. I couldn't go to work for anyone for six months."

"What's going on in Alaska?"

"I've worked three summers with the USGS on their project to finish the official Geological Map of the Territory of Alaska. Liberty and Shell and several of the big companies see potential for some great oil fields on the North Slope of the Bristol Range in North Alaska. There are oil rich source rocks, but the question is whether or not the quality of the potential reservoir rocks is good enough to provide the massive potential reservoir storage volume to justify the high cost of drilling in Alaska. Oil has to be sold to obtain any revenue or return on investment.

I would bet that it would take a discovery of at least one billion barrels to pay for a pipeline to move oil out of that extreme territory.

If I find good rocks this summer, I'll come back to Texas with a giant oil field drilling prospect in my hip pocket."

"Mike, that's exactly the prospect I want to drill. Come work for me when you get home."

If I find what I'm looking for, North Alaska will become a billion-barrel oil province, maybe several billion barrels. I can find somebody to drill it and give me a piece of the action. I was hoping it would be you. In any case, Mr. Phillips, it's sure been a pleasure to meet you."

"Well, Mike, if I come up with something that might change your mind, would you reconsider?"

"Sure, sir. Of course. I'm always ready to listen."

"We are destined to get together. I'll figure out a way to get you back here for good." They stood and shook hands.

Jordan sat staring at the photograph of the #3 Daisy Bradford Well on the wall behind his desk, tapping his fingers. After a few minutes, he turned in his chair and faced the wall behind him and picked up the mouthpiece of the Dictaphone sitting on his cadenza and began to dictate a letter. The letter was addressed to Mike Wharton in Austin, and in the letter, Jordan offered Mike a one percent overriding royalty in any prospect he originated that was successful in finding oil. He told him in the letter to follow through with his plan to go to Alaska and complete his field geological research. He closed by saying that after he was finished in Alaska, he looked forward to him formally beginning his employment as TOPCO'S Chief Geologist in Dallas.

Back home in Austin the following Tuesday afternoon, Mike Wharton opened a flat brown envelope addressed to him. The return address printed on the envelope was TOPCO in Dallas, and a spinning red top logo was under the name of the sender. After reading the letter, he whistled a long, slow whistle, and he read the letter again. He made a mental calculation of the value of a one percent overriding royalty in a one billion barrel oil discovery. Jordan Phillips had given him the opportunity to become a millionaire many times over.

CHAPTER THIRTY

S AM KNIGHT, CHARLOTTE'S druggist from Kilgore, would visit her in California several times a year if she'd send him the train ticket, but Sam's visits to see her became less frequent as the years passed. She didn't slow down in her desire for male companionship even though Sam slowed down coming to her. She needed to have a romantic place for trysts with new men, so Charlotte bought a cabana on the beach next to the Santa Monica Resort Hotel. She kept a full bar inside her cabana stocked with fine wine and premium spirits, and it had a bedroom and full bath in the back.

Aging and losing some of the spark of her youth, Charlotte felt a younger man could help her feel young again. It didn't take her long to find a carefree guy named Rollie Masters, the manager of the Santa Monica Resort Hotel next door to her cabana. He was at least ten years younger than Charlotte, maybe fifteen.

"Wow! Charlotte you've got a fun place on the beach. Look at that sunset! I'm glad to get to know you better. Can I fix you a drink?" Rollie said on their first evening together.

"Yes, Rollie Boy. Fix me a Yellow Tail. Vodka on the rocks with lots of rocks and a twist of lemon. I like my vodka frigid cold."

"Holding a frigid vodka makes your hands cold."

"Yes, but it makes everything else warm, doesn't it, darlin'?"

"Honey, you and I are made for each other, but we're gonna need some music out here on the beach. I'll get you some records and a new record player. We need Bing Crosby and Sinatra. I'll find them."

When the records were playing the kind of music she liked, she'd say, "Dance with me, Rollie. Hold me close, and let's dance."

The friendly hotel manager decided there was no reason he couldn't get close to this older lady with a cinnamon complexion and colored blonde hair and a ton of Texas oil money, so when she'd call Rollie Masters and tell him to meet her, he'd get there fast. Sometimes the afternoons in the cabana ran long into the night. Sometimes they ran into the next day or two. Rollie decided he would have no problem helping Charlotte enjoy her money.

"I am it, Charlotte. I'm the real thing. It's time for you to divorce that Texas oil guy so you and I can spend the rest of our lives together. He doesn't want you, and I'll take care of you. Divorce him. I'll get you a good lawyer, and you'll get half of everything he owns. We'll spend the rest of our lives together. Honey, babe, love, I don't want to ever leave you."

CHAPTER THIRTY-ONE

"JORDAN, THERE'S A man here in a uniform here who wants to see you, and he's got a gun," Merle said, walking into her boss' office after he had left his Management Committee meeting.

"What's that, Merle? Why would someone in a uniform with a gun come into my office?"

"He must be a peace officer. He's wearing a badge. I tried to find out what he wanted, but he ordered me to find you."

"Well, show him in."

Merle brought the man into Jordan Phillip's office. He was dressed in a khaki uniform with a badge on his chest, wearing a ten-gallon hat with a revolver in the holster on his belt. "Are you Jordan Phillips?"

"Yes, I am, and who are you?"

"I am a deputy constable of Dallas County, and I am here to serve this summons on Jordan Phillips." The constable held a paper in his right hand, and he opened it and began reading aloud: "'In the matter of Charlotte Sasakwa Phillips, plaintiff, versus Jordan Phillips, defendant, in the Petition for Divorce dated Tuesday June 12, 1952, you are hereby summoned to be present at a hearing at the Los Angeles County Courthouse on Wednesday June 18, 1951.'"

The constable told Jordan Phillips to sign the receipt of the document. When he had signed on the dotted line, he handed the original of the summons to Jordan Phillips and took the carbon copy and turned around and walked out of the office.

"Well, I'll be, Merle! She did it. She filed for divorce."

"Jordan, you knew this had to happen, eventually."

"Why now?"

"She's probably found some over-the-hill cowboy movie star and wants to get rid of you so she can get married."

"She's living the good life, and I take good care of her and Jan. She gets all the money she needs. What in the hell is the matter with her? Call that new lawyer right now."

Merle called Joe Anderson, the young lawyer here in Dallas that Ed Clark told Jordan to use. Joe Anderson wasn't a transaction lawyer. He wasn't a lobbyist. He was a people problems lawyer, and he had almost a perfect record in the court room. He had learned everything he knew about people problems law from his step-father, one of Texas's most famous litigators.

"Hey, Joe. It's Jordan Phillips. My wife just filed for divorce."

"Mr. Phillips, Ed told me about Mrs. Phillips, and he mentioned this possibility to me. This could cost you your company. You've got to pick up the phone now and call her and talk her out of filing. I'll bet you she's got one of those movie-star divorce lawyers, and those Hollywood lawyers can be as mean as junk yard dogs."

"It won't do any good to call, and I don't know how to talk her out of filing."

"That's simple, Mr. Phillips. Call her, and tell her you will cut off her money unless she pulls her filing. She will cry 'uncle' and tell you that she'll pull her divorce filing, then call me back, and you and I can have a good laugh."

"Good thinking, young man. You are absolutely right. I'll call her and cut her off." He hung up and called Merle and said, "Tell David Paterno to get in here."

"Come in here, David. She wants a divorce," Jordan said when David appeared at his office door. "I knew it would happen, but I have been fooling myself thinking I could put her off, but it's over. She filed."

"Mr. Phillips, it may not be over. Maybe she's just firing a shot across your bow, but you need a divorce lawyer."

"I know it, but, I've got this young lawyer Ed Clark told me about, Joe Anderson, and he's good. He's not only a divorce lawyer, but he can do any legal thing that anybody with people problems ever needs, and you never know what a harlot like Charlotte will do next. They take, and they take, and they keep on taking. Joe Anderson said I need to call Charlotte and sweet talk her out of filing."

"He's right."

"Why in the world would I talk to her? We haven't slept together for years. No marriage bed means no marriage."

"But, legally, you're married."

"Sure, and I'm her sugar daddy, and I pay all the bills. All I do is sign a bunch of blank checks, and Merle pays her bills I don't ever even want to know what she's spending all my money on."

"That's okay. You've got to try to work out some kind of deal with her. A divorce will put you in one hell of a financial squeeze."

"Well, to hell with that. My TOPCO stock is my separate property. It was mine before we got married."

"Well, you're right, you got your TOPCO stock before you married, and you'll say it's your separate property, but her lawyer will claim that not only is the stock half hers, but every asset you acquired after you two were married was acquired with community funds, and they'll say that makes her entitled to half of everything you own, like the 'Log Cabin' in East Texas and your residence here in Dallas on White Rock Lake and the mansion out in Beverly Hills. All of your Western art and your stocks and other investment portfolio would be community property. Half hers."

"I guess my stocks are worth at least twenty-five million. I don't know what my Charlie Russell and Remington paintings and the Remington sculptures are worth today. I ought to ask Tom Gilcrease. He'd know."

"Mr. Phillips, it'll cost the hell out of you if she goes through with this. You'd have to shut down your drilling program, and what about Jan? Have you taken care of Jan?"

"Jan has a five-million-dollar trust that's hers when she turns twenty-five. And no, by God, I am not going to stop wildcatting."

"You'll have to do some high financing if you buy off Miss Charlotte and still have fifty million more to spend on drilling your wildcats."

"Merle, get Charlotte on the phone."

Merle stood there shaking her head in disbelief. She'd been standing there in back of David Paterno listening to the whole bloody story. She went back to her desk and phoned Miss Charlotte and transferred the call to Jordan.

"Hello, Charlotte," Jordan said. "Why didn't you tell me you were going to file for divorce? What in the world's going on? I thought we had an arrangement. I have kept my side of our deal."

David and Merle remained quiet. Only Jordan could hear Miss Charlotte's response.

"The grass is not greener on the other side, Charlotte. You forget that I sign all those checks every month, but that's over now. I won't sign another check to you. You'll have to live without any money from me until your divorce goes through the courts. I'll fight it, and it might be years before you get another dime out of me. How are you going to eat without my checks?"

He stopped talking to take a breath. He listened for Miss Charlotte's response. She was silent until finally he asked her about Jan.

"I'll keep sending checks for Jan's school and for her trips to Europe and checks for her cars, and I'll pay for her new sailboat at Redondo Beach. Jan hasn't hired a team of lawyers like you, Charlotte."

Jordan paused again. He could hear Charlotte whispering to someone in the background, "He says he's going to stop sending the money."

Then more silence. Finally, Jordan said, "So if you're talking to your lawyer friend, c'mon, Charlotte, you've got your head screwed on wrong. Tell that lawyer to pull that filing, and then fire him." He listened to her response.

"Well, no wonder. You're crazy to use a free lawyer. I don't care if it's your neighbor. You'll get what you pay for. I shouldn't be telling you how stupid you're acting, but you're still legally my wife and the mother of my daughter, and I am still taking care of you and for God's sake, once I loved you. Let me tell you once and for all, don't keep sticking your head down a sink hole. I'll take care of you like I have done all these years, but I'm not send-ing you another dime until you pull that divorce filing."

After another telling pause while he listened to Charlotte, he said, "Well, good, I'm glad to hear you getting some sense. Leave well enough alone, and life out in Beverly Hills will be good."

"Yes, and tell my little girl hello for me and to come see me."

Then after another moment, he tersely replied, "Okay, that's good. Bye."

Merle said, "Jordan, I hate to tell you, but it's not over. She'll be back. You better get your house in order."

"I know it, Merle."

CHAPTER THIRTY-TWO

JULY 15, 1952 was a clear day in Alaska. Mike Wharton was bouncing around at 10,000 feet in the de Havilland Otter on the flight from Fairbanks to the bivouac point to meet the USGS geological field-mapping team on the north shoreline of Alaska. He double checked his seat belt and cinched it tighter for good measure. The flight plan took him over the Brooks Range across the North Slope down near an Inuit settlement on the shoreline. The radial engine roaring loudly as the craft buffeted through the winds of Anaktuvuk Pass. Mike sat in the back of the ten place amphibian next to a girl who looked like she might be pretty if he could see through the hat and scarf covering her head.

After about a half hour of flying, the girl turned to Mike and said, "Excuse me, my name is Joan Ambrose."

"Nice to meet you. I'm Mike. Mike Wharton. I'm a geologist. How about you? Why are you going to the North Shoreline of Alaska?"

"I'm here from Mines interning on a USGS surface-mapping crew. I need field work to complete my PhD dissertation. Are you with the USGS?"

"You could say I'm on loan to the Survey. I've finished up

with my doctorate at Texas University and have been with the Bureau a couple of years. You know, the Bureau of Economic Geology. It's like the State Geological Survey. Austin is the state capital. Can I call you Joan?"

"Of course, Mike. Call me Joan, but c'mon, everybody knows Austin's the capital of Texas."

"There can't be more than one USGS crew, so I guess we'll be working together. What's your paper on? The Carboniferous? Mississippian or Pennsylvanian?"

"Both. My advisor thinks the big Leduc discovery in Alberta means there's potential for reef builders in Alaska, and he wanted my thesis to be on the possibility of reef growth in the Carboniferous in Alaska, so here I am."

"Well, I don't know about reef growth up here. You might find some dolomites in the outcrops we'll be seeing, but the limestones I've seen have mostly had only fracture porosity. If that's all we find, the reef hunters will stay home in Alberta or down in Midland in the Permian Basin. What we need to find in Alaska is rock with big reservoir volume potential. Nothing small is commercial in Alaska."

"So if you are just on loan to the USGS, what's your real agenda up here?"

"I just told you. I'm looking for rock with large storage volume, and what I have seen tells me the best potential for large reservoirs could be the Triassic. With nearby source rocks loaded with hydrocarbons, a Triassic reservoir could be loaded with oil, but reservoirs in Alaska are going to have to hold billions of barrels of oil. With no infrastructure and the arctic climate, it will cost billions of dollars to sell the first barrel of oil."

"You got your work cut out for you. I hope I get to help you find the rock you're looking for."

"If you can paddle a canoe upstream to the foothills, I

imagine I can get you assigned to be my intern. It's really nice to meet you, but frankly, I'm surprised. I've never seen a woman on a geological field trip."

"The world is changing."

"We might spend three months in the wilderness."

"I can take it. Change with the world, or it will change without you."

"You're kind of a smart ass chick, aren't you?"

"If that's how you want to see me. I'm really not a smart ass, but being the only girl and the youngest of six kids with five older brothers, it's either be a smart ass or be wiped out." She said that with a slightly sexy smile. For that matter, Mike felt it was kind of sexy for a woman to be alone on a field trip for two or three months with a bunch of young males—geologists and Indian guides.

"Why would you volunteer to be the only woman alone in the wilderness with a crew of young males for half the summer?"

The plane slipped down quietly through the clouds toward a landing along the shoreline of North Alaska. "Let's get something straight. I'm a virgin. I'm saving myself for the man I marry if I ever find such a man. There's no male-female issue up here for me. I can handle any man I need to handle."

"I'm sorry, Miss Ambrose. I didn't intend to get that personal with you."

"Don't worry about it, Mike, but tell me, have you been here before?"

"This will be my third summer with the USGS. Before I start work with my new company, the C.E.O. wanted me to come back here and finish this project. Who knows, maybe someday I'll end up doing some exploration here."

"I'm slow but I finally get it. Your company sent you up here to find them a giant oil prospect."

"Who knows? We'll have to see what we find."

The pontoons of the float plane slapped down on the waters of the Beaufort Sea, and the plane water-taxied up to loading dock. The passengers exited the float plane into cold, twenty-degree temperature and a strong, biting north wind blowing at least forty miles an hour which brought the chill factor down to below freezing on a late summer day.

Mike was able to arrange for Joan Ambrose to be his intern and to paddle upstream on the Sadelrochit River in his canoe, one of a string of canoes from the USGS mapping team. They paddled hard and finally made camp the first night up past where the river became a stream.

The next day, they paddled farther until they reached a fork in the ever shrinking stream. The flotilla of canoes took the southeasterly fork and paddled a little further until the stream became too small to continue, and they tied their canoes to small pine trees on the side of the pool of cold spring water that was all that was left of the stream. They stashed provisions for the return trip down the river to the North shoreline of Alaska. Mike was careful to hide a couple of bottles of Champagne Brut in the gunny sack he sunk in the cold water and tied to the canoe.

The entire crew began their trek on foot, up the spring creek for several miles until they got to the springs that were feeding the spring creek. They kept on climbing up into the rocks of the foothills of the Sadelrochit Mountains above the tundra of the North Slope. When they got to the rocks, the geologists would begin the their tedious work, measuring and describing rock, inch by inch, all the way up from the first outcrop at the base of the foothills and over the crest of the Sadelrochits on up to the top of the Brooks Range.

The days were long, and sometimes the geologists had to scale steep cliff faces to get their job done. Other times, they squeezed through narrow cracks in the rock walls of the outcrops or had to force their way through fallen branches of the overgrown trails in the pine forests where the Eskimo guides hadn't done a very good job clearing trail with their wood cutters. There was too much work to expect perfection in clearing a trail or in doing anything in the cold and extreme north woods of Alaska.

At the end of the third day of scaling and describing the stratigraphy of each steep cliff, their climb brought them to a new and entirely different rock. Geologists knew that a change in the rock could mean they had crossed a contact between two different geological formations, one a dark carbonate and the other a mudstone. They stood at the base of this reddish mudstone cliff that must have been two hundred feet high. Obviously the tall cliff was entirely comprised of the same rock.

"Joan, describe this as a very fine grain, quarzitic mudstone, reddish to orange, no visible porosity or permeability. The few flat clam bivalves tells me this is Triassic. It's Sadelrochit Group, probably Ivishak equivalent. It has about as much porosity as a tombstone. There's zero reservoir volume in this rock. I hate to say this, but it looks like we can forget about the Triassic as an exploration target," Mike Wharton complained to his lady intern.

"Heck. That's too bad, Mike. So do we still need to climb the whole cliff and describe the entire outcrop?"

"Of course. Our orders are to compile a complete description of the geological section of the North Slope. We are not going to cheat one inch, so tombstone or not, let's climb. Write down in your notes exactly what I said: Triassic, Sadelrochit Group, Ivishak equivalent with zero reservoir quality." The two of them scaled the two hundred foot high cliff of tombstone rock. Mike talking and Joan writing down notes.

At night in the summertime, it was never completely dark. They could see the Aurora Borealis—the Northern Lights—and the wind always blew hard, and although it was summer, the temperature dropped below freezing almost every night.

The native guides would prepare dinner of Coho Salmon or rainbow trout or whatever fish they had caught that day, and after a hard day of climbing, the dinner would be welcomed by all. Around the campfire at night the geologists would talk about the rocks they had seen. There was always one small tent alongside all the men's sleeping bags so that the girl geologist could gain a little privacy.

Joan Ambrose and Mike Wharton became friendlier. She learned she could sort of tease Mike when they were alone, but sometimes their talk was serious geology.

"Mike, it won't be long and we will be at the top of the Brooks Range, and we'll turn around to go back down there," she said pointing north toward the blue waters of the Beaufort Sea between the shoreline and the horizon. "I can't help but wonder how terrible you must feel that we haven't found any good reservoir rock."

"Joan, this trip is not over till we get back to the bottom. I'm not giving up yet."

"It doesn't look good, and I can't help but feel sorry for you. You must be terribly disappointed."

"Look, I never give up. Until the chances are zero, I'm not giving up. I expect to return to Dallas with exactly what I'm looking for. Maybe we missed the good rock so far, and we'll find it on the way back down."

Mike Wharton and Joan Ambrose and the rest of the USGS geological mapping team reached the summit. On the return back down the mountains, the crew took a different route. They followed a more westerly trail down the mountains, around and back up to the lower summit of the Sadelrochits, and then back down toward the place they began when they ran into the ice-cold spring fed creek, then the trail doubled back along the creek until they finally reached the fork where the two small mountain streams merged together, right where they had stashed their canoes and provisions for the final leg of the trip home. It was there where they would board their canoes and float down the fast moving water only a short day back down to the sea, and the summer in Alaska would come to an end.

Mike and Joan lagged behind the other canoes. They were both disappointed not to have found the reservoir quality porosity needed in the rocks for Mike to recommend drilling for oil in Alaska. Mike got quieter and quieter as they got closer to the point of return. He was trying to think of an idea for another place to advise Jordan Phillips to explore for a giant oil field.

When the two geologists reached their canoe, Mike began the process of fixing what he presumed would be his last lunch ever with Joan, retrieving the champagne and two cans of Vienna sausage he had stashed in the cold spring water next to the canoe, looking forward to reminiscing with his new gal geologist friend about their time together. He doubted now if he'd have an excuse to meet with her again, since it looked like the idea of working together exploring for oil in Alaska would be chalked off to experience and just another dry hole.

"Mike, when we were coming back down the trail and reached the springs, I looked to the right up a game trail and saw a cliff that looked different. If it's okay with you, I'd like to walk back up there and go over and take a look at the face of that cliff. I'll let you alone to fix one of your famous Vienna sausage and Ritz Cracker sandwiches"

"Now, don't bad mouth my Ritz Cracker and Vienna Sausage sandwiches. Even stale Ritz Crackers will taste good with ice cold champagne, but sure, Joan, go back up there and look at that rock. Call me if you see anything I need to see"

"Mike, I'm sad. I was hoping we'd be celebrating finding good rock."

"Don't let dry holes get you down. That's show biz." Mike shrugged. "We'll keep looking. Maybe you'll find it up at that cliff you're going back to look at. Most surprises in geology are bad, but sometimes surprises can be good—real good. If I had my pipe and some tobacco, I'd walk back up to that cliff with you and light my pipe and lie down on the ground, blow a few smoke rings and look up the rocks all the way back to the top of the mountains, and I'd try my best to figure out where the good rock in North Alaska might be, but Mother Nature's hiding it like she's been hiding it through the ages."

Joan left him to walk back up the fork of the stream a half a mile to the little trail up to the cliff she'd seen on the way down. Mike started a campfire on the bank of the stream next to the canoe. After she walked back up the trail, she turned and walked over to the cliff. As she walked closer to the cliff, she stepped over more and more stones and pebbles, which all looked like pieces of the same rough brown grainy rock. She reached down and picked up a large pebble, and the rock floated up in her hand almost as light as a feather.

She kept walking up the trail until she reached the base of the cliff, and she could tell that was all the same tall and broken brown rock. Being a geologist, it was easy for her to tell that the pebbles on the trail she had walked on were the same rocks that formed the cliff. She made a mental description of the rock on the cliff, and the pebbles on the ground along the trail. Coarse grain, light, brownish, soft, loosely consolidated sand was how she described the rock. She broke a larger pebble in two, and the rock crumbled apart easily.

She rushed back down to the stream and back down the

stream toward Mike to where he could hear her cry, "Mike, come here! Come here now!"

Mike put down the Vienna sausage can and the old box of Ritz Crackers and ran as fast as he could up to where Joan was standing.

"What is it, Joan?"

"You won't believe it. Look at this rock. It's what we've been looking for all summer." She handed Mike a piece of the rock. "It's an unconsolidated, coarse grained sand. It crumbles when you try to break it. It's oil stained, and it must have a high carbon content. You can almost see the grease in the pore spaces."

Mike looked at the rock through his hand lens. "This is an excellent rock, but I don't understand it. This is the same formation that only a few miles east was nothing but a tombstone. Here it's a great reservoir rock. We found a happy surprise, didn't we? This is Triassic, in the Sadelrochit Group, and we have discovered one hell of a fan delta. It's exactly the rock we've been looking for! This rock could hold billions of barrels of oil."

"Mike, that cliff is over three hundred feet high. How much oil could a reservoir like this hold if it was three hundred feet thick?"

"Billions of barrels. It wouldn't have to cover that much area to hold billions of barrels of oil. If we can find this rock trapped, we'll find our giant oil field. I can't wait to tell Jordan Phillips. God bless you, Joan, for finding this rock."

They filled a sack with samples of the rock. They never stopped talking as they walked on back downstream for Mike's shore lunch.

As Mike fixed Joan a plate of Ritz Cracker and Vienna sausage sandwiches, and the flames of the fire rose higher and higher. Joan took one of the rocks she had collected and threw it into the fire, and their conversation was interrupted by the sharp popping sound almost like firecrackers on New Year's Day.

"Listen to that popping. Can you hear the hissing sound? That's gas being released from the rock with the heat from that fire causing the rock to explode. Now what do you smell? It's the odor of oil."

"I've never seen anything like this. Mike, this has been an incredible summer."

He filled two paper cups with ice cold champagne.

"Joan, I propose a toast to you and to our good fortune. Thank you for finding this good rock."

"But I only stumbled on this rock. You brought me here, Mike. Thanks for the champagne and for the toast."

The two geologists drank down the toast, and they continued to talk as they finished lunch. She lay back on the tarp Mike had spread on the ground. They drank more champagne and toasted the exciting future together they both felt lay ahead in Alaska. Joan lifted herself up on her arms and placed her face close to his and looked him straight in the eyes. "Mike, I'm liking you better the more I get to know you. I hope you don't mind if I kiss you." She kissed him on the lips. He returned her kiss and hugged her tight for one long magical moment.

CHAPTER THIRTY-THREE

BACK IN DALLAS in July, Jordan spoke to Joe Anderson. "These demand letters are driving me crazy, Joe. She pulled her divorce, but do I still have to furnish her copies of my personal bank statements and the TOPCO bank statements and all the other information she keeps demanding?"

"Mr. Phillips, if it keeps you out of the court house, do it. Don't worry about it. Furnish her whatever she wants," he told Jordan. "Someday you'll decide to go through with it and get rid of her once and for all. You might as well get yourself ready."

"Okay. We'll flood her with so much information she won't know what to do with it. I'll talk to you next week," he said as he hung up the phone.

Jordan got up and walked into his secretary's office and asked, "Merle, what are you doing?"

"I'm pulling together all that information you asked me to send her."

"Good. Joe says to go ahead and mail all the damn stuff to her."

"You must be feeling low, Jordan. I haven't seen you this down in a long time."

"Well, damn it, I'm only human. The jackal's applying the Chinese water torture."

"Why don't you get away? Go fishing. Get your mind off of her."

"I'll think about it, but it's late, Merle. I'm going home. I'll see you tomorrow if I'm still alive."

Jordan drove himself home. He went out on the veranda to rock in his rocking chair and look at the lake. He sipped his Dewar's on the rocks and listened to a record of George Gershwin on the Victrola, playing "Rhapsody in Blue" on the piano. Jordan waited for the bullfrogs to croak and for darkness to fall across White Rock Lake. He watched the mushy night blooms of the hydrilla plants that floated across the lake appear and smelled the slight odors of night on the lake.

"Sully, bring me another drink."

"Here it is, Boss," Sully said, handing Jordan another Dewar's.

"Thanks, Sully."

"Boss, can I ask you a question?"

"Sure, Sully. What'd you need?"

"What about Miz Charlotte? You hear anythin' from her?"

"Sully, she likes living out in Hollywood with all the movie stars and pretending she's something special. She wants to leave me for good. Says there's nothing about me worth promoting and that I sold her a false bill of goods about East Texas. I'll probably never see her again."

"Oh, I hates to hear that Boss, but Miz Charlotte, she the one who wrong. Not you. She done made a big mistake when she left East Texas, but what about Miss Jan. She loves you most."

"I miss my baby girl. I can't stand it if she grows up, and I never see her again." Jordan gazed out at the lake, watching the late sunlight gleaming on the water. "Sully, tell me about Herman."

"Yes, suh. Herman, he was the valedictorian of the colored high school, and he's doing jus' fine in doctor school, thanks to you for gettin' him in. Annie an' me are sure proud of Herman."

"Sully, that's fine. What kind of doctor is Herman going to be?"

"He's working on being a surgeon. They told him the best place for a colored doctor to learn how to sew people up is the emergency room, sewing up the brothers who gets cut on Saturday nights."

"Tell Herman I want him to drive me to East Texas someday for one last time to see Chirp."

"Why you say the last time, Boss? You and Mister Chirp got lots more years together."

"No, Sully, Chirp and me, we're both reaching the end of the line. I love Chirp, and I need to see him."

"Mister Phillips, Herman is home studying his books tonight. I'll ask him. I bet he can take you to East Texas tomorrow."

The next day, Herman drove Jordan in his Ford Fairlane the ninety-five miles to Gladewater to have lunch with Chirp Branscum at the Green Hut. Jordan was quiet. He looked out the window as they passed into the beautiful and solemn Piney Woods. He thought about his first stormy day in East Texas and him seeing the raging Sabine and the water moccasins twenty-five years before. Back then, he had nothing but a dream and water soaked boots. He made his dream become real. The lush Piney Woods and Mrs. Daisy Bradford's farm had been good to him. He managed a smile. It would be good to see Chirp.

Herman pulled up and parked the car in the Green Hut parking next to the chain link fence around an oil well that was pumping hard, producing a little oil and a lot of salt water—one of four wells still producing out of the six oil wells Casey Agrelius had drilled twenty-five years ago outside his hamburger joint.

"Herman, I'm sorry you can't come in and eat with me. Casey never did have a colored dining room. I'll bring you a hamburger and some fries out to the car that you can eat on the way back to Dallas. While you're out here, why don't you listen to Gordon McClendon, the Old Scotsman's broadcast of the baseball game?"

"I can't listen to the game today. I have to study for my gastro-enterology finals," Herman said as he pulled out a thick textbook.

Jordan left Herman in the car and walked on into the Green Hut. He found a table and sat down. Casey Agrelius, the hamburger joint's Greek owner, walked over and greeted him. The place smelled the same.

"Welcome home, Jordan. We don't see much of you around Gladewater anymore. It's sure an honor having the Chairman of the Board of the Wall of Honor back at the Green Hut."

"Come on, Casey. Get off of the Wall of Honor stuff. Your wall is getting full of other pictures. I hope they help you sell hamburgers."

The Wall of Honor was a bunch of grainy photographs of the oil boom. Framed copies of old, fading newspaper clippings were either nailed on or pinned with thumb tacks. In the middle of the wall hung two large black-and-white photograph portraits that had been hung above bronze plaques that told about the subjects of the portraits. Both of the portraits were gathering dust and starting to fade. One of the portraits was of Jordan Phillips as a smiling young man about thirty years old standing by an oil well Christmas tree with his hands holding the master valve open and the well flowing a four-inch stream of pipeline oil thirty feet or more out from the wellhead. The other photo was a formal portrait of C. W. Austin, the head of the oil loan department and Vice President of the Republic National Bank in Dallas. C. W. was Casey Agrelius's banker, and a photograph of Casey's banker struck Jordan Phillips as a "stick your tongue out and shoot you the finger" kind of joke.

"I never heard of anybody hanging a picture of their banker on the wall. Did you have your tongue in your cheek?"

"If you think I'd be selling hamburgers without the six oil wells in my parking lot that C. W. loaned me the money to drill, you got another think coming."

"Well, okay. Leave C. W. on the wall, but dammit, Casey, take me down."

"What the hell, Jordan? If it hadn't been for you, everybody 'round here would be on the government dole."

"But it's over, Case. I don't want to think about this oil field anymore. Just fix me a hamburger with extra tomatoes and French fries."

"Your hamburger's on the way, and your picture's staying on the wall. Look, here comes Chirp."

"Hello, men. Sorry I'm late." Chirp sat down. "Jordan, you okay? You look pissed. What brings you to Gladewater? Why didn't you call me first?"

"Tomatoes, Chirp. Tomatoes."

"Tomatoes? What are you talking about?"

"I wanted tomatoes. Casey's burgers are better than any burgers because of all those tomatoes. Isn't that right, Case?"

"That's right, Jordan," Casey said. "Lots of tomatoes. The old Greek Way, but what in the hell made you think about tomatoes?"

"Well, like Chirpie said, the ice cream in my life turned to shit. Everything has turned to shit except a Green Hut hamburger, and it's because of all the tomatoes that your hamburgers are still ice cream. I also needed to talk to you and Chirp one last time."

"Jordan, what in the hell is this one last time stuff?"

"Nothing's worth a damn anymore."

"What's the matter?"

"Look there." He stood up and walked over to the window and pointed outside. "Look how hard your well is pumping, Casey. You're lucky if you're getting five barrels. Before I moved to Dallas, that well was nothing but one piece of pipe sticking out of the ground with a valve on it not any bigger than you'd need for a garden hose. A five-year-old kid could unscrew that valve, and the well would flow its allowable of pure pipeline oil in ten minutes.

Now it takes a huge pumping unit that covers three parking places, and it never stops pumping. I never saw anything like the way this oil field's going to water." He turned around and went back to sit down with Chirp. He sat in front of his plate of a hamburger and French fries.

"Well, so what else's new?" Chirp said. "Look, man, you still got hundreds of flowing wells out in the Fairway, and someday they'll be worth a fortune. What in the damn hell are you worried about?"

Jordan could see that Chirp was showing his age, almost seventy-five years old. Except for some gray hair, he hadn't changed much since he first met him thirty-five years ago back in the Seminole Field in Oklahoma.

"When those Fairway wells are worth all the money you're talking about, it'll be long after I'm dead and gone and Charlotte has taken over. Case, bring me some ketchup."

"I thought you put her on hold. Can't you make a deal with her and get her off your mind?"

"She'll never let me rest, and she'll never work anything out with me. I'm going to have to sell everything and pay her off." He turned the almost empty bottle of ketchup over and pounded on the bottom so the last drop of the ketchup would run out of the bottle and on to his French fries. He ate one fry. Just one fry.

"For once, I wish you'd let me talk to you about somethin' that's botherin' me."

"What's that?"

"That Railroad Commission lawyer you hired."

"You mean David Paterno?"

"Watch him."

"Why?"

"He's over here nosing around the other day. Did he tell you he's coming to East Texas?"

"No, but that's alright. I made him my number two man. I guess he wants to know more about our leases over here."

"Damn it, he should have told you before he came over here, and he should've called me to tell me he was coming. I'm sorry I mentioned it. There's plenty of good things happening. Tell me about your plan to find a new oil field. I heard you were hiring some geologists."

"Well, I have. I hired a UT geologist with both a Master's and a doctoral degree. He's smart, and he's got a lead on an area in Alaska where he thinks he can find an elephant of an oil field. He'll find me some big oil if I can keep drilling."

"Don't you have to spend big money to find big oil?"

"Of course, Chirp. Look, I can find the oil. If I dig the wells and spend the money it takes and drill behind the best geology, I'll find the oil, but if I can't keep drilling, what's the point? I might as well cash it in, and I don't see how it's ever going to happen. Not after Charlotte gets her hands on my bank account. I'll just quit drilling and sell out."

"Damn it, Jordan. I never thought I'd hear you talk like a quitter."

"The problem is I don't have any hope for anything. Nothing. It's a black time."

"I never seen you so long in the face. You haven't taken but one bite of your hamburger, not even with all those tomatoes."

"I'm not hungry, but Chirp, you're right. I don't know why I came over here to Gladewater other than to see you. I had to get away from Dallas. When I'm in Dallas, all I can think about is the millions of dollars I'll have to pay her when she finally files for divorce. I came over here to get away from all that Charlotte baloney, and when I get over here, all I hear is more depressing stuff about how the oil field is going to water. Where is the fun in the oil field anymore? Where is the adventure?"

"Jordan, stop talking like this. Go home, and tell Merle to get you out of town. Go somewhere, and forget all this."

"Maybe I should go fishing, and you can get ready for more of David Paterno. He's smart, and I'm turning it all over to him."

"Jordan, for Christ's sake, that would be the stupidest mistake you ever made. You've got to get away. Go fishing. Let Merle handle the business, and I'll drive over to Dallas and help her, but don't give that damn Yankee lawyer anything. He is a damn shyster, and you've got to give him his walking papers."

Jordan stood up and handed Casey Agrelius a twenty-dollar bill to cover everyone's lunch. He didn't say another word. Casey gave Jordan a big Greek hug. Chirp stood up with Jordan and walked with him out to his car, still telling his old friend to get away to go fishing.

Jordan took the lunch he'd ordered for Herman with him to his car—a paper plate filled with a hamburger with everything on it and with extra tomatoes and French fries smothered in catsup.

Herman started driving his boss and his benefactor home to Dallas with one hand on the steering wheel, eating his hamburger with his other hand. As he drove this man he loved home to Dallas, Herman couldn't think of anything but how much he owed to Jordan Phillips for enrolling him in medical school and paying all the costs of his education.

Herman had never seen this great man so despondent and so obviously in serious trouble. "Mr. Phillips, are you feeling all right?" Herman said, turning his head back briefly to glance at his passenger in the back seat.

"I'm all right, Herman. Thanks for asking. I guess it's not hard for you to tell that my problems are weighing me down."

"Sir, I just hope you know I'm here to help you when you need me. I'll quit medical school and spend all my time with you. I want you to get over what's bothering you and get back to being your old self."

"Thanks, Herman. The best thing you can do to make me happy is to finish medical school and become a doctor. That would make me happier than anything I know."

"Sir, can I give you my first doctor's prescription?"

"Sure, of course. Lord only knows I need some doctor's orders."

"The cure for worry and anxiety is action. In my psychology class, the main thing I learned is, if you're depressed, you need to move away from passive dependency and become proactive and assertive. Remember how you were when you were a young man and you discovered the big oil field. That's how you need to be now. My first doctor's prescription is for you to get the wrinkles out of your soul. Take a break and come back fighting. Find yourself that new oil field. You'll forget about what's been worrying you, and, Mr. Phillips, I'll always be here to help you."

"Thank you, Dr. Morris. I feel better already."

Herman drove on into Dallas past Buckner's Orphanage and turned north toward White Rock Lake. Sully, waiting for his boy to bring his boss home, met them when they drove into the driveway. He walked Jordan around the house to the veranda overlooking the lake to his rocking chair where his Dewar's on the Rocks was waiting.

Jordan, as he always did, sat in his rocking chair and sipped his scotch and looked at the lake rocking himself to sleep, listening to George Gershwin.

He slept there quietly until Sully woke him and helped him get in bed.

CHAPTER THIRTY-FOUR

"MORNING, BOSS. I hope this'll be a better day for you," Merle said.

"Jordan, listen to me. You need to get away from Dallas. Get your mind off these things."

"It wouldn't help, Merle," he said, standing there without moving. He closed his eyes and massaged his temples.

"Jordan, stop it. Look at me and listen. Why are you so worried, and why are you so mad? You need to go fishing in Cuba. I'll get in touch with Carlos and reserve his boat for you for a month."

Jordan turned away from Merle and went over to the window. He looked down thirty floors and stared at the street. He looked over toward the Dallas City Hall and then looked down at his feet.

Merle's face flushed with the concern. He closed his eyes and ran his hand through his hair and then shook his head violently, as if rejecting some horrendously obscene proposal.

Finally, he looked back up at Merle, sighed, and said, "Merle, you're right. Send a telegram to Havana, and get word to Carlos that I'm coming."

"Jordan, you'll come back a different person. Stay down there for two or three months. I'll deposit the oil runs and mail you the bank balances every Friday."

"No one takes care of me like you, Merle. I'll sign enough checks to get you through the time I'm gone, and you can give them to David Paterno, and tell accounting to send him the invoices to pay while I'm gone."

"Jordan, you shouldn't leave any blank checks with him. Not if they're signed. There's something strange about that man."

"Chirp felt the same way. Told me the same thing. I'll leave the signed checks with you. Handle the bill paying however you want like we did back in Gladewater."

"What about the new geologist you hired? When does he come to work?"

"Last of September, after he finishes his geology field trip to Alaska. You might as well write him and tell him the deal's off. Tell him I won't be drilling, not after I sell out and pay off Charlotte."

"Jordan, I'm not going to let you make decisions like that. Not now. You go down to Cuba. Carlos will have your scotch and your cigars. Catch some fish, and get your mind off Charlotte, and when you come back to Dallas, you won't be talking about selling out."

CHAPTER THIRTY-FIVE

CARLOS WAS A sometime fishing guide for Ernest Hemingway when Papa was having a big party. Hemingway had even said that Carlos was the model for the character Santiago, the hero of *The Old Man and the Sea*. In August, the waters of the Gulf Stream in the Florida Strait between Florida and Cuba were the Holy Grail for marlin fishermen.

However, if Jordan needed to catch fish to get over his funk, he had a problem. The marlin weren't hitting. After three weeks of hard fishing, neither Jordan nor Carlos had a single hit. Jordan was feeling like Santiago, who at the start of Hemingway's novel had gone 89 days without a catch.

Jordan said to Carlos, "We've been fishing too many days without catching a fish."

"*Espero, Señor Jordan. Espero. Nunca se sabe cuando el papagrande pescado weel heet.*"

Carlos and Jordan sat backwards facing the waters behind the boat with their lines far out, trolling slowly, and rising high and falling low with each swell of the Gulf Stream. The August afternoon temperature was rising, and the fishermen were becoming sweatier and more frustrated. After an hour, the swells rolling from the southeast became taller and the clouds became darker. Carlos asked his fisherman, "*Señor Jordan, estas listo para conocer a tu creador?*

"No, Señor Carlos. No. Why would you ask me if I'm ready to meet my maker? I'm ready to meet my marlin."

"Fish not biting *y viento caliente blowing del Sur signa grande viento viene,*" Carlos said, switching more to English and pointing to the southeast. "*Este año,* this year, *los storms mas malo. Mira en el horizon a el los clouds, negro, y mas grande,* much bigger, *y tenemos que volver al marina.* We must return to the harbor. If we stay here, we must be prepared to meet our maker."

Without regard for his fisherman's wishes, Carlos pulled in his line continuing to talk about the benefits to man of patience and deliberation and most of all, what fishing meant to life. He spoke passionately in Spanish.

Jordan Phillips was having trouble understanding Carlos, but he understood the unusual passion with which Carlos spoke. He realized how important being a fisherman was to Carlos.

Carlos started his sixty horsepower Mercury outboard engine. He pointed the twenty-five-foot boat in the direction of Havana Harbor. "Señor Phillips, this weather is turning bad. I must take you home. *Hoy es su ultimo dia conmigo y quiero prepararte en la playa la mas mejor comida de todo su vida, fresca del mar.*

"I am sorry that today is your last day to fish with me this year, but thank God, each day you fish adds a day to your life. On the way home, I'll take you to the beach and prepare the finest shore lunch you have ever had in your life. While we ride across the tops of the swells of the Gulf Stream, you can sit back and enjoy *tu cerveza fria.*" Carlos opened the ice box and uncapped an ice cold Hatuey Beer and handed it to Jordan.

Someone had told Jordan that once long ago Carlos had

studied philosophy at the University of Madrid. Thanks to Carlos, Jordan was learning how to live again.

Carlos almost reached the shoreline of Cuba twenty-five miles from the Havana harbor when he turned his little boat ninety degrees and almost ran it straight into the shore on a beautiful and hidden coral beach. He climbed out of his boat and held his hand to help Jordan step out with him on to the narrow coral sand beach.

He remembered how good it always felt to stretch his legs, so he took a walk along the coral shore. Carlos made ceviche and fried their red snapper filet to make their shore lunch as Jordan walked along the narrow ledge above the beach. After a while, he found himself a quarter mile or so from Carlos' campfire. He stepped down on coral so slick he almost lost his balance. A brown sheen covered the coral rock. He soon could tell that the viscous liquid he was stepping on was slowly oozing out of the rock, but the interesting phenomenon was the strong smell of rotten eggs that filled the air. He reached down and rubbed his fingers in the ooze and stuck a finger in his mouth to taste the rotten eggs, and he didn't taste rotten eggs, he tasted oil.

His mind drifted back to Pennsylvania when he was a boy fishing with his dad. His dad showed him the oil springs and told him how the Indians used the oil to caulk their canoes, and his daddy had told him how Edwin Drake drilled the first oil well in the world next to the stream where the oil springs were flowing.

Jordan had just discovered a flowing oil seep.

CHAPTER THIRTY-SIX

"MERLE, I'M BACK. Babe, is it good to see you!" Jordan gave Merle a big bear hug. "Here's something from Havana." He handed her a box wrapped in green paper tied with wide yellow ribbon.

"It's good to have you back, Jordan. We missed you." Merle opened the present and held the light-green, low-cut silk dancing dress up to the light to look at it, and she saw nothing more than two threads for shoulder straps. "You didn't have to give me this. I don't know where I'll wear it, but it might be fun. Thanks, Jordan."

"It's good to be home."

"You look like your old self. Thank God."

"We didn't catch one fish, but Carlos showed me how to be happy with nothing more than a little boat and a big fishing pole."

"Well, God bless that man."

"Listen to this, Merle. The oil field gods were looking out for me in Cuba. On the beach where Carlos stopped to fix my final shore lunch, I found oil flowing out of the ground. Can you believe that? Now, I'm going to go back down to Cuba and drill, and find me an oil field!"

"Thank God, Jordan, you got your Midas touch back."

"Now that I'm back in Dallas I can only think of one thing," he said, pointing his right index finger straight up.

"What're you thinking?"

"About drilling in Cuba, and when our new geologist gets here, maybe I'll be thinking about drilling in Alaska too. I can't wait to get started drilling."

"He got back Friday, and all of your guys are waiting for you in the conference room right now."

"I can't wait to tell them." Jordan hurried to the Executive Conference Room.

David Paterno and Sam Knight were seated at the conference table. They stood when their boss entered.

"Welcome home, Mr. Phillips. I hope you caught some fish," David said.

"I missed you guys, and it's good to be back. I can't wait to talk about drilling our wildcats. Where's Mike Wharton?"

"He's in his office," Sam said.

"Why isn't he here in this meeting?"

"Well, sir, we didn't know you wanted him to sit on the Management Committee."

"What do you mean? He's our Chief Geologist." He yelled for his secretary. "Merle, tell Mike Wharton to get in this conference room."

"Of course, Mr. Phillips."

"Excuse me, Mr. Phillips. Before you left for Cuba, how much money were you saying you wanted to budget to make TOPCO a full-fledged exploration company?" David asked.

"David, we can't budget the exact amount until we know where we're going to drill, but I imagine it we'll be spending something around fifty million dollars."

"That's what we thought you said."

"It's not your job to worry about money. You handle the leasing and the contracts."

"Well, sir, I can't help but wonder where the money's coming from."

"Thank you, David. What I wanted to tell you about is that I found a place to drill down in Cuba where we can find an oil field if you can tie up the land we need to drill on down there. Let's eat lunch, and I'll tell you what I found, then we'll let Mike tell us about Alaska. Merle, bring the sandwiches in. We'll talk while we eat."

While they were waiting for Merle to serve lunch, Jordan started to talk about what he had found in Cuba. Mike Wharton entered the conference room.

"Hello, Mike. Welcome to Dallas. It looks like you survived the bears and the mosquitos."

"Yes, sir. Being my first Management Committee meeting, I didn't know when you wanted my report on Alaska."

"Let's hear it after I tell about Cuba. I can't wait to learn what you found in Alaska."

David spoke up, "Mike, we want to hear what you found in Alaska, but the first item on the agenda is to hear from Mr. Phillips about Cuba. I try to manage the agenda, and I'll call on you when it's your turn to have the floor with the Management Committee."

"Speak up whenever you want to, Mike. I'm excited about the oil seep I found in Cuba, but I can't wait to hear about Alaska. If we decide to get leases in both Alaska and Cuba, David, you're going to be busy. Really busy."

"Sir, this is the first I've heard about any drilling in Cuba," said David.

"The story on Cuba is simple. I found an oil seep on the beach east of Havana. Oil was oozing out of the ground. Many of the world's major oil fields are found next to oil seeps. I want to drill a well next to those oil seeps, but, David, how are you going to get the rights for us to drill in Cuba?"

"Sir, I can get rights to drill anywhere, especially in Cuba," David said, lying through his teeth. He didn't know how in the hell he was going to get a license to drill in Cuba, but he would have to find out how. "How much money do you want to budget for drilling in Cuba, Mr. Phillips?"

"We need to get Sam to get us some cost estimates, but if you figure we'll need to have several oil wells completed, and the basic production facilities, I'd say we ought to budget at least fifteen million dollars, maybe twenty million."

"So, you want to start your program of exploratory drilling with only fifteen or twenty million in Cuba?"

"Whatever it takes, David."

Merle brought a large tray carrying four plates of lunch for the attendees of the Management Committee Meeting. She gave every one a plate with a fried catfish sandwich on toast and hush puppies.

"Mike," Jordan said as the group was finishing eating their lunch, "Tell us about Alaska."

"My report may take more than a couple of minutes."

"I'm all ears," the boss said.

His lawyer and his petroleum engineer did not want to listen to a green geologist who had never found a drop of oil tell them how to find a giant oil field.

David looked at his watch and stood up to leave the room.

"Excuse me, sir. I need to make an important phone call at one o'clock. I'll be right back."

Sam butted in. "Mr. Phillips, I don't know anything about operating in Alaska, so if you don't mind I'll excuse myself from the meeting. I've got to get a rig moving on to a location at Carthage."

"David, leave and make your phone call if it's so important. But, be back here in five minutes. If we decide to buy oil and gas leases in both Cuba and in Alaska, getting that land will be your responsibility. Sam, I told you I need you to move to Dallas to supervise our drilling operations wherever they might be. That means anywhere in the world, and the world includes Cuba and Alaska. I want you to hear Mike's report from the beginning. That's the only way for you to start your Alaska learning curve. Please stay here and listen. I'm betting Mike finds a prospect for us to drill in Alaska."

Sam didn't say another word. He sat back down in his chair at the conference table taking sips of black coffee, looking bored as hell.

Mike Wharton stood at an easel with a pointer in his hand, pointing at the map of Alaska. "Sir, we've uncovered an excellent geologic lead, and I'm very hopeful that with the seismic coverage we need we'll confirm a drilling prospect with a billion barrels or more reserve exposure."

"Are you serious? A billion barrels?" asked Jordan.

Yes, sir. A billion barrels. Now let me be clear, sir. I am talking about exposure."

"I understand, Mike. You're not talking about money in the bank. You're talking about potential. What we have a chance of finding if we hit oil."

"Yes, sir."

David and Sam looked at each other, both of them turning their heads back and forth, exchanging smirks.

"Mr. Phillips, I am here to tell you that we found an incredibly good rock at the surface of the ground in Alaska. If we find that rock on a structure in the subsurface, it could be a reservoir loaded with oil."

"How are we going to find that structure?"

"We'll find it with the seismograph, Mr. Phillips."

"Where'll we get the seismic?"

"We'll either shoot it ourselves or participate in a group shoot with the majors. They're all active up there, and there will be a lot of seismic shot this winter."

"You mean we've got competition?"

"Oh, I don't know. Sometimes it's good to have the majors in there, sometimes it helps."

"How's that?"

"There's always data flowing out of major company projects. Often there is no action, and except for a couple of the big boys, like BP and The Liberty Company, the majors can be slow as hell. Look at this map," he said. "This area's called the North Slope of Alaska because it slopes north off the Brooks Range into the Beaufort Sea and it hits the ocean right here at this bay named Prudhoe Bay."

"Prudhoe Bay?"

"Yes, sir, Prudhoe Bay," he said, with his pointer on the map.

"Where's your best prospect? Where do you want to acquire the seismic?"

"Should be in this general area," he said again pointing on the map to the area on shore south of Prudhoe Bay.

"I recommend we call our prospect The Prudhoe Bay Prospect. We need to shoot a line of seismic from the Colville River over to the shoreline at Prudhoe Bay. I engaged this lady geologist to help me cost the seismic, and she estimates that we'll need to spend about three million dollars to get enough coverage to confirm a structure large enough to hold an economic volume of oil. If we see what we're looking for, then we'll need to file for leases on a hundred thousand acres or more. We can probably be drilling in a couple of years."

"How much will the leases and the well in Alaska cost?"

"I would say in addition to the three million for the seismic, we would need to budget another three million for the leases and then six million for drilling the well, sir, but I'll leave the engineering and the well costing up to Sam."

David spoke up, "What you are saying is that if all the costs are included Mr. Phillips needs to budget about twelve million to explore in North Alaska?"

"No, that's not all," Mike said. "If we really want access to all the major companies' data, we'll not only need to buy into their group shoot, but we really need to buy a piece of a wildcat they are drilling on what they says is the largest anticline ever drilled in the history of oil exploration."

"Where is this anticline?" asked Jordan.

"The Colville River runs on top of it. They call it The Colville High."

"So how much will buying this other seismic and buying into this other wildcat on the Colville High cost TOPCO?" asked David.

"It'll cost another three million dollars."

"So," David said, "that takes the Alaska budget to fifteen million?"

"That's right. Fifteen million should be enough for Alaska," Mike Wharton said.

Jordan spoke up. "Mike, I'm proud this is all coming together for you, and are you really talking about a billion barrels exposure?"

"My gut tells me there's a high probability to find at least a billion barrels, but we can't define the potential until we have the seismic and the seismic needs to image a trap. I hold out hope that if a trap is imaged that it will be big enough to hold more than a billion barrels, but getting the seismic is only the beginning of a process that may or may not end up giving TOPCO a giant oil field."

"Okay, let's go for it. David, lets budget the first three million for Alaska, with an out if the three million for seismic is a bust. I'm hoping and praying that won't happen and we'll spend the whole fifteen million in Alaska. Now, David, you get that Cuban contract and we'll find our first big oil field in Cuba, and in two or three more years we'll find our giant field in Alaska. We're off to a good start to be a real oil company, which is what I want to do."

"If you are talking about fifteen million or twenty million dollars in Cuba and another fifteen million dollars in Alaska. I don't see how in the hell you can finance all this drilling, Mr. Phillips."

"David, it may end up being forty million or even fifty million dollars before we find our big oil field, but let me warn you not to get yourself all hot and bothered over my finances. We have work to do. Get those leases in Cuba, and get them in Alaska. We'll shoot the seismic and drill those wells. TOPCO will always be drilling in East Texas, and who knows where else."

David didn't agree with one thing the man said, but he was paid to buy oil and gas leases wherever Jordan Phillips wanted to drill for oil, whether in Cuba or in Alaska.

CHAPTER THIRTY-SEVEN

DAVID WALKED DOWN the hall to his office, wondering three things. How in the hell was he going to get a license for TOPCO to drill for oil in Cuba? How was he going to file for oil leases in the Alaska Territory? Where was Jordan Phillips going to get forty or fifty million dollars or however much money he would need to spend on all this crazy drilling?

As he walked to his office, light bulbs went off in his mind. He remembered exactly how he could get anything he wanted from the Cuban government. He closed the door to his office and picked up the telephone on his desk and called his cousin, Angelo Lambrisi, Jr., back at his family law firm in New Jersey.

"Hello, Angelo. How're things in New Jersey?"

"My God. I can't believe it's my deadbeat cowboy cousin from Texas."

"Angelo, don't give me any shit."

"Look, David, here's the deal. We're up here waiting patiently for you to pay back all that money you owe us for financing your law school? Is that ever going to happen? We need your money, David. You're getting rich down in Texas, and we're all going broke."

"That's what happens when you let your only clients go to hell. Jeez, Ang, my student loan is gonna get paid off in spades. Wait'll you hear why I called."

"Make it good."

"I'm trying to figure out how to do business in Cuba. Didn't you go to Havana with Dad and Uncle Angelo when they went to that conference in Havana in '46 after the war?"

"Yep. Sure did. Damn'dest two weeks I ever spent. I kept notes of the meeting for Dad and Uncle David. At night, Frankie was singing in the Casino, and during the day, the families argued over who was going to get which new casino location, but anywhere people vacationed they agreed would be fertile ground for a Casino. When people go on vacations, they gamble. Florida, Nevada, California, and Havana, everywhere. That meeting led to Lansky getting his pot full in Havana. He doled himself the Havana franchise, but man, it was the nights I remember best."

"What happened?"

"The Cuban gals were unbelievable. They could dance your feet off with rhythm that made your head spin, and then they'd hit the sacks and screw all night. The dancing and the Beat of the Mambo and the Cha-Cha-Cha, the card games, and the slot machines were nothing like what happened afterwards when everyone hurried to get the best seats for the late show at the Shanghai Theatre. It was crazy. Gals would go up on the stage and take their clothes off and the crowd would choose one out of six or seven naked gals, and the gal they'd choose would be the lucky one who got to take on Superman, and the gals had never seen anything like Superman. It was unbelievable, but the gals would cheer 'im on. The funniest night was when a group of U.S. Congressmen were fighting us to see who could get the best front-row seats, but you didn't call me to talk about Superman. What'd you call for, David?"

"Angelo, this company I work for is the largest independent oil producer in Texas. The owner is this guy named Jordan Phillips."

"The guy on that cover of *Life* magazine that you sent me?"

"That's him. In Texas, he's what they call a wildcatter. It's a complicated story, but now he has decided he wants to drill for oil in Cuba."

"So that's why you're talking about Havana?"

"I need to talk to someone that knows how to do a business deal with the Cuban government and get a contract to drill for oil down in Cuba. You have any ideas how to do business there?"

"I can probably get you whatever you want with one phone call."

"That's what I figured."

"When do you want to go to Havana?"

"As soon as you fix me up."

"If you get an oil-drilling contract, there will be lawyers. Get us the law business, and as long as our split of the referral fees is still our deal, I'll fix you up in Havana."

"Sure, it's the same deal. Fifty-fifty on any referrals which I get sent to the firm, and your fifty is a credit against my receivable. Call me when you have it worked out."

"Damn it. Fifty percent is too much for you. I guess it's a deal, and I have to live with it, but don't you get too far from a phone. I may be calling you back real quick."

In less than two hours, Angelo Lambrisi, Jr., called back. He told David if he would appear at the front desk of the Hotel Nacional in Havana the next Monday at exactly noon, the chances were ninety percent that he'd get the contract he wanted from the Cuban government.

David immediately went into Jordan Phillips's office. "Excuse me, Mr. Phillips. I have some information you need to hear."

"What've you got, David?"

"I can get drilling rights for the company in Cuba."

"David, you never fail to amaze me. The next best thing I

ever did since buying that geological map from Doc Berry was to hire you. Tell me about it."

"I have an appointment in Havana next Monday."

"Music to my ears. I'll arrange for the plane. "

"Mr. Phillips, I expect that when I get to Cuba, I'll actually be talking to President Batista."

"Good. I like presidents. I'll like President Batista when I get to know him. Ask him if he would want to fish for marlin with Carlos and me after I find him a big oil field."

CHAPTER THIRTY-EIGHT

D AVID FLEW FROM Dallas to Havana the following Monday morning in TOPCO'S DC-3 with the bright red spinning top painted on the tail. The rest of the plane was painted the same oily green that all of TOPCO'S Christmas trees and pumping units and oil tanks in the oil field were painted. With so many oil wells belonging to TOPCO, all painted that same oily green, TOPCO green had become a famous color throughout the Texas oil patch.

When he climbed out of the plane at the Havana airport, David felt like he was walking into a steam room. He shielded his face with his hands and squinted his eyes to protect himself from the glare of the bright tropical sun. Warm gusts of the trade winds did not cool his brow.

At exactly noon, David walked up to the front desk of the Hotel Nacional. The room clerk welcomed him to Cuba and handed him an envelope containing a handwritten note and a key to his room. The note said, "Welcome to Cuba, Mr. Paterno. Your presence is requested immediately at Suite Number 930." The note was not signed.

When the elevator door opened on the ninth floor, Suite 930 was directly across the hall. He had never seen a hotel room with

a doorbell. He rang the doorbell, and the door was opened immediately by a small dark man with a baby face, dressed in white
from head to toe in a long-sleeved white silk Guayabera hanging
outside white pants. He was wearing white shoes and socks. This
man seemed to David to be a Cuban manservant for the resident
of Suite 930.

The Cuban butler smiled and said to him, "Welcome to
Havana, Señor Paterno. *Por favor, viene conmigo.* Please follow
me." He led David from the front door down a short hallway
to a sliding glass door that opened on to a large awning-cov-
ered balcony.

David could see this was no ordinary hotel suite. It was filled
with what appeared to be an important collection of the art of old
Spanish Masters. Maybe an El Greco and one or two Goyas. It
was obvious that someone of wealth lived in these quarters.

David followed the butler out on to the balcony. The prissy
little manservant stopped and pointed at a man in a white linen
suit sitting the other side of the balcony at a table under an open
umbrella. When David looked at the man in the white suit waiting for him, he could see the wall of the balcony behind him and
over the wall he could see the white sands of the beach and the
blue water of the Gulf of Mexico.

His host was not Cuban. He had a pock-marked olive complexion and was wearing large round black horn-rimmed sun-
glasses with dark lenses. When he stood to meet David, it was
obvious that he was a very small man, and his dominating presence was made obvious by his intense, steely eyes. He extended
his hand, saying "Welcome to Havana, David. My name is Meyer
Lansky. You have a strong family resemblance to your father. God
rest his soul. He was a fine man. We all loved him. Please accept
my deepest sympathy for the loss you and your mother and all
your family have suffered."

Meyer Lansky was legendary. His father often talked around the dinner table about his organizational talents and how he had brought stability and unity to the interfamily relationships of several of the family businesses who were clients of his father's law firm. Above all, Meyer Lansky had become the Czar of Casino Gambling in Havana.

Lansky moved his arm in a crude half circle and pointed to the empty chair where David was to sit. "David, please won't you join me for lunch."

"Thank you, Mr. Lansky. Thank you. My father often spoke highly of you. I'm honored to meet you. He told me many times how you were the key to the success of several of his most important clients."

"I understand from your cousin that you are working for an oil company in Dallas. Am I correct in that your oil company is interested in drilling for oil in Cuba?"

"Yes, sir."

"That will be no problem to arrange. After our lunch my limousine will be in front of the hotel at one fifteen waiting to take you to the office of the President. You will first meet with the President's Chief of Staff. He will inform you that the President is favorably disposed to granting your company a license to explore for oil on Cuban lands. Shortly after that, President Batista will enter the room and he will confirm to you that the Cuban Congress will approve your oil and gas contract. He will be with you for only a short time. If you wish to say anything to him, you must speak loud and fast if you want to get your message to him before he leaves the room. However, he will express to you that he welcomes the opportunity to bring an American oil company into Cuba. Is there anything else I can do for you?"

"Mr. Lansky, I am amazed at your efficiency. I can't thank you enough for helping me. Please tell me how I can repay you."

"David, please do not give a thought to repaying me. I am only continuing a relationship between our families, your father's and mine. Our relationship started generations ago in the old country, and it has continued on this side of the Atlantic. It has been a relationship which has been very profitable for both of us. Would you like a rum?"

"I'd love a rum. Will I see you again before I return to Texas?"

"Yes, David, we need to talk before you return to Texas. Please come back to my suite at sunset. I will show you an entirely different Gulf of Mexico. Look out there now at the bright noontime sun reflecting off the dark grey waters of the Gulf. As the sun sets in the evening, it turns red, and the sky and the Gulf waters will turn a stark deep blue. Everything is better in Havana at night. The rum tastes better at night, and of course, nothing is better than the beat of the drums and the urgency of the Cuban women at night. Come back at sunset, and we will talk about your meeting with the President. I may be able to help you finalize your transaction."

David was learning that there was more complexity to Meyer Lansky than met the eye. The two sipped their Daiquiris and ate their lunch. David listened as Meyer Lansky talked about the old days and the business transactions with David's father and how the law that Lansky's ancestors lived by in the old country was the law of tradition and that the traditions between the families would never end. Lansky emphasized to David the tradition that no one should ever participate in a business transaction that did not include a provision for compensation for himself.

After lunch, David went down to the lobby. On the sidewalk, he found a doorman holding open the door of a long, black limousine for him. The limousine was escorted by two Cuban policemen on motorcycles, sirens blaring. A feeling of immense self-importance crept over David Paterno, Jr.

The meeting in the president's office seemed scripted. In the five minutes he stayed in the outer office conference room with David, President Fulgencio Batista did exactly as Meyer Lansky said he would. He informed his guest that the Government of Cuba would be happy to grant an oil-drilling license to David's oil company. It didn't take long for David to realize that Meyer Lansky made the business decisions for the President of Cuba.

The long black limousine with the police escort sped David back to the Hotel Nacional. It was only mid-afternoon. He had been asked to return to Meyer Lansky's suite at sunset, so he had time to spare.

He discovered that the accommodations reserved for him were not like an ordinary hotel room. It was a luxuriously appointed suite, complete with a fully stocked bar including Dom Perigon champagne. The refrigerator was filled with several bottles of Puligny Montrachet, Meursault and other fine white Burgundies. There was an array of light and dark Bacardi rums on the glass shelves above the bar in front of the mirror. Sitting on the bar counter top was a variety of other premium spirits. Too many choices and not enough time, David thought.

Throwing caution to the wind, he decided to let the evening begin. He opened a bottle of light rum, poured two shots into a glass and added three ounces of fresh squeezed lime juice and a couple of pinches of fresh mint and two tablespoons of Cuban sugar. He pounded the mix into a powder and shook it hard over the ice in the shaker and poured himself a Mojito on the rocks. He drank it down with one long slow sip, and immediately mixed another.

David was happy. His oil deal was a done deal. He deserved to have some fun.

He walked through the other rooms in his suite and into his bedroom where he noticed that someone had unpacked his clothes and hung them in the closet with two new heavily starched white linen Cuban Guayaberas hanging on the clothes rack, an obvious gift someone had left for him. He appreciated such niceties.

David shook himself another ice cold Mojito. With a fresh Mojito in hand, he walked through the French doors out onto his suite's balcony. His eyes immediately focused on the breasts of an olive-skinned Latin beauty sunbathing on the beach. As if on cue, when he looked down at her, she raised her body off the towel and reached her arms behind her to untie the top of her bathing suit to let it drop to the ground and expose her large round breasts while she made eye contact with him.

Another girl lay next to her, face down on her towel, but he couldn't take his eyes off the Latin beauty with her body pushed up and frozen like a statue of a Greek Goddess with her nipples pointing straight at him.

David had promised Meyer Lansky he would meet him before sunset, so he gave the girl on the beach the thumbs up sign, and she nodded her head to say yes, and he walked back into his bedroom and poured himself another shot of rum.

As he was leaving before six o'clock to return to Meyer Lansky's suite, David noticed a tall mirror on the wall next to the bed, and he saw a tiny thread of wire looping from the bottom of the mirror almost all the way down to the floor and back up to reenter the wall below the base of the mirror, obviously wire providing electricity to light the mirror. A fantasy crossed his mind of the pleasure he would feel if he looked into that mirror and saw the reflection of the naked body of the beauty he'd seen on the beach. The night was young, and the best was yet to come.

At six o'clock as instructed, David returned to Meyer Lansky's suite, wearing one of the starched new white Guayaberas that had been hung in his closet. The royal treatment he had received in

Havana, the audience with the president of Cuba, obtaining the rights for his company to drill for oil in Cuba, and the pride he felt in becoming aware of the longtime relationship between his family and the man who controlled both the president and the casinos in Cuba made David feel important.

These feelings of importance and grandeur were solidified with each shot of rum. He became bulletproof, but it was early enough for him in the day to wonder what Meyer Lansky really wanted. He didn't expect to learn the answer as soon as he did.

"Welcome, David. Come in and have a drink. I hope you were satisfied with your meeting," Lansky said as he took a sip of an ice cold martini in a frosted martini glass, straight up with two olives, his usual.

"Thank you, Mr. Lansky. Just as you said, the meeting went smoothly. The President said we could have the oil contract."

"Walk outside with me, and I'll show you a Cuban sunset. Your timing is perfect, just before the sun sets. Would you like a Martini?"

"I have already started on rum, so would you mind if I had a Mojito?"

"Of course not, David. Francisco, bring Mr. Paterno a mojito." He said turning to his butler. "Yes, David, I know all about your meeting. It went fine. I hope you are pleased to do business with Cuba." They walked out on to the balcony.

"Look at that sunset." Lansky gestured with his opened hands toward the setting sun. "You've never seen a sunset as bright or as red or water as deep blue as the Gulf of Mexico off Havana."

"At Sandy Hook, at sunset, we see the lights of the city come on as darkness spreads across New York Harbor. In Texas, occasionally we have stunning sunsets, but rarely are those sunsets like this. I can see why you want to live in Havana."

The short, round Cuban butler came out on to the balcony

smiling and brought David an ice cold mojito in a frosted rum glass on a silver tray.

"Thank you, David. Let me correct one thing. I am not living in Havana because of the sunsets. I live here because of the money. And let me wish you good luck. Here's to lots of money when you drill for oil in Cuba." He raised his glass in a toast to David. David honored him in return with a nod of his head and raised his glass to toast him and took a sip of his rum.

"Thank you, Mr. Lansky. I apologize for implying a reason you might be in Havana. I meant no offense. Why you are in Havana is none of my business. It was a weak attempt to make small talk. I apologize. Yes, the president was eager to grant us the license to drill. He said to ask you about the contract."

"The president leaves his business decisions to me. I suggested that he grant you the same terms Venezuela granted to Creole Petroleum."

"I am not familiar with Venezuela's deal with Creole. By the way, this is the best and the coldest mojito I've ever tasted."

"David, remember, both mojitos and martinis are to be sipped, not drunk. I taught Francisco to make a martini the way a martini is supposed to be made—everything frozen and ice cold. That's the secret. The Venezuelan contract for your oil deal means your company will pay one million dollars cash up front and be granted a license on 25,000 hectares, or if that is not enough land, all your company has to do is ask for more land and more land can be provided. However, as my personal attorney has advised me, the license must be drilled to be earned. That's how I believe he phrased it."

David sipped his mojito. "It's not clear to me the size of the royalty Cuba is reserving or what percentage of the revenue my company will earn in the project."

"David, I know nothing about the oil business, so please

understand I am depending on my attorney in St Petersburg. He does have some oil and gas experience. He tells me that Cuba will retain the same royalty as Venezuela, a one-eighth royalty, twelve-and-a-half percent of the oil production. Also, he says, like Venezuela in its deal with Creole Petroleum, the contract will provide for an additional royalty of five percent of the production, but I hope you understand the reason for my interest in helping you."

"Of course, sir. That additional royalty you mention would be an overriding royalty. Overrides are normal in oil deals. Does that overriding royalty go to Cuba?"

"No, as in the Venezuelan deal with Creole, the overriding royalty will be handled differently. Most of that royalty will be divided between me and my partner in all my Cuban deals. I never do business without compensation for me, and it's no secret that my business partner in Cuba is President Bautista, but because of the old relationship of your family and mine, a part of the royalty will be reserved for you, but, David, what you have described is a very interesting opportunity. I have decided that I must own oil. I want to own oil in the ground. Tell me more about your company. I want to acquire your company."

"Sir, the name of the company is the Texas Oil Production Company, and its President and founder and owner of one hundred percent of the shares of stock in the company is Jordan Phillips, a man known as Texas' greatest wildcatter. He owns two thousand oil wells, and he is said to be worth one hundred million dollars and his company is not for sale."

"My God. These big guys always think they are bulletproof. I was not aware of his extreme wealth. Does he borrow his capital from a bank?"

"No. He doesn't borrow money. He pays cash for his capital expenditures."

"That's very interesting, David. Let's go inside, David. It's late. The sun has set. It's getting dark." Meyer Lansky walked back into his apartment into his game room. David followed him and they sat in the leather chairs pulled up to the bridge table.

"Mr. Lansky, how can I thank you enough? It's hard to believe that today I met with the President of Cuba, and he gave me the license to drill in Cuba."

"David, may I tell you the way things were between your father and me?"

"Yes, of course. Please do."

"Your father and I helped each other from the start. Our relationship grew with each transaction. Some deals were very small, and meaningless, but a long-term relationship like your father's and mine and, now, yours and mine, is a precious thing. There are unwritten traditions between our families that have lasted for many generations. Our families have been in many deals together. The traditions your father and I lived by originated long ago in the old country. Some of the deals were small and made little or no money, but on occasion when our deals worked, your father and I both got very rich. I owed much to your father, and by the way, he owed a lot to me."

"The most important tradition is that family relationships transcend the generations. Don't you find it interesting that you and I have inherited a relationship between our families that started generations ago?"

"Yes, of course. Mr. Lansky. That is a beautiful statement. It makes me proud to assume the mantle of a tradition that has continued for so long."

"David, your father and I were more than just friends. We were like brothers, your father and me, but I feel that you still don't realize what I am trying to tell you. Are you listening, David?"

"I think I understand, but please don't stop. Please continue."

"Take the oil contract in Cuba that you arranged for your company today. What did you get for yourself in that transaction? Zero. Nothing. Why didn't you arrange a participation in the deal for David Paterno, Jr.? You are like your father. Lawyers are terrible businessmen. I had to train your father and I will have to train you, but David, I feel that you are much more American than your father. You are too nice for your own good.'"

"Your company must pay one million dollars and an extra overriding royalty to acquire the rights to drill in Cuba. You will see all that in the contract you are taking back to Dallas. I, personally, will own one half of that five percent overriding royalty which means I will own two and a half percent of the deal free of any cost to me as my compensation for providing an important opportunity for my client, the state of Cuba. You must know that I don't work for free. You do not need to know how much of the one-million-dollar cash payment your company will pay will be mine, but it will not be insignificant. I am almost shocked that you showed no initiative to create a participation for yourself in both the overriding royalty and the one million dollars cash payment. Your company gets the contract for drilling its oil wells in Cuba only because of you. Why did you leave yourself out? May I teach you how the free market works?"

"Mr. Lansky, I am grateful for your concern about me. Perhaps if my father had not died so young he would have told me what you are now saying. Please continue."

"To start, David, let me inform you that I have arranged for you to be given one fifth of the five percent royalty. Granted, that's only a token contribution, and not large enough to fairly compensate you for your contribution. Some would only call compensation like that chicken feed. To me, it's not chicken feed. It's not even chicken shit, but, goddamn it, one point is better than the zero points you were prepared to take, and you are getting that not because of your initiative, but because of family tradition."

"Let me tell you that Cuba is obligated to pay a one-hundred-thousand-dollar legal referral fee out of the one million dollars cash your company will pay. Since you are an attorney, it is arguable that this referral fee is rightly yours. If you had been engaged in protecting yourself the way that is expected, you might have even negotiated a higher referral fee for yourself, but you hesitated, so you must take what you can get but, thanks to God, you will be getting a one percent overriding royalty and a one-hundred-thousand-dollar referral fee only because of the enduring relationship of your family's and mine."

"Good God. I can't believe a one percent overriding royalty and a hundred-thousand-dollar referral fee. That would truly be formidable. I don't deserve such extravagance. How can I justify keeping such compensation if I stay employed by Jordan Phillips? Is that ethical?"

"David, there you go again. Your mind is too small. The traditions we follow are governed by ethics, and yes, there is nothing more ethical than taking care of oneself first. Every successful business man knows to protect his own self-interest at all costs. You must start thinking bigger. You are underselling yourself, young man. As you will soon learn, I have a plan and my plan is for you and me to be partners. When the day inevitably comes that you must aggressively protect your own interest, and as my partner, you will be protecting my interest too, but I am not finished. May I ask you to continue to listen to me?"

"Of course, Mr. Lansky. I'll listen to you as long as you want to talk."

"David, I am trying to tell you that if the two of us work together as one, you will become even richer than your man Jordan Phillips, and I will become a richer man too. Then you will see why a one-percentage-point override and the one hundred thousand in cash you will receive are not worth the cost of the paper the money they signify is printed on. Not when compared to how much money you will make if you follow my plan," Lansky produced a smug smile. "You realize I have been very successful in building the Casino Industry in Havana. Last month, I deposited two million dollars into my personal accounts."

"My God. I was not aware of the magnitude of your success."

"In spite of that apparent success, I am faced with a questionable future. The Casino business in Havana could end in a moment's notice. Who knows when the Communist guerillas in the mountains will start a revolution? I must diversify into another business. David, quite simply, the bottom line is I want to get in the oil business and your company would provide a great entry for me."

"Well, yes, the oil business can be very rewarding. Are you saying that you want to invest in drilling with my company in the program to drill wildcats and search for new oil fields?"

"David, I don't take risks. We have been speaking about risk in drilling, and I understand that risk."

"Mr. Lansky, there are only two ways that I know to get into the oil business, to drill, or to buy oil reserves in the ground. Drilling is risky. Buying oil reserves is a very expensive and a tough way to make money."

"David, my plan is very simple. The way I will get into the oil business will be to acquire your company. I want to own one hundred percent of, how do you call it, The Texas Oil Producers?"

"Texas Oil Production Company. TOPCO. But if the plan you have been talking about is to buy my company, like I said earlier the company is not for sale. Jordan Phillips would never sell his company."

"No, David, I do not want to buy your company. I want to

take over your company. That is what I have been trying to tell you. It will take a combination of smart moves and hard work, but the path is clear for you and me to own the whole chicken farm with a thousand laying hens, and that is much better than eating only the chicken feed you are feeding on today."

"Mr. Lansky, I think I may be starting to understand you, but I don't understand your plan."

"Let me walk you through it. Tell me about that man. Does he have a strong financial statement?"

"As I said he is reportedly worth one hundred million dollars. He probably has never made a financial statement, but if he has a financial statement, it would be his private business. His company is owned by him and him alone."

"And you said he doesn't owe money to a bank?"

"That's right, he has never borrowed money."

"How will he pay for the wells he wants to drill in Cuba?"

"He has one million dollars cash in the bank and he receives another three million dollars a month in cash flow from oil. He will pay for his wells out of his cash on hand and his cash flow."

"Does he have other wells to drill other than Cuba?"

"Yes, he does. He's completely changing his historic way of doing business. He plans as much as fifty million dollars drilling wildcats in Cuba and in Alaska and drilling wherever else his geologists want him to drill for oil. You see, he is obsessed with finding his second giant oil field."

"Just a minute, David. Won't he need a bank to borrow the funds to drill all those wells?"

"Yes, of course he will need to borrow at least fifteen million dollars, maybe twenty, maybe more. He knows that and he asked me to arrange a line of credit with his bank."

"What about the risk of drilling dry holes?"

"Of course there is risk. His drilling is all wildcatting."

"You mean with about as much chance of success as you said like catching a wildcat in the forest?"

"Yes, sir. To be completely true, he could drill all dry holes and lose fifty million dollars."

"What you are telling me there is a risk that he fails. Failure leads to insolvency and bankruptcy. There is only one answer to that question, isn't there? Could Jordan Phillips lose everything?"

"Yes, of course he could."

"David, you will play a critical part in the execution of my plan. May I share it with you?"

"Of course, please do."

"You said that Jordan Phillips will need to borrow at least fifteen million dollars. Usually, entrepreneurs with wealth like his have no fear when they go on spending binges drilling mountain lions like he wants to do."

"Wildcats, Mr. Lansky, wildcats."

"Certainly, wildcats, but have you ever expressed your concerns to him about his taking such risks?"

"I have. I did last week just before I came to Cuba. I expressed caution to him about getting overextended financially"

"What did he say when you urged caution?"

"He told me that his finances were none of my business."

"When you go back to Dallas, let me give you some advice. Don't slow him down. In fact, push him to drill as many wells as he can drill. Force him to run out of cash. Force him to go to the bank."

"It's funny that you would say that, Mr. Lansky."

"Why is that, David?"

"Because that's exactly what our petroleum engineer said. He said Jordan Phillips is going broke and we should let him. He said we can pick up the pieces."

"Why would he say that?"

"Our engineer hates the ground Jordan Phillips walks on. He would love nothing better than watching Jordan Phillips go broke."

"David, you must get that line of credit for your company at a bank, and encourage Jordan Phillips to start his drilling program without any concern about financing, but you must get a new bank. Do not use the old bank in Dallas."

"The Republic Bank knows our oil reserves better than any other bank. It would be easy to mortgage our reserves with Republic."

"David, I own a bank. I want you to use my bank in Pennsylvania. Tell your boss that you found an Eastern bank giving money away to establish a new oil-loan business in Texas. My bank will make your man a loan on such terms that no one can turn him down. Can you get my banker some financial reports?"

"No. To my knowledge there are no financial reports on the company. Only bank balances. He gets a report on his bank balances every Friday. He signs a tax return every April, and that's all the financials he has. That's it. He would never let me or anybody else see his tax return or his bank balances."

"David, after you return to Dallas, you encourage your man to prepare an aggressive drilling budget and drill as many wells and spend as much of his money as he can as fast as he can drill. Our goal must be for him to spend all his cash drilling as fast as he can, then his old bank will refuse to expand his credit facility, and you can reach out and finalize a fresh and large new line of credit for your company with my bank in Pittsburg. This will be easy to do. That bank in Dallas has had a free ride without any worry except whether or not your boss deposits his oil checks in their bank every month. They will not be ready for the change in your boss's business plan, and I can promise you that the Dallas bank will refuse to finance an overextended budget of shooting wildcats. Your company will need a new bank, and my bank is the perfect bank. When you see my bank's loan papers you will know what Jordan Phillips will not know that when he writes his signature on my loan papers, his loan will automatically be in default, then my bank will take over your company and it will be ours."

David sat there in silence as the room grew darker by the second. He could hardly see Lansky's face now. "Mr. Lansky, it's drilling, not shooting, wildcats. Yes, of course, I am beginning to see what you've been trying to tell me."

"David, I hope you are remembering the first lesson that I have tried to teach you."

"I have learned so much tonight, Mr. Lansky. What are you referring to?"

"Take care of yourself first. What will be your compensation for your contribution to the transaction I have just outlined? After my bank takes over your company a new company with new principals must be formed to manage the foreclosed assets. You will become the Chief Executive Officer of that company. We will no longer need that silly name TOPCO any longer. We will name our new oil company 'Lansky and Paterno Oil and Gas Company' and call it LAPOGO for short. The new company will be owned equally by you and me. Fifty-percent will be mine and fifty-percent will be yours. How does that sound?"

"I see why my father thought so highly of you."

"David, now you see how I made your father very rich. If you follow me, I will make you very rich also, but tonight is the time for you to throw caution to the wind and enjoy yourself at the casino, then return to Dallas and put our plan into action and go to Pittsburg and meet my banker. The reward we receive will be enormous, and I look forward to sharing it with you. Do not wait. Together we will make this happen." The little man chuckled.

CHAPTER THIRTY-NINE

AT THE CASINO, the orchestra played the Samba, and David learned that he loved rum daiquiris better than Vodka martinis and that he loved the Samba better than the crap tables. He drank his rum and looked around the dance floor for a Latin beauty to fall in love with. When he found her, she had firm round breasts identical to the breasts he saw on the blonde on the beach. He moved close enough to her to reach around her and learn with his own hands that her breasts were as large as the breasts of the girl on the beach. She was that same girl. Maybe. It didn't really matter. She smiled at him and grabbed his arms and swung him around and pulled him close and opened her mouth and placed her lips over his. The beat of the music took control of their every movement and they danced the Samba, and between the dances, they drank rum.

Just after midnight, he grabbed her hand and pulled her behind him and staggered through the lobby of the hotel to the elevator. Her girlfriend was close behind. This motley threesome went together up the elevator, and the two girls laid him on his bed and removed his clothes and removed all their own clothes too. The two naked girls climbed all over David, caressing him, fondling him, kissing him, but it was useless. He was wasted and could not be brought back from dreamland.

David opened his eyes enough to see the blonde's girlfriend in the mirror removing her wig and revealing a bald head. She proved for sure that she was a he, and as drunk as David was, he could tell that the "girlfriend" had the round little fat face of Francisco, Meyer Lansky's Cuban butler. When drunk David realized it was Francisco lying on top of him belly to belly, kissing and fondling him, he sat up, vomited violently to the side of the bed, and then passed out once more. He looked like a corpse in a state of rigor mortis with his eyes wide and staring at the lighted mirror on the wall.

The next morning, Meyer Lansky picked up his phone and called his brother. "Jake, what did you get?"

"Got it all, every which way. That see-through mirror worked perfect. Your new partner is a fag forever," Jake Lansky, the manager of the Hotel Nacional, said. "Got it all on sixteen millimeter. Wanna see it, Bro?"

"Jake, you know I always want to look."

"I'll show you the movie tomorrow. It's a nice addition to your collection. Reminds me of the one we got of that senator that is planning to be the next president with the three gals in bed with him. By the way, I paid the gal her fifty bucks. Francisco got what exactly he was looking for, so he's okay."

CHAPTER FORTY

D AVID WOKE UP at four A.M. with a throbbing head. It kept getting worse, and it didn't take him long to know that he was fighting a world-class hangover. When he boarded TOPCO'S DC-3, the pain was in the middle of his head and pulsated with each step he took up the ladder into the plane. The airplane was Jordan Phillips's toy, but in the alcoholic mania of his hangover, David began to believe it was his own. After all, hadn't he obtained an enormous drilling concession from the President of Cuba?

The pain in his head wouldn't stop, not even with four Double Bloody Mary Hairs of the Dog he had asked the little red-headed stewardess to bring him.

Hoping that food might help, when the plane stopped to refuel in New Orleans, David ordered two New Orleans fried-shrimp Po' Boy sandwiches and a dozen fried oysters. He practically swallowed everything whole, but food didn't help either. After the plane left New Orleans and soared to the highest altitude of the trip, its sole passenger collapsed into a deep sleep until the plane began its initial descent into Dallas. A Technicolor nightmare made him wake with a scream. He had dreamed that a large female nipple was sticking in his right eye, and when he pulled back from that protrusion, he saw it was attached to the body of a naked dancing girl with the smiling face of Meyer Lansky's butler.

When his breathing calmed and he stopped shaking, David finally began to think about the business at hand, and he reflected on Meyer Lansky's agreement to give him half of the company if he could engineer the takeover of Jordan Phillip's company. It would be easy to do, and he was ready to get started, but first he had to recover from his world-class hangover.

When the plane landed in Dallas, David called Sam Knight from the airport hangar.

"Hey, Sam, I'm back. Find me two good-looking women and have them for me at the Carousel Club. I'll be there in thirty minutes. You get there first and have them put in the little private room in the back. Tell them to wait for me. By the way, I got the contract to drill from the president of Cuba, my new best friend."

"Good God, man. That is terrific."

Sam didn't know where to find any women that fast, so he called the bartender at the Carousel Club and told him to get him two blondes. It didn't take David two hours to finish off those two girls in the back bedroom at the club where his hangover came to a glorious climax several times. Then it was over. He was ready to drink and go to work on Meyer Lansky's plan.

"What'd you want to talk to me about, David?" Sam Knight asked after they had ordered martinis.

"That boss of ours that has gone crazy to be drilling all these wildcats. It's going to wreck him and wreck his business, and it's going to wreck you and wreck me if we stay with him."

"Well, David, I don't know about his drilling, but the salt water in East Texas is driving him crazy. With nine hundred flowing oil wells in the Fairway, he doesn't have anything to worry about, yet he is so obsessed with finding another East Texas Field.

I hope it doesn't get him down, but you're right. He's going to spend himself broke trying to do it."

"If we want to save the company, we got to take it away from him. I've got a way to do it. We can pick up the pieces, and the company will be ours. We'll both become very rich."

CHAPTER FORTY-ONE

D AVID DIDN'T SHOW up at TOPCO'S office until after lunch, but he felt fine and was dressed a little too formal in a blue suit and a sky blue tie. His tardiness had delayed the start of Jordan Phillips's Monday Management Meeting, but Jordan was anxious to hear about his results in Cuba, and his Cuba report was first on the agenda.

David began performing like a second-rate stage performer. He stood and acted out his meeting with the president—with a few embellishments. He talked about his new best friend, the President of Cuba, without attempting to hide any brag in his voice. Never a word was spoken by David of his father's relationship with Meyer Lansky, the real reason for David's success in Cuba.

"I love that deal, David. Congratulations on getting it. When can we sign it up?" Jordan asked.

"Right now. Here are the papers." He handed two copies of the contract to Jordan. "If you're ready to go with it, sign both of these copies, and give them back to me with a check for the one million dollars, and I'll return it to Cuba, then you can drill your well down there whenever you're ready."

Jordan turned to Sam. "Sam, when can you move a rig down to Cuba?"

"Probably three months."

"That's too slow. Get it there quicker. What about the costs? Any estimate?"

"I figure five wells down there next to your oil seeps could be put into the tanks for about five million, but the rotten egg smell means it's probably sour crude. If it is, we'll have to get the oil over to the big Shell plant in Jamaica, which is a big capital expense, or you need to come up with 30,000 barrels a day of sour crude to justify Shell or somebody else building a refinery in Cuba. We'll need to drill at least fifteen wells to get 30,000 barrels a day."

"That's okay. Get that rig down there, and start digging."

Jordan Phillips signed both copies of the Cuban deal contracts and the copy of the TOPCO internal check request. He didn't read any of the papers he signed because he had an attorney to read legal papers. His attorney to read those papers was David Paterno, Jr, who was to be the payee of a check for one million dollars after he approved Jordan Phillips's signing the papers.

Sam Knight, Jr., went to Cuba and stayed until he had drilled fifteen oil wells. The first oil well TOPCO drilled in Cuba was completed on the pump for three thousand barrels of nineteen gravity sour crude a day. Exactly as Sam Knight, Jr., had predicted, there was no purchaser for heavy sour crude oil in Cuba. The only way for TOPCO to get any revenue from the Cuban oil wells was to spend the money to drill enough oil wells required and produce enough sour crude oil in Cuba to make the investment in a sour crude refinery in Cuba economic and profitable.

TOPCO invested the twenty million more dollars drilling fifteen oil wells in Cuba. Although not one barrel of this oil could be sold, these fifteen new oil wells meant that TOPCO increased its oil production capability by 30,000 barrels a day, and it has proven oil reserves were increased by one hundred million barrels. The finding cost of this oil was only twenty cents a barrel. Jordan Phillips had begun the execution of his master plan to turn his oil production company into a substantial oil and gas exploration company. He had found a nice shallow oil field in Cuba. Jordan was satisfied that he was on the path of finding another East Texas Oil Field.

However, Jordan Phillips had no way of knowing that Meyer Lansky and David Paterno, Jr., had initiated their evil conspiracy to take his prime jewels away from him.

Drilling in Cuba was the first time since East Texas that TOPCO had borrowed money to drill oil wells. With bank balances still full of cash as ordered by his boss, David Paterno borrowed fifteen million from the Republic National Bank for TOPCO to drill its wells in Cuba.

CHAPTER FORTY-TWO

"MAY I SPEAK to Mike Wharton?" Joan Ambrose said to the switch board operator at TOPCO's office in Dallas.

"Hello, Joan," Mike said.

"Mike, they're putting that seismic northeast of Colville up to the shoreline at Prudhoe Bay on the market. We'll have to move fast to buy it, and if we like what we see, we can be first in line to buy the leases."

"Joan, we'll be looking at the crumbs the big boys leave behind, but those big company guys have fallen in love with their elephant: the Colville High. I'll take the crumbs they leave behind and find the oil."

"Two million dollars for all the lines is what we it will cost if we buy it. I think I can talk them into a two-week exclusive to check it out."

"Call them and tie up the two weeks for TOPCO and get the data. I'll tell Mr. Phillips to get ready to write the two million if we like what we see."

"I'll make the call, but, Mike, how about you and me? Are we ever going to talk about us?"

"I'll call you at nine tonight, honey."

"That's six Anchorage time. I'll be waiting by the phone. If you don't call me, I'm calling you."

"Joan, you know how I feel. I can't wait to talk all night, if you'll let me talk that long," Mike said to his lady geologist, shaking his head and smiling as he hung up the phone. He looked up and saw that his boss had just walked into his office.

Mike stood up. "Hello, Mr. Phillips. How's everything going?"

"I'm feeling good, Mike, but I need to catch up on Alaska."

"I just learned from Joan that those east-west lines running from the Colville High to the shoreline at Prudhoe Bay are being put on the shelf for sale. My gut tells me those lines will image a closure that needs to be drilled."

"Can we take a look before we have to write the check?"

"Yes, sir, but Joan could only talk them into two weeks. We have to say yes or no today regarding if we are okay with starting the two week period or if we want to forget it and be another bridegroom left at the church."

Jordan shook his head, "Well, Mike, do it, of course. Look at it, and buy it."

"I figured you'd want to look, sir, and I told her to get it. In a couple of hours, she'll be picking up the data in Anchorage and hot-shotting it down here to Dallas. The two week exclusive doesn't cost us a dime if we don't like what we see, but if we like it, in two weeks we've got to get them a check for two million dollars."

Jordan grinned and said, "Nice work, Mike. I hope we pay them the two million dollars. I'm betting that'll be the best bargain we've ever gotten. I still don't understand those major oil companies. Why are they dumping that seismic now?"

"Two reasons. First, their bean counters have told the big companies that with the four dry holes they've drilled, it's time get some revenue into a failed exploration program in Alaska. Selling that seismic puts revenue on the Alaska program books, and they don't want to drill anymore in Alaska after they dig their well on that big anticline, the Colville High. If Colville is their fifth dry hole, they can tell their shareholders not to worry because they've already given up on Alaska and taken their marbles home."

"So, what you're saying is they couldn't care less about the little jewel we might see, even if it might be a better place to drill?"

"You're sure right, Mr. Phillips, but we'll never know for sure until we buy the seismic and drill the closure I hope we're going to see."

Joan picked up the material in Alaska and flew to Dallas to hand deliver the data to Mike. She unrolled the copies of the seismic lines and secured them flat on the drafting table with paper weights, and she and Mike looked at them together. The first east-west line they looked at started on the west side of the Colville High and proceeded east up and over the large Colville High with regional dip off the top of that anticline to the northeast toward the shoreline of Prudhoe Bay.

They had already seen the seismic over Colville so that large area was no surprise, but they were both surprised to see a different structural picture next to Prudhoe Bay than a geologist would expect to see.

"Wow! Look at that reversal. The regional dip is off Colville to the northeast, and it should continue to the east-northeast, but look at that. That is an unquestionable western dip back to Colville away from the shoreline."

"Mike, it's a serious closure. And," he pointed to where the shoreline of Prudhoe Bay would fall on the seismic line, "look here under the shoreline there's some kind of termination. Good

Lord! Couldn't a trap that size hold the billions of barrels of oil we need to have to make it work in Alaska?"

"You got it, babe. Exactly right. The only way to find out is to buy the leases and move in a drilling rig then drill a hole and find out."

CHAPTER FORTY-THREE

I T WAS TIME for Jordan to decide about Alaska.

"That's right, David. It's twenty million for Cuba, but we have no problem with our financing. We won't need to borrow as much money as it looked like we would." Jordan turned to Mike Wharton, who had just come into the conference room. "Mike, when do we need to plan to start spending dollars on the Alaska Project?"

"We got the five-million cash call from BP for the Colville High participation for the seismic and the 10 percent interest in the wildcat they're going to drill, but now we've got to come up with another two million to buy the other seismic and, like you said you wanted to do, control your own one-hundred-percent owned prospect in Alaska. So that's seven million for Alaska so far."

"How much more should we budget for buying the leases and drilling the one hundred percent well on the prospect by the shoreline next to Prudhoe Bay?"

"It'll be at least five million for the land and five million for the well."

"That's only fifteen million for Alaska. I thought we'd end up with spending real money in Alaska, so raise it to twenty million." Jordan said.

Shaking his head and rubbing his eyes like he did sometimes when he was under stress, David's frown turned into a little smile. He thought about how Jordan Phillips was spending all this money. "Mr. Phillips, running this business has always been your responsibility. I can see why you have been so successful and have found so much oil. Spending that kind of money should increase the odds of your finding a new big oil field. Nice work, Boss!"

Jordan grinned like a madman from David's perspective. "Let's add enough of a contingency to round off our budget at fifty million dollars."

"Fifty million dollars is a good round number," said David. "Mr. Phillips, may I congratulate you? You couldn't have conceived a more brilliant strategy to build your company into the most successful oil-finding company in the business."

"After the Shell refinery is finished in Cuba, we should pick up a couple of million in cash flow at least, and our reserves and bank borrowing base should increase incrementally in value, but why don't you start the conversation with C. W. about increasing the Republic line?" Jordan said.

"Mr. Austin retired last summer. I already talked to the new oil V.P., and he'll only increase our line by ten million, but sir, I can get a twenty-five million line from a bank in Pittsburg that's trying to move into oil banking in Texas."

"Well, then do it. Let's get to drilling." Jordan Phillips slapped the top of his conference table and swung around in his plush leather swivel chair like a little boy.

After the Management Committee meeting ended, David Paterno returned to his office and placed two long distance phone calls. The first call was to the Hotel Nacional in Havana, Cuba, where he asked to be connected to Suite Number 930.

"Meyer Lansky."

"Hello, Mr. Lansky, this is David Paterno."

"How are you, David?"

"Things are going well. I hope it's a pretty day in Havana."

"It is a typical fall day. I hope you have good news for me, David."

"Sir, I do. I was able to get him to finalize his drilling budget at fifty million dollars."

"Wonderful, David. That should eliminate any Texas bank loaning him the money he will need."

"Yes, sir, it already has. The next call I make will be to your bank in Pittsburg."

"Congratulations, David. You are making great progress. The future holds great promise for you and me."

"I have to come to Havana to go over the company's Cuban drilling results with the Cuban Government's Commerce Department. Would there be time for me to drop by to see you and say hello?"

"Of course, David. Please don't ever come to Havana without seeing me."

When his call to Havana ended, David placed a call to the First Pittsburg National Bank of Pittsburg, Pennsylvania. He asked to speak to the President of the Bank.

"Hello, Mr. Leibowitz. This is David Paterno. It was good to meet you last month. I want to tell you that my company is ready for a twenty-five-million-dollar line of credit. I'll get you the property descriptions in Gregg County so you can prepare the mortgage and Deed of Trust."

"Thank you for calling, Mr. Paterno. As you know, I have been waiting for this call. Are you sure that twenty-five million is enough? When do you expect to make the first draw on the loan?"

"It depends on the rate of cash burn and how fast he drills."

"That's fine, Mr. Paterno. We must get the papers filed and perfect our lien immediately. If you will send the property descriptions, my legal department will draw up the papers and return them to you, then the money will be available for your company to draw down when it needs the money."

"Thanks, Mr. Leibowitz. It's a good feeling to have the financing secured before embarking on such a program, if you know what I mean."

"I know what you mean, Mr. Paterno."

CHAPTER FORTY-FOUR

MEYER LANSKY WAS dressed all in white.

"It's hot out here, David. You need a Panama hat from J. Lock's in London. I will get you one. Everybody needs a Panama hat in Havana. So how are things going in Dallas?"

"He's doing exactly what you said he would do, spending money he doesn't have."

"When can we foreclose?"

"Possibly in three, maybe four months."

"It must happen sooner."

"We don't have control over the timing of most items in the oil field. It might take nine months."

Lansky was usually placid, but now his face flushed as he spoke evenly, slowly. "I don't want to wait nine months. I'm not having a goddamn baby." David noticed for the first time how small and yellow and sharp-looking Lansky's teeth were.

"But, sir, doesn't your bank own the mortgage?"

"Yes. My bank has the mortgage, and when my bank's mortgage documents are signed by the borrower, the mortgaged properties are mine. I don't know a goddamn thing about the oil business, but I know something about mortgages. This Jordan Phillips is crazy for drilling fifty million dollars' worth of oil wells without having his financing arranged, then mortgaging his family jewels to a bank owned by Meyer Lansky. For God's sake, David, I can't believe why anyone could be as stupid as Jordan Phillips?" Lansky emitted a nasty little laugh.

"He's a Texas oil man. They trust other oil people like brothers. These Texans did oil deals with people without anything in writing. Just a handshake. They believe a man's word is his bond, but their bond is nothing like the tradition that your family and mine still honor."

"David, I'm glad you finally understand the depth of our family relationship across many generations."

"Mr. Lansky, may I ask you some questions about your plan?"

"We have gone over it. What else is there to discuss?"

"You said I was to be included for fifty percent of the surviving company after the foreclosure on TOPCO'S assets. Would it be appropriate for me to ask you to confirm our fifty-fifty split in writing? I will be happy to prepare the papers to form our new corporation: LAPOCO, Lansky and Paterno Oil Company. What a great name for an oil company. With a name like that, we can grow into the largest of the independent oil companies operating in the United States. If we ever decide to refine crude oil and market LAPOCO Gasoline, we will sell as much gasoline as any major oil company. I'd feel so much better holding a stock certificate in my hand.

"No. Goddamn it, David. You're asking me to do something for one purpose only—to make you feel better. That's bullshit, doing something only to make you feel better that would violate another of many traditions between our families. Like your Texas oil men, your father and I never had any written agreement. My word is as good as the bond you talk about between the oil wildcatters. David, you will become very rich from this deal. You never need anything in writing in any deal with Meyer Lansky."

What David was heard was, "If you're a good little boy, you might get a nice big piece of cake. It won't be half the cake though." David was hearing now that Lansky's bank had tied up TOPCO'S legacy East Texas Fairway oil wells under its mortgage. Lansky didn't need him anymore.

There was a big difference between making a lot of money and getting rich and owning half of a company the size of TOPCO— hundreds of millions of dollars. David also realized that whatever percentage Lanksy might give him had a high probability of shrinkage. That meant his potential share under Lansky's deal could turn out to be zero.

There was nothing else for David to say. With deep reticence, he shook Meyer Lansky's hand. He left him to return to Dallas, knowing that he could only become very wealthy man if he took the ball in his own hands and took over control of TOPCO on his own. It was time to forget about any association with Lansky. To hell with Meyer Lansky.

When he got back to Dallas, he called California. "Mo, this is David Paterno, Jr."

"Well, David, I haven't talked to you in years. How's that piss ant cousin Angelo doing? Haven't seen him since Chicago. Don't tell me you need L.A. counsel. You in trouble with some woman?"

"Well, maybe, maybe not. I'm the number two man in this Texas Oil Company in Dallas, and the owner has the trouble with his L.A. woman. I'm trying to help her find a Christmas present for her old man. He's going down the tube broke, and he's almost toast. I want you to help her with the coup d' gras. Can you form me a California corporation? It'll be an oil company."

"Sure. Why not? What do you want to name it?"

"I don't care. You pick a name. Just have 'oil' in the name."

"How about 'Sunset Production'?"

"Sounds like a moving-picture company. Make it 'Sunset Oil.'"

"Who'll own it?"

"I'll own fifty-one percent."

"What about the wife?"

"She'll own forty-nine percent."

"Send me a thousand dollars, and I'll form a California corporation. You need to come out here, and bring your fingers with you. You can't start a California company unless you pick up a fountain pen and sign the papers in California before a California notary, with you as the Founding Chief Executive Officer. I still don't understand why you need the wife."

"It's complicated. I have to cut her in on the new company because of her claim to half the old company as her community property."

"So what's that for?"

"You'll find out later. Show my name as the founder if you have to, then, after the corporation is formed and in good standing, take my name off of everything. List someone else as the Chief Executive Officer, someone who could execute any court filings that might be made on behalf of Sunset Oil."

"Who would that be?"

"The wife, Charlotte Sasawka Phillips. Having the wife in the take-over company makes the big picture work. She claims he screwed her out of her community property—half the stock in his oil company, which is total bullshit because he got his stock before he married her, but I can use her claim to bring him down. You'll see what I mean when we get there. There may be other legal issues that require work by you."

"What are you talking about, David?"

"I have other plans for Sunset Oil."

"Like what?"

"You'll know when it happens."

"For God sake, David, if I'm setting up a new corporation for you I need to know what in the hell you're doing."

"Can a California corporation throw a Texas company into bankruptcy?"

"If it's a creditor, it doesn't make any difference where it's domiciled."

"Okay, then do it like I said."

"Look, David, if you have all these plans, I need to know where to contact you twenty-four hours a day."

"My office or my apartment, and you have those numbers, Mo."

"I need another number if you aren't home or at the office. What's your favorite restaurant or bar?"

"The only place I might go is a dive called the Carousel Club. Here's the number: 23446."

"I hope to hell you know what you're doing. Having the wife owning part of your company could create problems for you."

"Go ahead, and paper the deal. Send your damn law bills to my apartment. I'll be out in L.A. soon and sign everything."

David hung up the phone and called his legal assistant into his office. Jackson Farrar had just passed the Texas Bar Exam. "Jackson, don't you agree with me that TOPCO should have a decent law library?"

"Yes, sir, Mr. Paterno. I've been wondering where your law books were."

"Why don't you call East Publishing Company, and tell them we want to buy a complete set of the Black Statute, Code and Constitution volumes and any other volumes they would recommend for a first-class law firm."

"How much are you prepared to spend, Mr. Paterno?"

"Try to keep it under fifty thousand dollars. No, go higher if you have to, and, Jackson, have the publisher make the invoice out to TOPCO in care of me."

"Yes, sir."

"One other thing. Have them engrave the cover of each volume."

"How do you want to have them engraved, Mr. Paterno? 'Law Library, Texas Oil Producing Company'?"

"No, these books will be mine and they should be engraved: 'David Aldo Paterno, Junior, Esquire.'"

"Yes, sir." Jackson Farrar couldn't understand David Paterno and his law library, but he ordered the law books. He didn't know yet that three creditors that were owed money were needed in order for an involuntary bankruptcy to be filed. Since David would be sure that none of invoices ever got paid, it wouldn't take long for East Publishing Company to be an unpaid creditor of TOPCO'S, and David knew who to use for the other two creditors.

David's phone rang. "Hello, Mr. Paterno. This is Barry Shapiro. I am the Executive Vice President of the First Pittsburg Bank in Pittsburg, Pennsylvania."

"Yes, Mr. Shapiro. How may I help you?"

"I am the Chief Lending Officer for this bank. As I believe you know, we have the mortgage on your company's oil properties in what county? Oh, yes, it's Gregg County, Texas. We notice that you have not drawn anything down on that loan."

"Yes, our cash burn rate is such that it we don't need to make a draw yet."

"That's understandable, Mr. Paterno. However, we would like to suggest that you take a draw of, say, ten million dollars. We need to show an increase in our total loans. It would be helpful if you could request that draw today, then we want to suggest that you take another similar draw next month."

"Certainly, I understand."

"Thank you, Mr. Paterno. May I consider this conversation your verbal request for the ten million dollar draw?"

"Of course. Please do."

"The draw will be funded by wire transfer."

David hung up the telephone. He knew Lansky was speeding up the foreclosure process, and he would have to get moving if he wanted to win the race.

CHAPTER FORTY-FIVE

JORDAN PHILLIPS ASKED his attorney and land manager, "How about the land on the Prudhoe Bay prospect? Did you buy all the leases we need, David?"

"Yes, sir, we did, but we had to pay five million. We had to go through the auction process. The trick is to pay off six or eight guys to draw for leases and bid, but they all have to be paid off and there's always one guy that runs the show and he gets paid off the most. That's the drill."

"I don't know that drill, but I assume it's legal?"

"Sure, it's legal. It's the game you play to get those leases. Everybody plays it."

"So do we have our hundred thousand acres?"

"We ended up with one-hundred and six thousand acres."

"Are they one-eighth leases?"

"Yes, sir. Are you thinking about giving out any overrides?"

"I don't give overrides, David."

"What about Mike Wharton?"

"He has a special arrangement. This Alaska prospect was his idea. He wouldn't join us without the incentive of the override. I thought you knew that, David. I'll tell you what: if we hit oil in Alaska, you'll get a bonus that'll double your annual salary."

"That would be nice, Mr. Phillips," said David Paterno. "I would prefer an override, but I understand." He really didn't give a damn because, when he took over TOPCO, he was going to fire Mike Wharton and screw him out of his override anyway.

"When does Sam think he can start drilling up in Alaska, David?"

"He said Loffland Brothers can have a rig on that location about the first week of December."

"I'm ready, and you can write this down and take it to the bank. The #1 Prudhoe Bay-State of Alaska is going to hit."

"Sir, it either hits or you lose another fifteen million dollars."

CHAPTER FORTY-SIX

LIBERTY OIL'S TOP management always had a hard time with the guest list for their annual hunt—except for Jordan Phillips, who was always invited. Invitations to the Liberty Hunt were coveted by the top independent oil men in the business.

The company's annual get together on its eighty-thousand acre lease in Duval County was a time of camaraderie when the men could drink whiskey and talk oilfield together in the brush country of South Texas, where almost everything bit you, stuck you, or made you bleed. The rattlesnakes, scorpions and cactus took care of that.

For the past five years, Rex Davis had been Liberty's C.E.O. He started a tradition of inviting one other major oil company C.E.O. to join him as co-host. This year he invited Leonard "Mc" McCullum, the C.E.O. of Continental Oil.

Liberty was one of the first oil companies to use geologists to find oil. Except for Humble Oil, Liberty was the only major company to own oil and gas leases in the East Texas Oil Field when it was discovered by Jordan Phillips. The guests at the Liberty Annual Hunt were independent oil men—oil producers that didn't refine oil or sell gasoline like the major oil companies because they didn't have a vast nationwide network of filling stations.

Most of the hunters this year, except for two, arrived thrilled with the possibility of shooting an eighteen-point trophy white tail buck. George Coates and Wordie Gorman, never brought a deer rifle to a deer hunt. Coatsie arrived early with his dog man driving his Chrysler station wagon, pulling a trailer carrying Blondie and a couple of other bird dogs. Wordie Gorman flew down in his Bonanza and landed on the dirt strip.

The two bird hunters slept later than the deer hunters. The early risers were awakened at four-thirty A.M. for hot coffee and a steaming breakfast of crisp bacon, chorizo and two eggs over easy, with corn tortillas and salsa, then off with their guides to their blinds when it was still pitch black, an hour before sunrise with plenty of time to hear the last nightly yelps of coyotes waking up the sun.

The bird hunters would have breakfast at a reasonable hour and then leave camp and spend the day behind the dogs, hoping to find at least twenty coveys of bobwhite quail. Pat Rutherford arrived late from his ranch in Frio County. He already had his daily limit shooting birds back at his place before he left, but Pat would never miss the camaraderie and the spirit of friendship he felt around the campfire when he was with his brother wildcatters at the Liberty hunt.

Rex Davis greeted his guests. The burning mesquite logs popped and hissed. "Gentlemen, welcome to Liberty's Annual South Texas Hunt. We're glad to see you all here once again this year. We hope that tomorrow's hunt will be better than today's. George, I can't wait for you to tell us how many coveys it took before you and Wordie bagged your limits, but, we want you to tell us how many wells you're going to drill at Berclair."

"Davis, I thought you and Mc knew I don't talk business

during playtime, especially not about Berclair. I'll tell you what I'll do, you tell us how thick the pay was in Liberty's well at Northeast Thompsonville, and I'll talk about Berclair. But, if you're going to ask me my secrets, why don't you ask Rutherford when he's going to find another Conroe? Or, ask Gorman about his little oil field in Jim Hogg County that he won't let anybody know will end up being one big oil field."

Jordan was quiet and stared into the fire. Oblivious to the chatter he sipped a scotch. Mired in his thoughts.

Wordie Gorman raised his hand and said, "What about Earl? Why don't you ask Earl about him and Rutherford and their drilling company trying to undercut my drilling bids?"

"Wordie, our rigs are too big to drill the shallow wells you drill. We'd rather find oil than make money drilling wells," Earl Rowe said.

"Okay, guys, we want you all to have a great time this year. You all know the drill. Have a drink or two, and we'll go into the dining tent and eat some Armstrong Ranch steaks so tender you can cut them with a fork. Just let me or any of my guys know if you need anything. We're here to have a good time."

The talk went on around the campfire. Orion's Belt and the Big Dipper and millions of bright stars lit the clear and cool nighttime sky in South Texas as darkness fell. Competitors became drinking Buddies. Memories and oil deals were made.

Everybody sitting around the campfire was waiting for Jordan Phillips to brag about his new oil field in Cuba. They kept kidding him about his rabbit's foot, how it worked in East Texas and how it sounded like it was still working in Cuba. Nobody realized that Jordan Phillips was on the edge. No one knew the great wildcatter was gambling his fortune in the search for another East Texas Oil Field.

"Davis, I was once a sugar engineer in Cuba and I'm ready

to go back down to Havana and drill some oil wells. If Jordan Phillips here, will first tell us the straight skinny about his oil field in Cuba," George Coates said.

Jordan Phillips hadn't said a word, and he was never going to talk about his oil field in Cuba. But, as he sat there, he thought to himself about how he was either going to be richer than he had ever been, or, lose everything and be just another old broke wildcatter. He knew that whatever happened to him was totally out of his control. He knew the only thing that he could do was to keep the drill bit turning to the right in his well in Alaska, and when it reached total depth, he'd either strike big oil again, or he'd go completely broke.

So, Jordan kept his mouth shut. He took another sip of his scotch, and stared at the burning logs. He let George Coates's questions about Cuba blow over him like the warm smoke wafting from the fire.

"Well, Jordan's not talking about Cuba." George continued, "So, Rex, tell us what Liberty's doing on the other side of the King Ranch at Premont. Tell us about Seeligson Field. Is Liberty or the Sun Company going to operate the Seeligson Unit. I hear about those secret unitization committee meetings in San Antonio, trying to figure out how to get the Seeligsons to unitize each pay sand into it's own unit."

"It's no secret Sun will operate the unit, and when it's unitized the production will double. But, it will never happen if we can't get those Seeligsons to let us unitize the field the way it ought to be unitized."

Listening in silence, Jordan Phillips surprised everyone by sitting straight up and started to talk. He looked around the circle into the eyes of each hunter, saying, "Tom Slick. Do what Tom Slick did," and, then he repeated what he had said, loud and clear.

"Jordan? Why'd you say Tom Slick?" Rex Davis asked,

bewildered. And everyone else was stunned too...hearing words that absolutely made no sense come out of Jordan Phillips' mouth.

Jordan spoke again. "Tom Slick chose Arthur Seeligson to be the Executor of his Estate. Mr. Slick would never have chosen Arthur Seeligson to be the Executor of his estate if he hadn't known that Arthur and his brother Lamar were the best lawyers around. You Big Boys better be smart and take whatever deal the Seeligson's give you if you want to unitize their oil field. If you don't, you'll end up with the short end of the stick."

"Jordan Phillips how in the world do you know anything about Tom Slick?" Rex Davis asked.

"I'm from the Pennsylvania oil field, Rex. I heard about Tom Slick in the oil field ever since I was a kid back in Pennsylvania, when my dad told me Tom Slick had gone to Oklahoma and discovered a big oil field at Cushing. And, anybody who ever watched Tom Slick in the oil field learned the secret of how he found so much oil. His secret was to start drilling and never quit until he struck oil. He kept finding one field after the other and, he never stopped drilling. Tom Slick was the greatest oil finder there ever was."

And, that was that. Jordan Phillips shut his mouth and stared back into the fire and watched the smoke. Except for the sizzling of the burning mesquite, no one heard anything around the campfire for that quiet moment, or, maybe in between the crackling, the chirping of a cricket. Or the occasional shrill of a Mexican whip-poor-will.

Finally, a tall black man in a large white chef's hat came out of the camp house ringing a cowbell, singing, "Soup's on. Soup's on. Come and get yall's steaks. They's hot, and they's ready to eat." Last in the line to enter the dining shack, Jordan Phillips stopped when Rex Davis touched his shoulder. "Can I talk to you out here privately for a minute, Jordan?"

"Sure, Rex. What's on your mind?"

"My guys tell me you're up there in the North Slope play."

"We sure are."

"I think you had a piece of BP and Sinclair's well on the Colville High."

"We did. Ten percent."

"We had twenty percent."

"I understand it reached Total Depth a couple of weeks ago, and it was about the driest dry hole ever drilled in Alaska. My geologist said it was hard to explain how a structure as big as Colville could have been so dry. What did your guys think?"

"You know, they say the Colville High was the largest closure ever drilled anywhere in the world, and, yes, it was as dry as a dry hole can be. I haven't heard the full story yet. I know I'll hear all the excuses like the timing of structural movement and all those other esoteric geologic alibies. It could have been an elephant oil field."

"Is that what you wanted to talk to me about, Rex?"

"No, not really. I hear you bought an acreage spread east of the Colville High below the shoreline at Prudhoe Bay."

"Yes, about 125,000 acres. What about it?"

"We like it. We participated in the seismic, but like the other big companies, that big dry hole was all it took, and we decided against any more exploration in Alaska. But after I took another look at that seismic with our Alaska geophysicists. That termination has to mean there's a trap under your acreage. I decided I wasn't going to chicken out of Alaska, so, we'd like to offer to buy half your interest in your leases and drill our half with you. TOPCO can operate if you want to operate. Give me your price, and don't be bashful. We like it and we'll pay to get in it."

"Rex, our Prudhoe Bay Prospect is not for sale. I decided to keep the whole thing. It's too late anyway. We're already drilling. It's down to about 4,000 feet."

"We buy into drilling wells, but it sounds like you've got 8/8 fever. That's an incurable and often a terminal disease, but it doesn't hurt to ask."

"Last month, I would have bought your twenty percent in Colville," Jordan said.

"Jordan, like you said about your acreage at Prudhoe Bay, our interest in Colville was never for sale. Liberty doesn't sell. We're buyers. Hey, let's go eat a good steak."

"That's a deal I'll make with you anytime, Rex. Thanks for having me back this year."

"You'll be here as long as Liberty has its hunt, but I'm serious about Prudhoe Bay. Call me if you ever want to sell down any of it."

CHAPTER FORTY-SEVEN

"CAROUSEL LOUNGE," SAID the hostess into the phone, loud enough that she could be heard over the music and the buzz of lots of people talking.

"Jack Ruby, please."

"Of course," she said, turning away from the phone and yelling, "Sparky, it's for you." She handed the phone to the greasy faced fat man.

"Thanks, Baby. Hello. Sparky here."

"Sparky. This is Lansky."

"Well, how in the hell are you, Boss? Things still booming in Havana?"

"Just keep sending those rich Texans down here to blow their oil money in my casinos, and you won't hear one complaint out of me."

"When can I come down and see you, Boss?"

"Take care of a little job I got for you, and come on down and play with me."

"What can I do for you, Mr. Lansky?"

"You know anybody from an oil company named TOPCO?"

"If he drinks a lot I probably know him. What's his name?"

"David Paterno."

"Nope. Never heard of any David Paterno, but I have a

customer I think works for that company. He usually drops in here on Wednesdays. A big guy, an oil field type. Some nights he drinks a lot, and the bartenders love him. Sometimes he brings women with him or sometimes he picks this gal up here. I can't tell who is the hornier: him or her. You can't tell what motivates a woman if screwin' is her business. I don't know how much he pays her, but he always takes her somewhere and I presume he fucks her."

"What's his name?"

"Just a minute while I ask Dooley." He hollers to the bartender, "Dooley, what's the name of the oil company guy who comes in Wednesdays with that red-headed hooker? Drinks scotch, double Dewar's on the rocks."

"Sam Knight. At least four drinks two or three nights a week. Gave me his business card once. Let's see if can find it in this drawer...Yeah, here it is. Manager of Operations and Chief Engineer. TOPCO. Red spinning top on the card."

The phone was quiet. All Meyer Lansky could hear over the phone was the bartender yelling, and Louis Armstrong singing "Mack the Knife."

Jack Ruby put the receiver back up to his ear. "Name's Sam Knight. His card says he works for a company called TOPCO. I've heard about that company. It's owned by a guy named Jordan Phillips."

In the background, Lansky could hear Satchmo's gargling of the words, "Hey, the line forms, on the right, dear, now that Mackey's back in town."

"Oh yeah, Boss, I almost forgot. Sometimes there's a dark guy with slick black hair meets up with him. Mid-thirties, flat belly. Doesn't say much, and, jeez, you know, when he talks, he sounds like he's from the east coast, ya know, New Yawk or Joisey."

"He's the one. His father was a lawyer for me back in the old days. His name is David Paterno, Jr. I want you to get to know all you can about Paterno and Knight. Where they live, what kinds of cars they drive, who they're fucking, their usual schedule, those kinds of things. Do you know anything about this guy, Jordan Phillips?"

"Only that he's supposed to be the richest man in Dallas, maybe Texas."

"You get to be these two oil guys' best friend and find out everything you can about what they think about their boss. Put a tail on them. Learn how to find them quickly when I tell you to find them."

"Easy peesy, Boss."

"Try to find out how much I can depend on that Sam guy if I need him, but that New Jersey guy is bad news. I may need you to take him out."

"What? Take him out? What's going on, Boss?"

"Jack, don't you know the rule? Don't fuck with Meyer Lansky."

"I got it, Boss. That's why I am here to help when you need it. I'll find out all you need to know in a week or two for sure. Don't fuckin' worry 'bout that."

"Good, Jack. If you need any long green, just call Jake and give him the word."

"Good. And, Jack, there's one other thing."

"What's that, Boss?"

"There's a fifty G bonus for you if you find out something about these guys that helps me. If you find anything I don't already know that helps me, Bingo! I will pay you the long green. It'll be my call. This is between you and me. Nobody needs to know about this little transaction."

"Of course, Boss."

"If it works, you can take your choice of where you go next, Vegas, or hell, I could use you down here in Havana after we get rid of Castro, but, Jack, this is exactly why I wanted you in Dallas."

CHAPTER FORTY-EIGHT

S HE HATED TO say it, but sometimes she couldn't take that young stud Rollie Masters all the time, and she'd yearn for the slower times when her old boyfriend from Kilgore would come and take care of her in slow, smooth way. Since Sam Knight hadn't seen her Cabana on the beach at Santa Monica, she called him on the phone and begged him to come see her. When he received the train ticket, he came.

"Why don't you come more often, Sam?" Charlotte said as he was stirring her Tom Collins on the covered porch of her Cabana.

"I'm getting old, Charlotte. Tell me if this is too sweet for you, honey."

"You can't do anything too sweet for me, Sam, and you're not too old." She grabbed him and kissed him. "Why don't you sell that drug store and move out here with me?"

He put both arms around her and squeezed her tight and said, "My old-lady customers need me back at the drug store in Kilgore. I got to make a livin'."

"No, you don't. Not out here. I've got plenty of money and you can work for me, baby." She grabbed him again and kissed him harder.

He pulled back from her kiss and said, "But, Charlotte, that's Jordan's money."

"Sam, when I get through with him, half of his money will be mine. The only reason he found oil is because of me. I ought to be the one they thank for finding that oil field."

"Charlotte, I don't know. My wife's been dead for years, and I'm old. I feel guilty about what you and I have been doing to Jordan all these years, but there's nothing I can do about all those years. All I can do is stop it now. You need a young stud."

"Sam, don't talk that way. I want to be with you. Tell me when you're coming back to see me."

"Never, Charlotte. It's over." Sam left the Cabana on the beach and returned to Kilgore.

CHAPTER FORTY-NINE

I T HAD BEEN a tradition for many years for the Knight family to gather to celebrate Thanksgiving. Sam, Jr., his two brothers, Walter and Bob Knight, and their wives, Fran and Jane, and their collective three sons and two daughters met in Kilgore with the family patriarch, Sam Knight, Sr., now in his seventies and having health issues. The tradition always included the ritual of listening on the radio to the annual Texas versus Texas A&M Turkey Day football game.

Sam Jr.'s two sisters-in-law always arrived early at the Knight family home and put a turkey stuffed with corn bread dressing in the oven to bake. They'd use Mama Knight's recipe for Lady Baltimore Cake and make their kids' favorite dessert. At noon, all of the family would gather at the table and hold hands, while Sam Knight, Sr., gave thanks to God for his family and for the gathering of his clan another year.

To finish off their feast, they'd bring in the Knight family's old scratched wooden ice-cream freezer with the can filled with frozen homemade vanilla ice cream that the boys had turned before lunch. As the feast ended, everyone had a full stomach and a spirit full of happiness and love.

After lunch, the girls and their mothers cleared the table

and went into the kitchen to wash dishes while the men and the boys went into the living room and all six of them lay flat on the floor listening to the play-by-play of the football game on WFAA Radio with the melodious voice of Kern Tips calling the game as he had for years. The oil well outside the living room window was pumping so much water—and making so much noise as a result—that to hear the game they turned the volume on the radio up as loud as it would go.

The Turkey Day game was a blow out for the Texas Longhorns: 27-0. The credit for the victory went to the Longhorn's new coach, Darrell Royal, who had been an All-American Quarterback under Bud Wilkinson at University of Oklahoma, so the whipping of the Aggies by the Horns broke up the Knights' Thanksgiving Day celebration earlier than usual, and the two married Knight brothers and their wives and their kids said goodbye to Big Sam and to Uncle Brother Sam, Jr., and left before the end of the third quarter.

Being alone with his dad gave Sam, Jr., an opportunity to confront his dad about his investment thirty years ago in TOPCO. He had always thought that Jordan Phillips had taken his dad to the cleaners.

"Yes, son, the money invested by me and two others allowed him to keep drilling and drill his discovery well, but that investment was the best investment I ever made."

"What do you mean, Dad? He found the Black Giant with your money, and then he forced you out for peanuts. He screwed you when he bought that stock back from you. Just look how much that stock would be worth if you still owned it."

"Sam, Jordan is a good man. You really don't know what in the hell you're talking about. I invested five thousand dollars and when he bought me out he paid me seventy-five thousand dollars. One of the best deals I ever made."

"But, Dad, if he hadn't screwed you out of your interest in his company with all that Fairway production, today you'd be worth a fortune."

"Listen to me, son. Jordan Phillips is one of the most honest people I've ever known. He begged me not to sell out. We almost had to force him to buy us out. Didn't you know all this? And he made all three of us original investors agree in writing that we thought it was a fair deal, and he gave us a whole year to change our minds and get all of our money back too."

"I never knew that."

"Well, son, you know it now."

"Why didn't you tell me?"

"You didn't ask."

"I don't know what to do now. I've been wrong all these years."

"Listen to me, Sam. Jordan Phillips gave you a plum job when you graduated from A&M. When none of the companies were hiring engineers you got a good job, and you've learned the business and made a good living in a job you would have never had if it wasn't for Jordan Phillips."

"I can't believe it, Dad. I can't believe it. No one ever told me the real story."

Sam Knight, Jr., realized that all the resentment and hatred that had been building in his mind about Jordan Phillips was wrong. How could he ever face Jordan Phillips? What would he do with all the guilt that was buried in his soul? Maybe the knowledge of his dad's trust and admiration of the man he had hated would help save him. Maybe a stronger bond would grow between himself and his own father.

On the Sunday of Thanksgiving weekend, Sam Knight, Jr., was sitting next to his father where the Knight family always prayed at the First Baptist Church during the eleven o'clock service. They were praying the Lord's Prayer when Sam looked at his father, and his father looked back at him and they both smiled, then Sam Knight, Sr.,'s head dropped into his son's lap. He was dead of a massive heart attack.

Three days later, Sam Knight, Sr.,'s funeral was held at the First Baptist Church in Kilgore at 11:00 AM. There was a reception in the Church parlor, and Jordan Phillips stood in the receiving line working his way up to pay his respects to Sam Knight's three sons and their families, especially to Sam, Jr.

"Thank you for being here, Mr. Phillips. My brothers and I appreciate your coming from Dallas."

"Sam, your dad was one of my oldest and best friends in East Texas. I had to pay my respects to him and offer my sympathy to you and your brothers and their families during this period of mourning for your great loss."

"Thank you, sir, but I need to apologize to you. You need to know that for many years, I have had the wrong impression about your repurchase of my father's stock in TOPCO. To be honest with you, I thought you had stolen that stock from him, but on Thanksgiving Day, he told me how honest and fair you had been."

"Sam, I felt the same way about your dad."

"Thank you, Mr. Phillips. I know you realize that I'm leaving for Alaska the day after tomorrow. I'm going to start the well on the North Slope."

"That's good, Sam. I'm glad you'll be there. It'll be in good hands."

"Loffland Brothers has fine equipment and good people, but I'll be there and I'll get that well finished right, but I have something I must talk to you about before I leave for Alaska."

"What's that?"

"I don't know how to say it, except to tell you to watch out for someone."

"Watch out for who?"

"David Paterno."

"Why David?"

"I can't really say for sure. I don't have all the details. I'll find out more and I'll call you." Sam, Jr. closed his eyes and looked down, shaking his head, squeezing both hands into fists, and crying real tears.

"Sam, don't worry about the company. This is the day we remember the life of wonderful dad. There'll be another day to worry about David Paterno."

"Thank you, sir, but you must hear me." He lowered his voice into a whisper so no one standing nearby could hear. "Something happened after he went to Cuba. After he has a few drinks, he feels important and starts talking about how you are going broke, and then he tells me he is standing by to pick up the pieces."

Jordan was shocked. The more he heard about David Paterno, the angrier he became. His face turned red, and he said, "Good God, I hope I have time to fix this, but, Sam, today, my prayers are with you and your family and your father."

Standing tall, distinguished and handsome with a full head of greying hair, Jordan Phillips turned away from Sam Knight, Jr., and walked out of the church to the limousine that was waiting to return him to Dallas.

CHAPTER FIFTY

D RILLING FIFTEEN NEW oil wells capable of producing a total of fifteen thousand barrels a day of sulfur oil and having a piece of the biggest dry hole ever
drilled in the world on the Colville High in Alaska, then paying
the bonus to buy oil and gas leases on more than one hundred
thousand acres and paying the cash call required to get a drilling
rig to move in and start drilling on the Prudhoe Bay Prospect
south of the north shoreline of Alaska meant that on Wednesday,
December 10th, 1958, TOPCO and Jordan had spent almost
fifty million dollars looking for new oil. Not a drop of oil had
been sold in Cuba, and not a penny of new oil revenue had been
deposited in TOPCO'S bank account since the spending of all
this money started.

On this Wednesday, Merle also placed on her boss's desk a
check request covering another five million dollar cash call from
the drilling contractor on the well in Alaska.

"This is the big one, Merle. Spending this money will take
care of all our problems. In about four weeks, this well should be
down, and we should strike oil in Alaska."

But this cash burn was shrinking TOPCO'S bank account,
and Jordan Phillips knew it. Happiness was a positive cash flow.

With this cash situation, there was no way for him to be happy. He never forgot what he had learned years ago: if a wildcatter had the patience to let the drill bit keep turning to the right and making hole, it will finally strike oil. Great happiness will always follow. At least that's what he hoped.

Jordan didn't quit thirty-eight years ago in East Texas, and he discovered the largest oil field in the world. He wasn't quitting now. He signed the check for the five million dollars and handed it back to Merle. The well would keep drilling on TOPCO'S one-hundred percent owned Prudhoe Bay Prospect. Jordan Phillips was still in control of his company, but being in control did not resolve the problem that he had begun to learn would be worse for him than the most expensive dry hole: David Paterno, Jr.

CHAPTER FIFTY-ONE

WHILE IN THE process of a routine client account review in preparation for a coming audit by the bank examiners, the auditors for the Pittsburg Bank had discovered that TOPCO had failed to furnish the bank copies of the state oil production reports and oil run tickets as required under the terms of TOPCO'S mortgage of its East Texas oil wells to the Pittsburg Bank. This "failure to furnish" required reports placed TOPCO in technical default of its loan agreement.

The only reason TOPCO had enough cash to pay the five-million-dollar cash call to the drilling contractor and keep drilling in Alaska was because of the cash draw of ten million dollars against the Pittsburg loan. David had requested the draw, but he failed to disclose the draw on the loan to Jordan Phillips. This was Paterno's initial move in his race with Meyer Lansky to be the first to take over TOPCO.

Not one of the five invoices that had been sent to TOPCO by the East Publishing Company every month for five months for the fifty thousand dollar purchase of law books had been paid. Since they had been sent to David Paterno's attention, Paterno had filed them in File 13: the trash can. The East Publishing

Company account with TOPCO was one of several of TOPCO'S accounts now in arrears.

On Thursday morning, when Merle was pouring herself a cup of coffee in the company break room, TOPCO's chief accountant was standing next to her. He asked Merle, "What do you think about the ten million dollar draw on the Pittsburg bank loan?"

"That's the first I've heard of that."

"Did you know," the accountant continued, "about the bank's notice in the letter we got yesterday was that the company's loan is in default because of failure to furnish copies of the state production reports on the East Texas properties as required in the loan document?"

Merle recoiled. She immediately went to Jordan's office and told her boss everything she had just learned.

"What's going on, Merle? Why didn't Paterno tell me about that draw? There's no excuse for not sending those copies of the monthly production reports. Tell Paterno to get in here now."

David came in and stood in front of his desk. Jordan wondered who this person really was. He was no longer the sharp young Railroad Commission lawyer he hired. David stood dressed in his dark blue suit with his sky blue tie, and he stared at Jordan with his hair disheveled and piercing baggy eyes and the touch of a sinister smile on his lips.

"David, what are you doing to this company?"

"I'm trying to do my job to keep you out of trouble, not only with the Railroad Commission but with the bank in Pennsylvania. All those reports are required routinely under our mortgage."

"Then why didn't you send them? Get me a copy of that mortgage. I want to see what I signed. We should have stayed with Republic Bank. I never had to read a Republic Bank mortgage."

"But you never had a mortgage with Republic. You only had some unsecured loans with Republic, Mr. Phillips."

"Well, get one right now. I have never read bank stuff, but I'll tell you one thing. D&M estimated the net barrels we discovered in Cuba at a hundred million barrels with a PV-10 Value of twenty million dollars. Any bank would give us a substantial boost in our loan value with those reserves, so get that Yankee bank to increase our line of credit to twenty million, or go to Republic and borrow the money and pay them off. David, what are you doing? Are you still on my side? I don't understand it. What are you thinking?"

"I am the only person associated with you who is trying to help you. I hate to tell you this, but Sam Knight is a terrible threat to you. Your drilling engineer thinks you stole his father's stock in TOPCO from him. He's mad as hell at you. I'd watch him if I were you."

"Sam's father's dead, and Sam knows the real story. Sam knows now how well I took care of his dad. You're out of your mind, David. Quit worrying about Sam. Get my line of credit increased with all those new reserves we proved up in Cuba. Oh, and is the rumor correct? You've decided I am going broke, and you're waiting to pick up the pieces, for God's sake?"

David spoke calmly. To Jordan, he seemed more a robot than a human being. "I know more about TOPCO'S financing than anyone. More than you. I'm the person getting your drilling financed. I am surprised you don't appreciate how much I am helping you. Sam Knight lied to you that I was expecting your downfall. You should fire him, and you don't need to go back to Republic Bank. You should be thanking me for finding a bank when you needed a bank."

"David, this is today, not yesterday. Fix what we have to fix to be okay with that Pittsburg bank. Get me the money I need to keep drilling. Don't waste another minute of my day. Go to

Republic and give them the D&M report on the reserves in Cuba. Get enough money to take us out of the Pennsylvania bank."

Jordan knew it was time to circle the wagons. He told Merle to get Joe Anderson on the phone.

"Joe, I got a problem."

"What's up, Mr. Phillips?"

"That New Jersey Railroad Commission lawyer. You know, you met him. He's my in-house lawyer, and he's from New Jersey. I hired him because I needed an oil and gas lawyer, and I liked him so much."

"David Paterno?"

"Yeah. He's trying to take me down. He got me into this Yankee bank in Pennsylvania, and they're talking about calling my loan, saying we haven't filed some reports. I need to get Republic to take them out."

"Have you talked to your banker at Republic?"

"C. W. Austin's retired. I, personally, don't know a soul over there at Republic Bank anymore. I told Paterno to handle my banking."

"Don't you worry. I'll help Merle, and we can handle everything. You go find C. W., and tell him he needs to get off the golf course and take care of an old buddy," said Joe Anderson. "I will get you the best private investigator in Texas, and he will get everything there is to know on your New Jersey lawyer, but a word of advice for you is you better give that asshole his walking papers before it's too late."

CHAPTER FIFTY-TWO

"MRS. PHILLIPS, MY name is David Paterno. I am a lawyer with your husband's oil company."

"What in the world are you calling me for?" Charlotte asked.

"I happen to be in Los Angeles, and I'd like to talk to you about your husband."

"Why? What's going on?" Charlotte sat in her library at her home on Beverly Drive.

"I prefer not to discuss this matter over the telephone. May I make an appointment to drop by your home to see you?"

"I suppose. This afternoon would be fine. Say, four o'clock?"

A tall British butler in a white coat escorted David Paterno out to the swimming pool to meet Mrs. Jordan Phillips in the garden behind her Beverly Hills home. David introduced himself. Charlotte Phillips was dressed in a long, blue indigo garden dress, appropriate for a clear eighty-degree mid-December day in Beverly Hills. She sat at one of the tables on the tile patio that surrounded the pool. She sat in a position where the large umbrella in the table would shade her skin from the bright rays of the sun.

"Thank you for seeing me this afternoon, Mrs. Phillips."

Charlotte Phillips held out her hand, and, without rising,

said, "Nice to meet you, Mr. Paterno, but as I mentioned on the phone, I cannot understand why my husband's attorney from Dallas would want to see me."

"I think you may need to refile for divorce, Mrs. Phillips, and very soon. To be quite frank and above board, Mrs. Phillips, your husband is losing his mind."

"What?"

"Mrs. Phillips, the principal symptom of a manic-depressive condition is spend-thriftiness. Jordan Phillips is spending his money like crazy drilling for oil. He has set a goal of spending fifty million dollars trying to find a new oil field, and he has spent almost exactly that amount with no financial return. If spending fifty million dollars is not being a spendthrift then nobody is a spendthrift."

"What can we do, Mr. Paterno? I am not prepared to live a life of poverty."

"I have a plan. That's why I came to L.A. I'd like to tell you about my plan, which will save most of his fortune for you, Mrs. Phillips.

"Please tell me what we are going to do about Jordan?"

"We must move quickly before the entire company is lost. There is only one way we can stop his crazy spending. Immediately after the first of January, your husband will be hit with a surprise. We will form a new company, and on January second, it will force TOPCO into bankruptcy and take over its assets. That's the only way to stop him. And you, Mrs. Phillips, will be President and Chief Executive Officer of the new company."

Charlotte's chin rose. Her face brightened. "Of course, I have always thought I needed to return to Texas and run the business. After all, I was the brains behind all the oil he found in East Texas. I can do a much better job of running the business than he has."

"Mrs. Phillips, with your half interest in the community property, your ownership in the new company will qualify Sunset

Oil Production Company to be one of the three creditors to file the involuntary bankruptcy, and this will give our new company a preferential right to take TOPCO's assets out of bankruptcy. You really won't need to worry about running the day-to-day oil field operations of the company. I'll own stock in the new company. You'll be the president, and I'll work for you and be your Executive Vice President. I'll see that your checks are always sent to you every month to you in California or wherever in the world you may be."

"Tell me more, Mr. Paterno."

"It will be automatic. When we pull the trigger and file the involuntary bankruptcy, this mindless extravagance will come to an end. There is an immense fortune waiting for you if we keep this man who has gone insane from losing it."

"Oh, my Lord, I can't believe all this. Mr. Paterno, you are a Godsend. Lord, you deserve to own some stock in the new company. You will deserve everything you can get. How can I ever thank you, Mr. Paterno?"

"I am owed no thanks. I'll receive something more valuable than any stock in the new company. There is no better reward than the satisfaction I will receive from helping a person as vulnerable as you are."

"So what do we need to do next?"

"Really, there's not much to it. You'll need to sign some papers, which a lawyer will bring here to you. That's all you'll do. The new corporation will be formed. The lawyer I engaged to help out here in California is Maurice Caesarius. He'll bring the papers in the next day or two."

"It's so important that we move as fast as we can so we can save the business. I just hope it's not too late."

"There is still time, but we must move" David Paterno said as Jan Phillips walked up to the table by the pool in her black bikini.

"Mr. Paterno, I'd like you to meet my daughter, Jan Phillips."

"Miss Phillips, my name is David Paterno, Executive Vice President and General Counsel of your father's oil company in Dallas. It's a pleasure to meet you."

"It's nice to meet you," Jan Phillips said. "But how in the world can my father's lawyer help Mother and me?"

"Mr. Paterno, you realize that on New Year's Day, my Jan will be twenty-five years old."

"Of course. I know that on her twenty-fifth birthday, she is eligible to take down the five million dollars from her trust in the Republic Bank. I have already done groundwork at the bank, and January second will be the big pay day for Jan."

"I'm planning to go to Dallas and spend the New Year holiday with Daddy and go to the bank on the second to transfer my money to my bank out here in L.A."

"I'll be happy to take you to the bank, and I'd love to show you around Dallas."

"Thank you, but I don't need any help with that bank. I might take you up on showing me around Dallas though. Why don't you call me at Daddy's after I get there on the thirtieth?"

With that, David Paterno exited Charlotte Phillips's home and returned to Dallas.

Jan swam, and her mother went into the house and called Rollie Masters.

"Rollie, I've got to talk to you. Meet me out at the cabana at six. You can't believe what's about to happen. I'm taking over the oil business. I'm getting everything. I'll be the most important woman in Texas. From now on, you won't have anything else to do but take care of me."

CHAPTER FIFTY-THREE

"JOE, HAS YOUR private investigator learned anything yet about David Paterno?"

"Not much yet. He found a guy to run the traps back in New Jersey. It takes time. He'll find people that know the family. He'll check courthouse records for everything under the sun: births, deaths, and police and fire records. Their criminal records will be checked, and even traffic fines and parking tickets. You name it. He'll find everything. He's already found out one thing strange."

"What's that?"

"He's got a source with Braniff at Love Field. Paterno went to L.A. last Sunday and came back Tuesday. Why would he go out there?"

"It wasn't at my request. He wasn't doing TOPCO business."

"I should get the P.I.'s report after New Year's, and we'll know a lot more about your guy."

CHAPTER FIFTY-FOUR

THE SMELL IN the back of the joint was like a bus-station bathroom, and the smoke was so thick it made your eyes burn. David didn't like the Carousel Club when he was sober, but he needed a drink, and the place would be okay as soon as he got a buzz on.

It was dark and smoky and hard for his eyes to adjust, then there she was—a redhead sitting at a little round table in the back of the club. He could tell who she was because of her full lips and her red hair and breasts just large enough to be interesting. He sauntered over and sat down beside her and ordered a martini, Plymouth Gin, straight up, one drop of thick frozen Vermouth and an olive. The record player was scratching out the sound of Frankie Laine singing "Mule Train."

"Hello, Betty."

"Hello, Yankee Man."

"You miss Sam?" David took a sip of his martini.

"Hell no," she said as she reached over, pinched his cheeks, and looked into his eyes. She planted a wet kiss on his lips. She didn't stop her kiss until he pushed her back.

"Sam's gone to dig a well in Alaska. He'll have a white Christmas, you can bet your ass," David said.

"Is there a David over here, David Paterno?" It was the bartender calling out as he walked around the club, holding a piece of paper in his hand.

"I'm David Paterno."

"You got a phone call. Says to tell you it's your lawyer 'Moe' from L.A."

"Okay. I'm coming."

David went to the bar and picked up the telephone.

"David Paterno here. Sure. Hello, Moe. Yep, mail the papers to my apartment here. Send them air mail, special delivery. I'll get 'em in time. I'm pulling the trigger next week, the day after New Year's Day. It's going to happen. Thanks. Yeah, she'll be here in Dallas tomorrow, Jordan Phillips's daughter, Jan. She's coming to get her trust money. Happy New Year to you, too, Moe."

David took the second sip of his first martini. It wasn't just a sip. He finished it.

"Barkeep, make me another martini."

"Still with gin? Straight up, a drop of cold vermouth, and an olive?"

"Yeah, Plymouth Gin. Not just cold, but be sure its frozen vermouth. You're smart, barkeep."

The bartender handed him his second martini, and he took his first sip.

The bartender said, "And what's your favorite song?"

"Play Tommy Edward's 'It's All in the Game' if you got it."

"Course, I love it," the bartender said as he took the Frankie Laine record off the Victrola and replaced it with the Tommy Edwards tune. He turned up the volume loud enough for everybody to hear Tommy Edwards croon, "It's all in the wonderful game of love."

David turned away and took his martini with him back to the table. He walked up to the red head and looked straight down to the bottom of her deep cleavage. "Nice pair of lungs, honey." She turned her lips up to his, and he kissed her.

"Hey, Yankee Man, you'll do 'til Sammy gets back," she said rubbing the front of his zipper. After the kiss was over she said, "Wow! I don't care if Sammy Boy ever comes back."

"I doubt that, babe. But who knows? Need another drink?"

"As the song says, birds do it, bees do it, even bar gals do it, but I need a drink first."

While she was talking, Jack Ruby entered the front door of his club and went up to the bar and sat down on a stool.

David Paterno downed his martini, stood up and walked out. "Enjoy your drink, babe. It's time for me to go. I got a lot to do. Goodbye, for now."

After David was gone, the bartender spoke to Jack Ruby. "Hey, boss man. See that guy that was back there with Betty and just left?"

"Yeah?"

"That's him."

"Who?"

"David Paterno."

"Sam's buddy?"

"A few minutes ago, he got this call from L.A. I answered the phone, and the guy calling said he wanted to talk to David Paterno and for me to tell him it was his attorney Moe callin' from L.A."

"Moe?"

"Yeah, Moe."

"What'd they talk about?"

"All I could hear was him saying was somethin' about 'pulling the trigger' the day after New Year's."

"That all he said?"

"He said something like, 'She's comin' to Dallas tomorrow.' I asked him who in the hell 'she' was."

"What'd he say?"

"Jan Phillips. Jordan Phillips's daughter."

"Thanks. This is yours," Jack Ruby handed his bartender a brand-new crisp one-thousand dollar bill, then turned away from the bar and went into his office in the back of the club and closed the door.

He placed a long-distance phone call. When Meyer Lansky answered, Jack Ruby said, "The New Jersey guy just got a call right here at the joint less than an hour ago. Some attorney named Moe from L.A. wanted to talk to him."

"There's only one Moe attorney in L.A. Moe Caesarius."

"That's right. Everybody in Chicago knew Moe."

"What'd they talk about?"

"All the barkeep could hear Paterno saying on the phone was he was pulling the trigger the day after New Year's.

"Say anything else?"

"He said something else that didn't mean a thing to me."

"What was it?"

"'He said Jan Phillips is coming to Dallas tomorrow."

"Who's she?"

"She's Jordan Phillip's daughter."

"That's all I need. Thank you, Jack. That son of a bitch is double crossing me. Take him out. Take him out quick. Do that quickly, and instead of fifty, you get a hundred big ones." Lansky hung up the phone.

Then Lansky ordered the hotel operator to get his brother on the phone.

"Jake" was how his brother answered all his phone calls.

"Jake, find those pictures that you took through that two-way mirror."

"Which pictures, I've got a bunch? The senator with the three babes all over him?"

"No. Fernando and that whore climbing all over that wasted New Jersey lawyer."

"Got 'em right on top of the stack."

"Enlarge the worst one and mail it by air mail, special delivery, to January Phillips, in care of Jordan Phillips, Dallas, Texas."

"What kind of greeting card shall I write?"

"Just say, 'Happy New Year, Jan. Beware of Danger. Fernando loves him.'"

CHAPTER FIFTY-FIVE

ABOUT SIX O'CLOCK that evening, Jordan's phone rang at home.

"Sorry about all the static, Boss," Sam Knight, Jr., said. "Can you hear me?"

"I can hear you okay. Is it cold up there, Sam?"

"Forty-seven below zero, and the wind must be blowing sixty miles an hour. It's a full-blown blizzard."

"How are we running?"

"The damn well is running as low as hell. We're at 7,956 and were supposed to be in the Colville Group, but the samples look like we're still way up in the Sagavankirktok. It looks like we're running 750 feet lower than we should be. If something doesn't happen quickly, we'll be so far off structure there's no way we can stop from drilling a dry hole."

Jordan had nothing to say. It was already pitch black outside, and he saw nothing but his reflection when he looked toward the window in his study. Finally, he spoke. "Let's hope the sample checkers are wrong. Keep on drilling. We'll learn they're wrong, and the shit will turn back to ice cream. Call me tomorrow, and tell me how the ice cream tastes."

"Thanks, Boss. Thank God for your faith. I hope you have a Happy New Year. By the way, I hope you can get me the score of the Cotton Bowl Game when I call on New Year's."

CHAPTER FIFTY-SIX

JAN PHILLIPS WAS yearning more for a reunion with her daddy than she was about getting her trust fund money.

Sully met Jan at Love Field in her father's four-door black Packard sedan.

"Thank you for picking me up, Sully, and thanks for taking such good care of Daddy." Sully loved greeting Jan, collecting her baggage, and taking her home to her daddy at his home on White Rock Lake, where Annie was waiting for her at the front door.

"Annie, I'm so glad to see you and Sully. I know you're both proud of Herman becoming a doctor. How is all the rest of your family doing back in East Texas?"

"Miss, Jan, they's all doin' good takin' care of the Cabin, but I guess you haven't heard. Earl died," she said, chewing her snuff.

"No, I haven't. I'm so sorry. Earl was a good man,"

"And, ma'am, I got to tell you, when we buried Earl, we almost had to bury Sully. He climbed into the grave with his brother, and he sang, and he prayed, and he wouldn't get out of Earl's grave for an hour."

"Well, bless Sully's heart." Talk of death caused Jan's anxiety to spike. "Where's Daddy?"

"Out sittin' an' lookin' at the lake like he do ever' day."

Jan hurried through the house to the veranda where her father was sitting looking out at the lake, rocking, and listening to his George Gershwin records. Her daddy rose from of his rocking chair and greeted his daughter with his arms outstretched. He gave her a big hug.

"Daddy, it's been too long."

"Darling, it's been hard having you grow up away from me. I can't believe you're going to be twenty-five. Where did the time go?"

"You seem so well, Daddy."

"I'm doing fine, and I'll be back on top of the world when this wildcat I'm drilling in Alaska comes in."

Sully brought Jan a glass of cold Puligny-Montrachet and the usual Dewar's for her father.

"What are you planning to do over New Year's while you're here waiting for your big payday?" her father asked her.

"Well, your lawyer, Mr. Paterno, wants to show me around Dallas."

"How'd you meet that guy?"

"He offered to help me get my trust money moved out to my bank in Beverly Hills."

"That's strange."

"Why, Daddy?"

"He didn't need to help you with that trust fund, and it's odd that he wouldn't tell me about talking to you. Did he go out to see you in Beverly Hills?"

"Not me, but Mother. I went over to Mother's to swim, and he was there talking to her. I told him I didn't need any help with my Dallas bank."

"Why would he be talking to your mother? He should never have gone to L.A. to talk to her without asking me."

"I don't know why he was there, but I know he was saying

something about you having business troubles. Dry holes or something. Aren't you drilling in Cuba or Alaska?"

"I found a good little oil field in Cuba, and I'm digging a wildcat in Alaska now. You know any well can be a dry hole. The well in Alaska is running low according to the geologists, but my gut tells me it could still be a big discovery. Maybe another Number 3 Daisy Bradford."

"Daddy, I believe in your gut more than anything. I'm with you forever until the bitter end. If your well comes in, we'll celebrate. If it's a dry hole, we'll sit down, just you and me, and we'll have a good cry. I would like to see Sam Knight, Jr., someday. When I'd return home to East Texas and make the rounds with you, I'd always see Sam, either at the Green Hut or at his daddy's drug store. Sam was always nice."

"Yes, Sam's running my drilling operations, but he's in Alaska drilling that wildcat well."

"Next time you talk to Sam, tell him I asked about him."

"I'll tell him for sure. He's one young man I don't mind you getting to know, but you don't need to know that New Jersey lawyer. You telling me he has been talking to your mother about my business is the last straw. I'm giving him his walking papers after the first."

CHAPTER FIFTY-SEVEN

ON NEW YEAR'S Eve morning, David Paterno's phone in his apartment rang at eight o'clock in the morning.

"Mr. Paterno, this is Charlotte Phillips in Beverly Hills." It was only six o'clock in California. "I have signed all those papers, and I would like for you to tell me exactly when you will activate our plan."

"Mrs. Phillips, the papers have been filed with the State of California and our new company is in business. I need to get you your stock certificate. My lawyer in L.A. should have already mailed the certificate to you."

"I am not calling about the stock certificate, Mr. Paterno. I am calling to ask you when you will take over my husband's company. I don't want him driving it any deeper in the ground. I can save it, and I am ready to go to work."

"Mrs. Phillips, here's the schedule. Keep this to yourself. The involuntary will be filed the day after New Year's Day, then the company will be yours to take over."

"That's exactly what I wanted to hear you say. Thank you." Charlotte hung up.

Before lunch on New Year's Eve, David Paterno called Jordan Phillips's mansion on White Rock Lake and asked to speak to

Miss Jan Phillips. "Jan," he said, "This is David Paterno. I told you I'd call you when you got to Dallas. Would you be interested in celebrating the New Year with me tonight?"

"Hello, Mr. Paterno. I was expecting your call. Thank you, but I'm busy tonight."

"You told me you'd see me when you were in Dallas over the holiday, and I've already made a reservation for dinner. Why don't you let me pick you up about seven, and I promise to make it an early evening."

"Alright. If you will bring me home after dinner, I'll join you tonight."

"Thank you, Jan. I'll see you at seven."

When they arrived at the Blue Room later that evening, David said, "Waiter, bring us two martinis, Plymouth Gin, straight up, each with an olive, and one drop of frozen vermouth. We'll watch the fireworks demonstration and drink more martinis and sing 'Auld Lang Syne' at midnight."

The martinis were served. He took a drink of his martini and immediately unloaded on Jan about her father, in what he believed was the best strategy to get her on his side. He found out in a very short time that he was wrong. "Jan, you need to hear the facts about the dollars your father is spending. I believe he is losing his mind. It's a sickness, this wildcatting. He's spent fifty-five million dollars looking for new oil without a dime of revenue coming back to him. He's drilling this wildcat well in Alaska, and he's got to meet a cash-call of five million dollars next week, and there isn't enough money in the bank to write that check. I hate to say it, Jan, but it's over for your dad."

"Good God, Mr. Paterno. What kind of New Year's celebration is this? I don't believe a word of what you are saying."

Jan never took a sip of her drink, although David had drunk his down and ordered a second.

"I haven't tasted my first cocktail, and you've ordered your second. Thank you for your time. Happy New Year and good evening. I am going home." Jan Phillips stood and walked away from the table with David Paterno staring at her in a state of shock.

CHAPTER FIFTY-EIGHT

ON NEW YEAR'S Day 1959, Jan Phillips woke up on her twenty-fifth birthday. Having not one sip of booze the night before, she felt terrific. She chuckled to herself, thinking what a terrible head David Paterno must have with having had two martinis in fifteen minutes before eight o'clock, and there was no telling how many he had when she left him.

Jan kept thinking about David saying that her father had gone out of his mind and was drilling his way into insolvency. If that was true, this sickness must have begun twenty-five years ago in East Texas, she thought. If he was insane with Wildcatter's Fever, it was certainly a fortuitous illness that had resulted in him finding more oil than any wildcatter in the world.

As he did every morning, when he first awoke on New Year's Day, Jordan Phillips turned on the radio on his bedside table. He immediately sat up in surprise when the announcer reported the stunning news about Cuba. Fidel Castro, the Communist Rebel, had overthrown the government of President Fulgencio Batista at midnight on New Year's Eve.

Batista had whisked his family out of Cuba by chartered plane, and Fidel Castro became the dictator. All the privately owned businesses and the private property in Cuba was to be owned by the Cuban State. Jordan knew that his oil field in Cuba was lost.

Jordan called Joe Anderson at his home. He didn't wish him Happy New Year, but he immediately told him to call Ed Clark in Austin and ask him to call Lyndon Johnson, now the majority leader of the Senate. He told Joe to tell Ed to tell Lyndon that it was a matter of national security for the United States government to protect TOPCO'S oil field in Cuba. He told him if Ed couldn't get Lyndon, to call Horace Busby and tell him to get word to Lyndon.

After Joe called Ed Clark, Ed placed a call to Jordan. He said, "Jordan, I already talked to Lyndon. There's not a snowball's chance in hell you can save your oil field. Lyndon's running for President. No Texan running for President can be seen as a lackey for a Texas oil man, and besides, why would Castro listen to him anyway?"

The situation was worse for Meyer Lansky. Shortly after the Batista family's airplane left the Havana Airport, and just before midnight, Meyer Lansky boarded a Twin Beechcraft for Florida. He had left seventeen million dollars behind in Cuban banks. The only way for Lansky to survive financially was to become a Texas Oil Man. As soon as he arrived in Florida, Lansky called Jack Ruby in Dallas.

"What about Paterno, Smoky? He's the only thing that could stop me from getting rich in Texas oil."

"Don't worry, Boss. The fun's about to start. Tell me about the revolution in Havana. Is the casino business finished?"

"It's over. Oh, and listen to what I just learned. That young senator running for President said there was no country in the world worse than Cuba because of Batista's policies, and he approved of Fidel Castro's proclamation in the Sierra Maestra calling for justice and, get this, getting rid of the corruption in Cuba. You know what he means by corruption?

"Tell me, Boss."

"One man's corruption is another man's honest business. No one ever got cheated out of a dime at any casino of mine. The son of a bitch wants to get rid of me."

"Those New Orleans guys have a plan to take out Castro, and if they do, you can get back into Havana," Jack Ruby said.

"Maybe, maybe not. Right now my business is to get that son of a bitch David Paterno taken out so my bank can foreclose on an oil mortgage in Texas, and when I do that, I'll be home free, and to hell with Havana."

"Don't worry about nothin', Boss. I hear you loud and clear. I got it handled. Paterno will be toast in a New York minute. And I mean burnt toast."

CHAPTER FIFTY-NINE

O N JANUARY THE second, Lansky called The First Pittsburg Bank at eight o'clock in the morning and asked to speak to Barry Shapiro, the Executive Vice President of the bank.

"Shapiro, this is Lansky. I'm impressed with you. You're on the job early. Have you foreclosed on that oil loan in Texas?"

"No, sir, we haven't."

"Why in the hell not?"

"The loan is not in full default yet, sir."

"I don't give a shit. Go ahead and foreclose. Read the loan document. Find any goddamn reason and foreclose. Didn't they fail to furnish copies of the state reports or some such shit?"

"We can probably foreclose on the twelfth. The company's first payment on the loan is due on that date."

"That's bullshit, Shapiro. Foreclose on the goddamn loan. Foreclose today."

At eight-thirty in the morning, David Paterno walked up to the front door of Jordan Phillips's mansion on White Rock Lake to get Jan Phillips to drive her downtown to the bank. Annie met him at the door.

"She's done already gone downtown. Sully took her, and she'll be back before noon."

David turned and left, fuming as he walked to his car. As hard as he had tried to insert himself into the lives of Jordan Phillips and his daughter, they would not let him in. No matter. The hell with both of them. David's plan to remove the old wild-catter from control of his business had begun. Only three days remained before the world of Jordan Phillips would be no more. David was ecstatic.

At the mansion on White Rock Lake, that afternoon, a United States postal truck delivered a large envelope stamped "Air Mail-Special Delivery." Jan opened the envelope and screamed so loud that Annie and Sully ran to her side. Her hands and her arms shook with fright. She was holding an enlarged black and white photograph and a handwritten note that said: "Happy New Year, Jan. Beware of danger. Fernando loves him."

Jan grabbed the black telephone and dialed her father's office. When Merle answered, Jan was still shaking so hard she could hardly talk.

"Merle, I opened this envelope delivered to me Special Delivery here at Dad's home. I saw it was from Havana. I am so frightened. What should I do?"

"What was in it?"

"There's this awful photograph and a handwritten note wishing me a Happy New Year and a warning to beware of danger." She was sobbing. "It's some kind of a threat."

"What was in the photograph?"

"A naked man and a naked woman trying to perform sexual acts on this passed out naked man lying on the bed."

Merle rushed in to his office and put Jordan Phillips on the phone to hear the story directly from his daughter.

"Jan, what happened? Merle's too upset to tell me."

Still shaking, Jan repeated the story.

"But, Daddy, what you really won't believe is what the photo is showing. The naked man passed out on the bed was David Paterno."

"Lock all the doors to the house. Stay inside with Annie and Sully until I get there. Somebody is trying to kill you and me. We must find out who sent that photograph and take 'em out before they get us."

He hung up the phone. "Beware of danger," the note had said. Again, his thoughts automatically flashed back to East Texas and Daisy Bradford's old black Creole priestess singing out, "Treasure found, then disaster, disaster and death. My spirits speak only the truth."

"Jordan, be careful," Merle said. He left his office to drive home to be at his daughter's side.

After lunch, his phone at home rang. Joe Anderson was calling.

"Mr. Phillips, Merle called and told me the story of the photograph they sent to Jan. I need two copies of everything: the note and the photo. I'll get a copy to the Texas Rangers who are running the trace on Paterno. Someone is trying to stop Paterno from doing something. You are in the middle of a fight to the death."

"I'm aware of that. What do you suggest?"

"I called Austin, and the Texas Rangers are sending one of their top officers to come to Dallas and take care of you and Jan. This officer will be your driver, and he can protect you at all times until we figure this out."

"Joe, you're about to catch up with all the legends about your step father Jack around all the court houses in Texas. I'm learning that if any legal problem raises its head, I can count on you. Thank you, son."

"Of course you can count on me, sir. Always. I'll call you at five and catch up on how things went this afternoon."

Mid-afternoon, the Texas Ranger arrived in his white sedan with the black Lone Star of Texas on the doors on both sides of the vehicle.

"Mr. Phillips, I'm Captain Fred Deviney of the Texas Rangers, and I am here to protect you and Miss Phillips." He'd recently upgraded from his standard issue .38 to the .357 Magnum. His service revolver bulged out of his suit coat. "I'll be with you twenty-four hours a day, and I'll take you wherever you want to go. I will not let you out of my sight."

"Thank you, Captain. We appreciate your looking after us. Let's hope we get this matter cleared up, and we can all return to normal. It's good you're here."

Late that afternoon, Merle called. "Jordan, you got a call that I guess you need to return. It's from that banker at the Pittsburg bank."

Jordan sat in his library and placed the long-distance call.

"This is Jordan Phillips with TOPCO in Dallas. I understand you wanted to talk to me."

"Yes, I did, Mr. Phillips. I have been advised by my compliance people that I needed to alert you."

"What do you need to alert me about?"

"Technically, your company's loan has been in default for twenty days and your grace period expires on January the twelfth. Your first payment of three million dollars is due on that loan on that day, but with your loan in default, you need to know that it is likely that we will call your loan next week, and when we do, you must repay the full principal of ten million dollars, or we will have no alternative but to foreclose on the properties that secure the mortgage."

The banker heard only silence on Jordan Phillips's end of the line. After two full minutes, Jordan Phillips said, "If you're going to call our loan, why are you telling me, Mr. Shapiro?"

"I am going through a process required under Pennsylvania law. Full disclosure of pending foreclosure to the owner of the asset. That is the law in Pennsylvania, Mr. Phillips." And with that, the telephone conversation ended.

Jordan immediately called his Dallas lawyer to tell him about the impending foreclosure. Joe Anderson told Jordan to get in touch with his old banker at Republic National Bank immediately.

Merle patched C. W. Austin on to Jordan's line, and Jordan told his old banker the whole story.

"Well, Jordan, I can go back down there to the bank and try to lay the groundwork. At least you've got a few days."

"I'm supposed to have until the twelfth, but how can I trust those people?"

"You say your Alaska well should be down in a few days. Does your rabbit's foot still work?"

"I'm betting it still works. Thanks, C. W. You lay the groundwork with your banker buddies, and get ready. I'll call you when I know."

CHAPTER SIXTY

AFTER HIS CONVERSATION with C. W. Austin, Jordan phoned Sam Knight in Alaska. At the drill site, it was sixty degrees below zero, snowing hard, and the wind was blowing fifty miles an hour.

Jordan shouted into the phone, "Sam, I can't understand you. You're breaking up. How's it looking?"

"We...high..."

"What?"

"Running..."

"What?"

"Running...high. Call Jane...Fairbanks. Can't...from here..." Then all Jordan could hear was "blizzard."

"I wanted to tell you, Jan is spending New Year's with me, and she said to tell you hello. Did you hear that?"

"Heard...Jan my best...North Pole." Then the line went dead.

Next, Jordan phoned Mike Wharton at the office and told him, "I talked to Sam on his radio phone in that blizzard, and I couldn't understand hardly a word. He said talk to Jane. Did you get a drilling report yet today from Jane?"

"Yes, sir. She finally got through to me. They're drilling at 8,022 and getting some good shows. They're sure they're running high now. They ran a Drill Stem Test and got half a million cubic feet of gas and recovered 1,500 feet of oil in the pipe. It's a weak oil show, but it looks like we're back where we should be. It'll be a two or three days before we get down to the Lisburne, the main target."

"Thanks, Mike. That's the kind of news I needed to hear. What about that sand you liked that I can hardly pronounce, the Saddle Oxford?"

"Sadlerochit. That's what it's officially named in the geological world. We like it but nobody gave it much chance to be here, so we'll settle for a Lisburne well. "

"Thanks, Mike. Whatever produces is good for me. I just want one big initial flow rate. Frankly, I have a few other things to worry about. I guess you heard we lost our oil field in Cuba."

"Good God. What can we do about it?"

"Nothing. It's over. What I need is a big oil discovery in Alaska."

"Well, sir, it looks like you got one."

CHAPTER SIXTY-ONE

APTAIN DEVINEY DELIVERED Jordan Phillips to the Magnolia Petroleum Building and parked in Jordan's reserved parking place on the third floor of the parking garage at eight-fifteen Monday morning, the fifth of January. Captain Deviney waited for Jordan in his car, and Jordan went down in the garage elevator to the building lobby and then up to his office floor. When he went through the entrance to his office and into the reception room, he was caught by surprise when he was met by a Dallas County Deputy Sheriff in uniform with a pistol at his side, holding his hat in his hand.

Merle was standing next to the man in uniform, and she said, "Jordan, I don't know what to tell you, but…"

"Are you Jordan Phillips, the Chief Executive Officer of the Texas Oil Production Company?" asked the uniformed law officer.

"I certainly am."

Reading from a document held in both hands, the Deputy Sheriff said, "On behalf of the authority vested in me by the laws of the United States of America and the State of Texas, I hereby serve on the Texas Oil Producing Company this petition of Involuntary Bankruptcy, which has been filed by creditors of Texas Oil Producing Company because of said company's failure to timely pay its accounts payable to said creditors, who are Sunset Oil Production Company, a California corporation, East Publishing Company, a Delaware corporation, and Mrs. Jordan Phillips, nee Charlotte Sasawka. Copies of the notice have been duly served on the debtor by a Deputy Sheriff on this day. Official copies of the notice have been delivered contemporaneously to all known secured creditors of the debtor including the Pittsburg Bank, Pittsburg, Pennsylvania. You are directed to attend the first meeting of the Creditor's Committee on Tuesday, January 6th, nineteen-hundred and fifty-nine at 10:00 AM at the office of the law firm of O'Toole, Watson, and Mustavi."

The Deputy Sheriff handed the petition to Jordan Phillips.

"Please acknowledge your receipt of this petition by signing on this line."

Jordan calmly signed the receipt and handed it back to the Deputy Sheriff. The lawman replaced his hat on his head and exited TOPCO'S corporate office.

"Merle call Joe Anderson, and then get that New Jersey lawyer rat in my office."

"I can't do anything right now." Merle laid her head on her desk and wept. Jordan had never before seen Merle like this. She had always been his rock, so stoic and strong through all his problems. Her shoulders shook. Her head trembled. Her sobs became a high-pitched wail, and Jordan felt it, too. He leaned on the desk to steady himself. He took deep a breath and wiped beads of sweat off his brow.

When he felt his heart calm down, he picked up Merle's phone and called David Paterno's extension. "Get in here now," he barked.

David Paterno came into the Executive Suite and took the paper that had been served on him that Jordan was holding, and he read it with bloodshot eyes. He stood erect, a smirk on his face. He noticed Merle crying. Every black hair on his head was in place, and he smelled sickeningly sweet like a new shave at a barber shop. Probably to mask the smell of last night's booze, Jordan surmised. "Well, isn't this an interesting development? Maybe it's an opportunity in disguise," Paterno quipped.

"Opportunity? This is bankruptcy for TOPCO. What kind of opportunity is that?"

"When three unsecured creditors are owed money by a business, the three creditors can file a Chapter Eleven, Involuntary Bankruptcy on their debtor."

"How could TOPCO owe any money to a Sunset Oil Production Company, and how can Charlotte claim TOPCO owes her any money?"

"I suspect that Mrs. Phillips is claiming she has a community property interest in your TOPCO stock and that TOPCO owes her revenue from that. I imagine you can expect her to make a claim for a huge payment from TOPCO in the Bankruptcy Court."

"What about the East Publishing and a Sunset Oil Production Company? What is going on?"

"East Publishing Company sells law books, and they are saying that TOPCO bought some law books from them and never paid their bill."

"I never bought any law books."

"Sunset Oil Production Company must be owned by someone TOPCO owes money to. All the creditors will have representatives at the Creditor's Committee Meeting. You'll probably learn things at that meeting that will be unpleasant to learn."

"We'll see about that meeting. I need to talk to Joe Anderson. Paterno, you're excused. Merle, did you get Joe yet?"

"Yes, sir, here's Mr. Anderson. Go in your office and pick up your phone. You can shut the door and talk to him," Merle said, dabbing her eyes with a handkerchief, trying to pull herself together.

In his office with the door shut, Jordan asked, "Joe, did Merle send you a telecopy of the bankruptcy?"

"Mr. Phillips, I read it. It smells to high heaven. This afternoon, I'll be getting the Texas Rangers investigator's report. I'll bet we find out that Paterno is in the middle of this."

"What action do you recommend?"

"Go to that meeting, and find out what the hell is going on. Then we'll quash this phony bankruptcy."

"Unbelievable. Sickening to have to deal with a crook like this guy."

Around three o'clock, Joe Anderson called back.

"Mr. Phillips, here it is. Get this: Paterno's father was the lead attorney for the five Mafia families in Manhattan and New Jersey. He made a fortune for them and for himself."

"Good God."

"But listen to this. Do you know who the C.E.O. of Sunset Oil Production Company is?"

"No, of course not."

"Charlotte Sasawka Phillips. I couldn't believe it, so I had the P.I. call and get copies of the entire file from the California Corporation Commission. The Founding C.E.O. was David A. Paterno, Jr."

"Shit."

"He immediately removed his name as the founding Chief Executive Officer and replaced himself with your wife, obviously trying to hide his involvement, and he was using Charlotte to get the benefit of her community property claims. I have yet to figure out how Sunset Oil Production Company could be a creditor with standing to file an involuntary bankruptcy. We'll probably see her with a claim for conversion by you of her community property.

Conversion is theft you know, but whatever is going on, this is something like I have never seen except in my case books in law school, a clear case of criminal fraud by a New Jersey Lawyer too smart for his britches."

"Your plan of action?"

"I've got it handled. I called the Attorney General. He told me to go to the U.S Attorney in Dallas, and I've talked to him. He's brought in the FBI. If you execute an emergency affidavit, and we get it to them today, we can probably be granted an emergency hearing immediately, like later this afternoon and a federal judge will grant a warrant for Paterno's arrest. So when he attends that meeting tomorrow, he walks into a trap. The Federal Marshall will be there with the warrant and then your Executive Vice President and General Counsel will be arrested, and he'll be put in the slammer for the rest of his life, and that will be the end of the son of a bitch."

"Joe, you are a pure genius though I'd rather see that S.O.B. thrown in the Sabine with an old drill bit tied to his ankles. This will be an interesting meeting, that's for sure. I'll see you tomorrow after the meeting. Goodbye, Joe. And…"

"Yes, sir?"

"Thanks, Joe." Jordan hung up the phone and looked up at Merle.

"Mr. Phillips."

"Yes, Merle. What is it?"

"That Mr. Shapiro with the Pittsburg Bank wants you to call him. He said something about his bank foreclosing on our Gregg County properties and ordering Bell General to transfer direct payment of TOPCO'S share of the East Texas oil runs to his bank."

"Oh Lordy. Call C. W. Austin. He was going to wait until I called him, but he can't wait. He's got to surface today to join the Extermination."

CHAPTER SIXTY-TWO

"WHAT TIME IS it?"

"It's nine o'clock, Mr. Phillips."

"Then call Mike Wharton."

"'I will. You feeling any better?"

"Sure. It's over. We'll come out okay, but what about you, Merle?"

"I'm all right now that I see you landing on your two feet, like you always do."

"Well, you're beginning to look like your old self, Merle. I can't wait until I see a little of that old twinkle in your eyes. We've always made it through these messes, and we'll make it through this one too."

Jordan's phone rang. "Hello, Mike. Any drilling report?"

"Yes, sir. Joan finally got through to me. It's like the pony express between the drilling well and real telephones, but she said they hit this good oil sand at 8,210 and had excellent mud log shows and bright golden fluorescence in the samples, and the samples had excellent porosity. She says it's the Sadelrochit, and it looks like a massive fan delta sand build up. They're preparing to run a Drill Stem Test."

"Mike, that's what you predicted would happen. You are one helluva geologist. How's it running?"

"It's running high, exactly according to the seismic. It looks like we have our trap."

"Fantastic. I wish my other news was that great."

"Are there more problems, Mr. Phillips?"

"Nothing serious. Just some trivial business problems with some whiners and complainers, but it's being fixed. When will they have the test run?"

"I'd say they'll probably open the test tool in two days, maybe three, who knows, might be a week, what with that Arctic weather."

"Let me know as soon as you hear anything. Thanks, Mike. Goodbye." He turned to Merle. "What time is that Creditor's Committee meeting?"

"It's at ten, but you need to leave in fifteen minutes to be there by ten. There may still be morning traffic on the new expressway out to the Meadows Building. "

David Paterno's face appeared at Jordan's office door. "Mr. Phillips, it's time to leave for the meeting."

"I'll see you there, Paterno."

"Would you like to ride over there with me, sir?"

"No sir, I would not, but after the meeting we will talk about your actions as an officer of my business. You have a lot of explaining to do."

"I look forward to talking to you any time, Mr. Phillips."

Jordan Phillips and Dave Paterno left TOPCO'S office and rode down the elevator together to the lobby where they boarded the garage elevators and rode up to the third floor of the parking garage. No words were exchanged. The closest parking space to the elevator on the third floor had always been reserved for Jordan Phillips. Today, the Texas Ranger's car was parked in the space which said "Reserved for Jordan Phillips, President and

Chief Executive Officer." Ranger Captain Deviney looked sharp in his Texas Ranger's tan Stetson hat.

The parking space next to Jordan's parking space was where David Paterno's car was parked with a sign that said, "Reserved for David Paterno, Jr., Executive Vice President." The entire third floor of the Magnolia Petroleum Company Building garage was reserved for TOPCO employees.

As they walked up to the cars, David said, "You're being driven by a Texas Ranger? What's the reason for that, sir?"

"Ask the Governor. He wanted to give me protection."

"Protection from what?"

"Maybe against the evils of the world." Jordan opened the passenger front door and slid in the right front passenger seat with Captain Deviney seated behind the steering wheel.

David got into the driver's seat of his Lincoln Continental and put the key in the ignition to start his car.

An explosion blew both David Paterno's and the Texas Ranger's automobiles into several sections. It was loud enough to break the eardrums of anyone within fifty feet. Debris ricocheted off the concrete beams in the garage and flew out the 3rd floor of the building onto the street below. Pieces of burned cars and shattered glass littered the garage floor. Smoke and the odor of seared flesh permeated the area.

In less than one minute, the Magnolia Petroleum Company security guard was there. In three minutes, three policemen from the Dallas Police Department arrived. There was no sign of human life in the wreckages. The policemen couldn't pull the bodies of the three men out of the cars. They had to wait for equipment that could force the burned steel apart. Word soon spread that three persons had been killed in an explosion in the parking garage.

With sirens blaring, only a small fire truck was able to

navigate the sharp curves and corkscrews up to the third floor. Three ambulances waited. The doors to David Paterno's car were finally forced apart by the policemen, and the medics retrieved his body and placed it on the ambulance stretchers so it could be hauled to the city morgue. Soon, in the same manner, the bodies of Jordan Phillips and the Texas Ranger were removed from the wreckage of the Ranger's car.

The ambulances drove down the exit ramps of the parking garage to Basin Street. All three ambulances received calls on their radio phones.

"Base to ambulance numbers one, two, and three. Base to ambulances one, two, and three."

"Ambulance number one. Come in, base."

"Take those three bodies to the Parkland Emergency Room so they can be pronounced DOA before you take 'em to the morgue. You copy?"

"Ten four, I got a copy. To Parkland Emergency. Over and out."

The ambulances, with sirens blaring, sped to the Parkland Hospital emergency room. As the Medics were carrying the three stretchers into the emergency room, the loudspeaker blared out, "Doctor Morris. Code 10, Doctor Morris. Code 10, Doctor Morris, to triage, to triage."

A young black doctor responded to the call. He looked at the charred body of David Paterno, Jr., and checked his vitals.

"This man is gone. There's no pulse, and his blood pressure is zero. DOA." He stepped over to the law officer's body and gave the same verdict.

Then he looked at the body of the third victim. "I can't find any pulse here...No...there may be a tiny heartbeat. Nurse, take an EKG and give him a shot of adrenalin. His face is as black as mine, but I think I saw him take a breath."

The nurse took a warm wet towel and began to clean the smoke and ashes off the face. The young doctor was watching her, and when she was finished, he could clearly see that the man was Jordan Phillips.

"Mr. Phillips, can you hear me? Please respond, Mr. Phillips. It's Herman Morris. Please respond."

Herman gave Jordan's hand a slight squeeze. In a minute or so, the young black doctor felt a tiny squeeze in return. "Mr. Phillips, this is Herman. You'll be all right. Praise God Almighty, you are saved."

Jordan Phillips's eyes opened slightly, and he looked into Herman's eyes. The doctor thought he could see a slight smile.

CHAPTER SIXTY-THREE

THE INTENSIVE CARE nurses let both Jan and Merle go into Jordan's room.

Jan rushed to the hospital bed and quickly clutched her father's hand. She leaned forward kissed him on his cheek and spoke softly.

"Dad, Merle and I are here. We love you. I called Mom, and she is on the way from Los Angeles."

"I love you, baby," her father whispered faintly. "I'm lucky, aren't I? Can you believe that man?"

"Dad, that David Paterno was evil. Maybe he got what he deserved."

Herman entered. "Miss Phillips. Merle. It's good to see you both, but right now, I'm afraid it's time to let our patient rest, so I'll have to ask you to leave."

Her father's eyes closed. Jan watched him, uncertain of whether or not he was asleep. A machine made a soft, steady beeping sound. She looked at all the feeding tubes and devices measuring his vital statistics and thought how fragile and vulnerable he really was—just like any other human being. She felt him squeeze her hand. She smiled.

The next day, Charlotte Phillips arrived from Los Angeles.

On the way to the hospital, while Sully drove her in Jordan's Packard, she sat tall in the rear passenger seat next to her daughter with her chin held high. Dressed immaculately and wearing her diamonds she was more than excited to think that she would now be the one to own and control TOPCO. She started talking with self-importance. "With that lawyer gone, Jordan almost dead, and Sunset Oil Production Company taking over Jordan's bankrupt company, there is only one way to handle this. I am now truly an independent woman of means and have earned my overdue seat at the big boys table. I have decided I will move to Dallas and run my oil business the way it should have always been run."

"Mother, you don't know what you are talking about. You must wait and learn exactly what's going on. Daddy will heal. He will be fine, and he will never need you to run his oil business. Never."

Charlotte inhaled deeply, trying to control a surge of anger. "Nonsense, Jan," she barked. "It's over for him." She looked out at the streets of downtown Dallas. A shabbily dressed old woman—probably a cleaning lady or a fry cook in some cheap diner, Charlotte thought—shuffled along the sidewalk. Men in business suits and topcoats strode around her. Charlotte spoke evenly, softly. "I have waited too long. Your father ruined his business, he's a dreamer and he has gambled his fortune on foolish pursuits, and it would have never happened if I had taken control earlier."

"Here we are at the hospital. You can see Daddy yourself. Our first duty is to help him recover."

Jan took her mother into the Intensive Care Unit.

Charlotte approached the bed.

"Jordan, I'm here now."

Jordan was tired and in pain, but he was cognizant.

"Charlotte, why are you here?" he whispered in a gravelly voice.

"Mom, I'm going to wait in the hall. We're not supposed to stay long. Don't get into any kind of conversation. Daddy's got to rest. He doesn't have the strength yet to talk."

Jan stepped out.

"Jordan, I'm here to help you. You don't deserve anything like this. I've come to Dallas to run things for you." She saw his eyes close as he seemed to fall asleep. She wondered if he was really asleep or just ignoring her.

Charlotte studied the blinking and beeping machines surrounding his bed and the tubes that ran into his arms. His left arm and both of his legs were in casts and elevated by slings that came down from the ceiling. His forehead was bandaged. His face was bruised and swollen. She almost felt a twinge of regret for how she had treated him over the years. Almost.

Charlotte turned to leave her husband's hospital bed. She left Jordan sleeping. He fell into a deeper and deeper sleep until he was sleeping so deeply he began to dream. He dreamed of the words of a quaking, old lady's voice, singing, "Treasure found, then disaster, disaster and death. Beware...beware the future." It was a dream of a voice he heard thirty years ago—Daisy Bradford's ninety-year-old Creole maid singing the song her spirits sang to her, warning the wildcatter of trouble ahead.

CHAPTER SIXTY-FOUR

THREE DAYS LATER, Mike Wharton visited the hospital. Jordan was more alert.

"Mr. Phillips, do you feel good enough to hear the results of the Drill Stem Test of that thick sand that we found in the Sadlerochit?"

"Yes, Mike. Tell me," he whispered.

"The well flowed at the rate of two thousand barrels of oil a day on a half-inch choke."

Jordan's eyes were closed, but he smiled.

"Mr. Phillips, you have discovered a major oil field. I estimate that the ultimate recovery will be at least ten billion barrels. If that ends up to be correct, you will have found the largest oil field in the western hemisphere."

Jordan kept his smile and whispered, "Mike, no, I found the two largest oil fields. Don't forget East Texas."

The next day, Jordan was moved from Intensive Care into a private room. Merle was in his room by ten o'clock in the morning. She said, "You are a man in control, Jordan, and you control so many lives that the Lord needed you here on Earth longer."

"Now, Merle, you're making these things up. No one really needs me."

"Well, Rex Davis at Liberty Oil must need you. He keeps calling, wanting to know if I've been able to deliver his message yet."

"What does Rex want?"

"He said to tell you he heard about the Drill Stem Test, and he wants to buy Prudhoe Bay from you."

"Tell Mike to call Rex and sell Liberty half interest in Prudhoe Bay for one hundred million dollars."

In the next two days, the Texas Oil Production Company sold half interest in Prudhoe Bay. There was no better medicine for Jordan than Rex Davis bringing the papers for him to sign to his hospital bed and handing him a check payable to the Texas Oil Producing Company for one hundred million dollars.

Merle deposited the hundred-million-dollar check into TOPCO'S account at the Republic National Bank with instructions to wire transfer ten million dollars to the Pittsburg National Bank before the twelfth of January so that TOPCO'S loan balance would be zero.

The Bankruptcy Court threw out the phony bankruptcy. Meyer Lansky's dream of becoming a Texas oil man was shattered. He drifted around the world, rumored to be the leader of all organized crime and worth hundreds of millions of dollars, but, in reality, when he died, he had no more than an ordinary man.

Miss Charlotte had failed to achieve her dream. Jordan's star had risen again. TOPCO had no bank debt. It would become recognized as one of the largest of all the oil companies. The oil wells TOPCO owned would include not only the 900 flowing oil wells in the Fairway of the East Texas Oil Field but would soon also include a one-half interest in 1,100 flowing oil wells producing one and one-half million barrels of oil a day in Alaska in the Prudhoe Bay Oil Field. Jordan Phillips was a happy wildcatter, yet nothing made him happier than when his daughter Jan moved to Dallas to be near him.

Miss Charlotte had come to Dallas to gain control of her husband's business. Jordan Phillips forced her to recognize that once again his rabbit's foot worked, so her only remaining hope was to return to the man she had forsaken if he would take her back. She stood beside his bed in his private hospital room. "Jordan, I came to Dallas to be with you. I want to help you recover." She used a tissue to wipe away an alligator tear.

"Thank you for thinking of me, Charlotte."

"I'm coming back home to live with you forever, right here in Dallas."

Jordan swallowed hard, thoughts and emotions racing through his brain and body. She made him tired. She was standing there, sucking the air out of the room. She didn't know that her run was over.

"No, Charlotte. You made your choice, and I made mine. Long ago, I loved you, and I wanted you to go with me to Kilgore at the beginning so you could help me find oil. You hated the oil field, and you hated me, so you left me. So now, you can go to Hell for all I care, and stay there. I'm going back to the oil field... back home to the Piney Woods...back to East Texas."

Charlotte was stunned. She met Jordan's rejection the only way she knew. She simply shook her head, concluding that he was a fool. She was never to learn what many people knew: true happiness could not be found by anyone who loved no one but herself.

Jordan liked the fishing in the Florida Straits, so he spent most Augusts and Septembers in his remaining years fishing in the Gulf Stream for black marlin with his old friend Carlos as his fishing guide. Carlos had moved to Key West from Havana after Castro took over. Sometimes Jordan and Carlos caught Marlin.

AUTHOR'S NOTE

A WILDCATTER'S TREK: Love, Money, and Oil is intended to be a novel rich in the history of the oil field told through a yarn of a fictional wildcatter, Jordan Phillips, and how he learned that the wildcatter's trek could take him headlong into not only the support of his fellow wildcatter, but also into the greed that lurks within the hearts of others, sometimes those closest to him, who he never suspects would do anything to harm him, until he learned, in spades, how wrong he could be.

I felt qualified to write this story because I am a wildcatter myself. Next to the thrill of discovering a world-class oil field, a surprisingly satisfying highlight of my life has been the time I've spent writing this book. Remembering one hundred years of family legends of life in boom towns and my own years growing up in the oil field has been rewarding in many ways.

My great-grandfather and my grandfather drilled their first oil well in 1913 in the Cushing Field in Oklahoma, and my dad joined them after rough-necking his way through law school at the University of Oklahoma. So, I am fourth generation oil field. My three sons and my daughter are also immersed in oil, along with three grandsons and two grandsons-in-law and granddaughters-in-law, who are active in various skills and technologies in different segments of the oil and gas business.

As for me, I was born in the East Texas Oil Field during the "Last Great Boom" when 30,000 oil wells were drilled after an old wildcatter named Columbus M. "Dad" Joiner drilled the #3 Daisy Bradford, and, discovered the East Texas Oil Field. "Dad" Joiner drilled where a veterinarian, who claimed to be a geologist, guaranteed him he'd find the greatest oil field in the world. But his 'geologist', A. D., "Doc", Lloyd, must have known something about geology because finding the greatest oil field in the world is exactly what happened. We may never know if this "Keystone Cop" duo was, as some believe, on a mission to swindle their way into great riches or whether they were simply dreamers motivated by the grandest of fantasies, which surprised everybody, no one more than themselves, when their dream became reality.

My ambition was to evoke a story of the twists and turns in the life of a wildcatter as he drills and discovers oil. This story spins a fictional narrative of the wildcatter's emotions, his loves, and the threats he encounters in the quest for his fortune. But, there are many true oil field historical facts and real persons interwoven in this tale. An attempt is made to convey the elation that a real discovery well brings to an oil wildcatter, a classic feeling that keeps a wildcatter drilling the next well.

Oil springs around Baku in Azerbaijan and the Caspian Sea, and other places around the world have been continuously burning and worshipped by Fire Worshippers since prehistoric times, and the Chinese dug wells and ran bamboo rods to pump brine for thousands of years. Yet, in 1859 in Pennsylvania, the first oil well ever known to have been drilled to produce oil was by a promoter named George Bissell, who didn't realize he would become the first wildcatter. Bissel hired a railroad train conductor on sick leave named Edwin M. Drake to be the drilling superintendent of the "Drake Well." One reason Drake was hired was that he had a free pass to travel on the trains and George Bissell gave Drake the phony title of "Colonel" to impress the folks around Titusville. Drake drilled into oil at a depth of sixty feet.

Bissell had collected a sample of the oil that bubbled out of the rocks next to Oil Creek in Pennsylvania. The same rock oil the Indians had used for millennia to caulk their canoes. In the first known application of geoscience technology to drill for oil, Bissell engaged Benjamin Silliman, a scientist at Yale University to write a report for the Pennsylvania Rock Oil Company confirming that its rock oil would burn. This meant it would illuminate the streets of cities that were growing dark with the declining availability of whale oil.

The advent of the internal combustion engine resulted in the explosion of a new and different demand for a barrel of crude oil: the gasoline refined from it. Then the wildcatters saw how they might strike it rich, and they began their trek across America starting in Pennsylvania, drilling thousands of wildcat oil wells and finding new oil fields: Spindletop in Texas, Glenn Pool and Cushing in Oklahoma, and from Ohio to California then back to East Texas, and finally up to the North Slope of Alaska. Applying continuing advances in geoscience technology, they found one oil field after another, some giant oil fields and they drilled deeper, farther out into the wilderness. The wildcatters kept finding oil yet many failed, but some wildcatters got very rich.

My greatest thanks go to the readers who have enabled this story to be told.

-Gene Ames, Jr.

ACKNOWLEDGEMENTS

MEMORIES OF THE East Texas Oil Field persisted until I wrote this story about a wildcatter and the oil field. This adventure would have never been possible without the help of many people. It would impossible to thank everyone who helped. Consequently, I'd like to give my sincerest thanks to my friends who contributed in so many different ways to my completion of this effort to tell a story about the oil field. Thank you, everyone, for helping.

I want to thank both the families of the wildcatters mentioned in this story, and, of those wildcatters not mentioned by name. This story is a tribute to every wildcatter in America who joined the trek of the wildcatter to find the oil that made America the most prosperous economy in the world. I'm sorry it's impossible to mention the name of every great wildcatter who took the risks and kept drilling and made those years the glory days of oil in America.

I want to thank Herbert Hunt, a great wildcatter and geologist himself, for sharing memories of his father, H. L. Hunt, and the famous transaction in which Mr. Hunt "bailed out" Columbus M. "Dad" Joiner after Dad "oversold" his promotion of the discovery of the East Texas Oil Field.

Ralph Cox, Ft. Worth, Texas, was manager of Operations for Atlantic Richfield in Alaska during the development of the Prudhoe

Bay Oil Field. Ralph oversaw the initial development of the largest oil field in the Western Hemisphere before retiring from ARCO as Vice-Chairman. I want to thank Ralph for reading my manuscript and offering some suggestions that I tried to use to improve the accuracy of the description of Prudhoe Bay, and Alaska. And, I can't fail to ask Ralph and his former colleagues at Arco to forgive my taking the liberties of fiction writing in fudging the timing of the discovery of Prudhoe Bay Oil Field to fit my story. Leighton Steward, formerly a research geologist with Shell Oil Company, then, CEO of Louisiana Land, and Exploration Company, a great oil finder, and the author of the best seller, Sugar Busters, was, always, available to give advice when I needed it.

Two persons deserving special thanks are John Kerr and Rich Curtin, both of whom metamorphosed from a pinnacle of success in their respective fields of law and research, into successful published authors of popular books. John and Rich took great time out of their busy schedules to read every word in early versions of an immature, pretty awful, first draft of my story. I want to thank John and Rich for their advice and counsel, an important key to my completing this endeavor.

And, I hope Scott Petty, Jr. realizes the importance to me of the historical information he supplied regarding the contribution of his father and uncle, Scott Petty, Sr., and Dabney Petty, to the science of oil finding with their innovative scientific breakthroughs in seismic and geophysical technology that made geophysics so important in the science of finding oil.

There are many others I must mention, Tom Ewing, PhD, Frontera Exploration; and, Bonnie Weise, Consulting Geologist, of San Antonio, Texas, who led the Venus Oil Company Exploration Team to earn industry recognition as "trend leaders" in the Downdip Yegua Play of the Upper Gulf Coast. Also, I want to thank Robert Blodgett, PhD, consulting geologist in Anchorage,

Alaska. Someday, I hope to meet both Gil Mull, the godfather of geological studies of the North Slope and Prudhoe Bay, and, John M. Sweet and thank him for writing his history of "The Discovery of Prudhoe Bay". Bruce Wells, Executive Director of the American Oil & Gas Historical Society was a great source of oil field historical information and, I urge anyone interested in preserving oil field history to make a contribution to the AOGHS.

The oil boom is gone, but I still have old friends in East Texas that I must remember, like Jack Phillips in Gladewater, who is still drilling for oil and gas, and John Glass, Jr., and the Glass family in Tyler, and, Duel Glass, a grand-nephew of Daisy Bradford, who takes care of Daisy's farm, and the farm house where his Aunt Daisy looked down the hill a couple of hundred yards at Dad Joiner's discovery well, the Number Three Daisy Bradford, which is still there today pumping oil almost 90 years after that fateful day when oil gushed over the top of the derrick and opened up a new era in Texas. Many of my East Texas friends and associates, have gone to the Happy Oil Field Hunting Ground, and they are missed, especially Tom Calhoun, Jim Beavers, Mike and Pat Hazel, and Mack Rankin, and many others.

I wish I could locate Herman, my first best friend when I was four years old. The last I heard of Herman was when I was told he was a doctor in Fort Worth. Herman, if you are still around, and read this, please give me a call. Herman's mother was our family housekeeper.

This book would never have been finished without the patience and help of my writing coach, Mark Spencer, Dean of the School of Arts and Humanities at the University of Arkansas at Monticello in Monticello, Arkansas, an award winning published writer of note. I also must thank Mark's daughter, Bronte Spencer Pearson, for her help in copy editing, and completing the manuscript.

My brother George's and my father, Gene Ames, Sr., was

among generation number three, of six generations of the Ames family in the oil business over more than a hundred years. Our Dad was a great oil man. He was a great people person, who loved people and people loved him. Unbeknownst to most, he was a catalyst that contributed to a couple of large oil companies happening. Many of the incidents in this book actually happened to him. He was blown off the catwalk of his refinery and he broke both feet and all of his exposed flesh was badly burned. He was a scratch golfer who was the founder of one of the best golf courses in the oil field in East Texas, but, he left a round of golf with his golf partner John Henderson the afternoon they heard the blast of the New London school explosion. They rushed to New London and spent hours stacking bodies of the school children who had died. When he followed his own father from Oklahoma to the great East Texas Boom, he took his bride, Pat, with him to Gladewater, where my brother and I were born. Our father established our family's presence in East Texas, and, I will always feel the Piney Woods is my home.

I want to thank all the other members of our family who, collectively, are the only reason this book was ever completed and published. Finally, I close by thanking the person who provided my greatest support, Ellen Rhett Young Ames—my girlfriend since she was thirteen years old, and my wife for 61 years, who turned out to be my secret weapon as a writer. Ellen had the patience for several years to let me do my thing and try to write a book, probably thinking, like most, that I'd never finish. The truth is I would have never finished this book without her. And, by the way, she knew better than me how the wildcatter's women should fit into this tale! Thank you, Ellen.

Gene Ames, Jr.

ABOUT THE AUTHOR

GENE AMES, JR., is fourth generation oil field. He is married to Ellen Rhett Young Ames, and they live in San Antonio, Texas. He was born in Gladewater, Texas in the East Texas Oil Boom where his father owned fractional working interests in producing oil wells and an interest in a gasoline plant. He and his family have been in the oil business starting back in Oklahoma, more than a hundred years ago.

Gene Ames, Jr., became interested in geology after spending four summers in Yellowstone National Park, observing and learning of the geological wonders of nature in the park. This experience included one summer as a Fire Control Aide for the National Park Service, cutting cords of wood with a hand-held cross-cut saw, clearing trails, all while serving on the Pre-Suppression Crew, the first responder fire fighter team to locate and evaluate the danger of new forest fires. He received a Bachelor of Science degree in Geology from the University of Texas at Austin, attended Law School at St. Mary's University School of Law and he completed the nine-week Smaller Company Management Program at the Harvard Graduate School of Business. He is an active petroleum geologist and independent oil producer and the owner of royalties and minerals in four states. As C.E.O. of Venus Oil Company he conceived and managed the execution of exploration programs which discovered and developed significant oil and gas reserves, included opening up the trillion-cubic-foot extension of the Expanded Yegua Play into the upper Gulf Coast of Texas with the discovery of the Vidor-Ames Field in Orange County. The exploration team under his management developed the concept of vast bypassed and undeveloped gas reserves in the Deep Cotton Valley Sands in the Vernon Field Area of North Central Louisiana. The American Association of Geologists reported the Vernon Field Area as a trillion-cubic-foot gas development and one of the largest gas fields developed in the lower 48 States in the first decade of the 21st century.

Today as managing partner of Compadre Energy, Ltd., Ames is actively seeking to acquire oil and gas fields, with bypassed undeveloped reserve potential while never stopping the search for unexplored giant frontier oil and gas reserve drilling prospects.

Gene Ames, Jr. has served as Chairman of both the Independent Petroleum Association of America ("IPAA"), which represents independent producers at the federal level in Washington, D.C. and the Texas Oil and Gas Association ("TXOGA"), an oil industry trade association at the state government level in Austin, Texas. He is a member of the Board of Directors and a former chairman of the Southwest Research Institute in San Antonio.

As IPAA Chairman, Ames played a leading role in the founding of the North American Prospect Exposition (NAPE) and he was a founder of the Petroleum Technology Transfer Council, which was established by the U.S. Department of Energy under the Administration of President George H. W. Bush. He has served as a member of the Advisory Council to the University of Texas Geology Foundation and as a member of the National Petroleum Council, the energy industry advisory council to the United States Secretary of Energy. He has received several prestigious national energy awards including the honor of being selected to receive the annual oil and gas industry honor as "Chief Roughneck." He is a member of the All-American Wildcatters, the American Association of Petroleum Geologists, the Society of Independent Earth Scientists and The South Texas Geological Society.

WORKS CITED

Ball, Max W. *This Fascinating Oil Business*. New York/
   Indianapolis: The Bobbs-Merrill Company, 1940. Print.

Bright, Lorine Zylks. *NEW LONDON, 1937, One Woman's
   Memory of Orange and Green*. Wichita Falls: Nortex Press,
   1977.

Burrough, Bryan. *The Big Rich: The Rise and Fall of the Greatest
   Oil Fortunes*. New York: The Penguin Press, 2009. Print.

Castaneda, Christopher and Joseph A. Pratt. *From Texas to the
   East, a Strategic History of Texas Eastern Corporation*. College
   Station: Texas A&M Press, 1993. Print.

Clark, James A. *Marrs McLean, a Biography*. Houston: Clark
   Book, Inc., 1969. Print.

Clark, James A. and Michel T. Halbouty. *The Last Boom*. New
   York: Random House, 1972. Print.

Coghlan, Howard. *By-Laws and Corporate Minutes, Texas Oil and
   Gas Products Company*. Gladewater, 1932. Print.

Eason, Al. *BOOM TOWN: Kilgore, Texas*. Kilgore: Chamber of
   Commerce, 1979. Print.

The East Texas Engineering Association. *The East Texas Oil Field,
   1930-1950*. Kilgore: Report for Member Companies, 1953.
   Print.

English, T.J. *Havana Nocturne.* New York: HarperCollins Publishers, 2008. Print.

Evans, Lewis. *Map of the Middle British Colonies in America. First Known Document to Show Oil at the Industry's Birthplace.* 1755. Philadelphia/New York: Ben Franklin Press and the Ethyl Corporation, 1953. Print.

Franks, Kenny A. *RAGTOWN, A History of the Greater Healdton-Hewitt Oil Field.* Oklahoma City: Oklahoma Heritage Association/Western Heritage Books, Inc., 1986. Print.

Giddens, Paul H. and Ida M. Tarbell. *The Birth of the Oil Industry.* New York: The MacMillan Company, 1938. Print.

Giddens, Paul H. *Pennsylvania Petroleum, 1750-1872.* Titusville: Pennsylvania Historical and Museum Commission, 1947. Print.

Haas, Michelle M. *Dad and Doc.* Rockport: Copano Bay Press, 2013. Print.

Hager, Dorsey. *Practical Oil Geology: The Application of Geology to Oil Field Problems-Primary Source Edition.* New York: McGraw-Hill Publishers of Books, 1915-1916. Print.

Harter, Harry. *East Texas Oil Parade.* San Antonio: The Naylor Company, 1934. Print.

Hatley, Allen G. *THE OIL FINDERS: A Collection of Stories about Exploration.* Utopia: Centex Press, 1995. Print.

Helgesen, Sally. *Wildcatters, a Story of Texans, Oil and Money.* Garden City: Doubleday & Company, Inc., 1981. Print.

Henry, J. T. *History of Petroleum, the Early and Later, Volume I and Volume II.* New York: Burt Franklin Research and Source Work Series 108, 1873. Print.

Hill, Margaret Hunt. *H. L. and Lyda, Growing Up in the H. L. Hunt and Lyda Bunker Hunt Family as Told by their Eldest Daughter.* Little Rock: August House, Inc., 1994. Print.

House, Boyce. *Oil Field Fury.* San Antonio: The Naylor Company, 1954. Print.

Hughes, Dudley J. *Oil in the Deep South, a History of the Oil Business in Mississippi, Alabama, and Florida, 1859-1945.* Jackson: University of Mississippi Press, 1993. Print.

Jackson, Elaine. *Lufkin, From Sawdust to Oil, a History of Lufkin Industries.* Lufkin/Houston: Gulf Publishing Company, 1982. Print.

Knowles, Ruth Sheldon. *The Greatest Gamblers, the Epic of American Oil Exploration.* 1959. New York/Norman: University of Oklahoma Press, 1978. Print.

Lawyer, L. C., et al. *Geophysics in the Affairs of Mankind, a Personalized History of Exploration Geophysics.* 2nd ed. Tulsa: Society of Exploration Geophysicists, 2001. Print.

Larson, Henrietta M. and Kenneth Wiggins Porter. *History of the Humble Oil and Refining, A Study of Industrial Growth.* New York: Harper and Brothers Publishers, 1959. Print.

McDaniel, Ruel. *Some Ran Hot.* Dallas: Regional Press, 1939. Print.

Milles, Ray. *King of the Wildcatters, the Life and Times of Tom Slick, 1883-1930.* College Station, Texas A&M Press, 1996. Print.

Milsten, David. *Thomas Gilcrease.* San Antonio: The Naylor Company, 1969. Print.

Olien, Roger M. and Diana Davids. *OIL BOOMS, Social Change in Five Texas Towns.* Lincoln/London: University of Nebraska Press, 1982. Print.

Owen, Edgar Wesley, under sponsorship of George H. Coates. *Trek of the Oil Finders: A History of Exploration for Petroleum.* Tulsa: The American Association of Petroleum Geologists, 1975. Print.

Petty, O. Scott. *Seismic Reflections, Reflections of the Formative*

Years of the Geophysical Exploration Industry. Houston, Texas: Geosource, Inc. 1976. Print.

Powers, Louis W. *The World Energy Dilemma.* Tulsa: Penn Well Corporation, 2012. Print.

Raab, Selwyn. *Five Families, The Rise, Decline and Resurgence of America's Most Powerful Mafia Empires.* New York: Thomas Dunne Books/St. Martin's Press, 2005. Print.

Roark, Garland. *Drill a Crooked Hole.* Garden City: Doubleday &
Company, 1968. Print.

Rose, Peter R. *Risk Analysis and Management of Petroleum Exploration Ventures.* Tulsa: The American Association of Petroleum Geologists, AAPG Methods in Exploration Series, No. 12, 2001. Print.

Silliman, B., Jr. *Report on the Rock Oil or Petroleum from Venango Co., Pennsylvania, With Special Reference to Its Use for Illumination and Other Purposes.* New Haven: J. H. Benham's Steam Power Press, 1855. Print. The Authors Library.

Sternbach, C. A., et al. *Discoverers of the 20th Century: Perfecting the Search.* Tulsa: The American Association of Petroleum Geologists, 2005. Print.

Sweet, John M. *Discovery at Prudhoe Bay, Mountain Men and Seismic Vision Drilled Black Gold.* Blaine/Surrey: Hancock House Publishers, 2008. Print.

Tunstill, Jack C. *Oil Legends of Fort Worth.* Fort Worth: The Fort Worth Petroleum Club, 1993. Print.

Warner, C. A. *Texas Oil and Gas since 1543.* Rockport: Copano Bay Press, 2007. Print.

Yergin, Daniel. *The Prize.* New York: Simon and Schuster, 1991. Print.

Yergin, Daniel. *The Quest.* New York: The Penguin Press, 2011. Print.